The Sky Falls Down

I0742432

The Sky Falls Down

An Anthology of Loss

Edited by Terry Whitebeach & Gina Mercer

The Sky Falls Down: An Anthology of Loss
ISBN 978 1 76041 730 7
Copyright © individual contributors 2019
Copyright © this collection Terry Whitebeach & Gina Mercer 2019
Cover photo © Barend Becker, used with permission
Extract from *The Orchard* by Drusilla Modjeska on page 13 reprinted by
permission of Pan Macmillan Australia Pty Ltd. © Drusilla Modjeska 1994

First published 2019 by
GINNINDERRA PRESS
PO Box 3461 Port Adelaide 5015 Australia
www.ginninderrapress.com.au

Contents

Foreword

There is no real preparation for the unfamiliar landscape of loss. We struggle to get our bearings in this new, confusing and unwanted landscape where everything familiar has lost meaning. We ache to return to the way things were before. When we suffer a significant loss, not only is the landscape unfamiliar, we can suddenly be lost to ourselves.

My brother Brenden's death through suicide shattered our lives in unspeakable ways. Unspeakable, because none of us had a clue what to say to each other. Like many post-war families, we didn't express emotions skilfully, or perhaps at all. The emotional tumult ravaged each of us who loved him in solitary and private ways. We had no language to articulate our shock, grief and despair. The pain of loss felt insurmountable. We were left behind, lost, uncertain how to live.

This beautiful collection of writings will meet you where you are. You'll find yourself reaching for particular pieces that somehow articulate how you're feeling – even before you've found the words to express it yourself.

The writers in this collection make meaning out of loss. They share, with insight and creativity, what they've learned. They send telling reports from the land of loss. They gift us the words we need most when we feel isolated, without hope.

May this book become both a friend and a warm companion to you as you traverse your particular landscape of loss.

Petrea King

Author of *Sometimes Hearts Have to Break*
Quest for Life Centre, Bundanoon,
www.questforlife.com.au

Introduction

Terry

There are cascades of loss that can feel overwhelming, never-ending. When my decade-long Central Australian adventure was interrupted by a debilitating neurological condition that temporarily robbed me of the use of my limbs, I spent months in hospital, before, still convalescent, I returned home – to a Tasmania I hardly recognised – to continue my recovery, and, subsequently, to be with my daughter during her life-threatening (but ultimately life-saving) surgeries and subsequent convalescence, then, with my sisters, to take on the long-term care of our elderly parents, both of whom had cancer.

My mother developed Alzheimer's and my father dementia, and so we entered the choppy ocean of ambiguous loss, where key relationships shift and change and the losses both present and impending must be navigated. Isolation, exhaustion and grief were my constant companions. There were bright moments of unexpected kindness and connection, but when 'the sky falls down' and the known world is obliterated, one can flounder about in very bleak seas.

Many times I have needed and welcomed the words of other writers to help me make sense of what I am experiencing and to reduce my sense of aloneness. I am always grateful for the feeling of recognition and affirmation these accounts offer, but when skilled writers transform painful and confusing narratives into art, there are the added gifts of pleasure, enrichment, meaning-making and, yes, joy.

It was in the wake of this deluge that I conceived the notion of gathering stories, essays and poems into an anthology of loss. During lunch with some fellow Tasmanian writers, I mentioned this idea to Gina and asked whether she'd be interested in collaborating on such a project.

Gina

I was immediately taken with the idea. A collection like this could, I thought, act as a meeting place, a site of connection. It could provide a community of companions where people, feeling disoriented and isolated by loss, might find recognition and solace.

Looking back, I realise that I was born into a household pervaded by loss, my father having been killed in a head-on collision while I was *in utero*. Loss was the air I breathed. It was my family's identity in the small fishing town where we lived. My mother was known as the Widow Mercer. Defined by her loss. Then, before I'd even gotten through my teens, my mum was killed by a passing car as she cycled along the Pacific Highway.

When I went to university, I received the Double Orphan's Pension (such a ridiculously Dickensian name). Again, defined by loss. What followed was a decade of navigating bleak and messy seas as I struggled to develop any sense of who I might be, where home might be. I felt bewildered, adrift, without guiding stars by which to navigate. What I love most about this anthology is the way each of the contributors gifts their hard-won and life-affirming knowledge to that bewildered teenager.

The longer we live, the broader our experience of loss. It can be utterly mundane, like losing your keys or a biro. It can be catastrophic. It can be cumulative. But every loss is in some ways disorienting – though to vastly differing degrees. The effect on your inner landscape can be equivalent to an earthquake. Everything you've known changes shape. Nothing can go back to the way it was before. My interest in exploring these disrupted landscapes was what made me so keen to collaborate on this project.

In response to our general call-out, we got an amazingly rich response from places as diverse as inner-city Melbourne, the Torres Strait, Manus Island, academia, a locked high-care aged facility, a remote bay in southern Tasmania. People wrote of mastectomy; loss of place through climate change; stillbirth; loss of language; amputation; being jilted; the multiple losses of becoming a refugee; so many diverse experiences of loss. Their words are moving, wry, insightful, powerful. The fact that so many people could create strong, beautiful work out of the experience of loss is a potent and inspiring message in itself.

Terry

Some losses may be celebrated, accommodated fairly equably, or even viewed humorously. There are such examples in this anthology. But in the depictions of more shattering losses, and the way we must learn 'how to live with any bigness of spirit when the soil from which it must flourish has shrunk to a small handful of loam…[and to accommodate] the emptiness that brings you slap up against that naked reflection in the mirror', as writer Drusilla Modjeska puts it, we face a stark, at times seemingly impossible, task. But, Modjeska assures us, 'by being forced to live within a curtailment not of one's own choosing, there can be a corresponding expansion in the heart's capacity'.[1] It is this 'expansion in the heart's capacity' that most aptly characterises the work of the writers in *The Sky Falls Down*: as both an invitation and a gift to the reader.

Gina

It's been a long haul, the making of this book. There have been multiple losses for each of us in the five years it has taken to make our way from that first conversation through to publication. But we persevered – inspired by the creative energy that brought these writings into existence. Our wish is that this book may speak to those navigating their own particular oceans of loss.

Terry Whitebeach
Gina Mercer

1. From *The Orchard* by Drusilla Modjeska, reprinted by permission of Pan Macmillan Australia Pty Ltd. © Drusilla Modjeska 1994.

While you were gone

While you were gone the sky fell down against the windows.
While you were gone our song cried so much I had to put it in
    another room.
While you were gone the telephone sulked and the muesli had an
    existential crisis.
While you were gone I worked night shift keeping the bed warm.
While you were gone I bought you a thousand gifts and took them all
    back again.
While you were gone a lot of tedious jobs knocked on the door and
    sold themselves to me.
While you were gone I remembered who I was without you.
While you were gone the grass grew as wildly as if time were passing.
While you were gone the mirror was a bit unkind.
While you were gone meals seemed twice as demanding, wine three
    times more dangerous.
While you were gone all the birds in the neighbourhood moved out.
While you were gone I almost watched American TV, that's how
    much I missed your voice.
While you were gone I didn't do a single crossword puzzle.
While you were gone my house was tidier, my accounts more
    balanced, my heart more tiny.
While you were gone the silence stretched so thin I could see through
    it, and
while you were gone I think something might have broken.

Debi Hamilton

It will not be enough

It's there in the water, in the shadow of the hull. A body of clear, voluminous jelly, encasing a brain-like orange mass. It is huge, greater than the length and breadth of your four-year-old body. The interior reflects the light in such a way that it appears to hold its own luminescence, while below it, clouds of billowing skirts contract and expand as it passes.

I clutch hold of your shoulders as you lean from the stern. I watch your face in profile – mesmerised by the way it is swimming, quivering towards the shore. In a lifetime of sailing I've seen larger jellyfish, but none quite so impressive. I wonder what kind of age it could be? How far it has travelled? Here in these sheltered waterways there's danger. Its passage between the rocky edge of the island where we made our fire and the larger island to the east, may be its last.

Leaning from the dinghy, my niece takes a ghostly photograph. It's the one we carry with us into the CSIRO, on the urban edge of the Derwent. Later, in the park across the road, I lean on a swing as I chat to one of the resident biologists on the phone. She has an accent, Canadian perhaps? Belonging to colder oceans. She is enthusiastic, grateful, her interest is contagious. This is exciting, this creature is new to southern waters. We've seen it passing where no one has before, this beautiful, foreign thing. She spells out its name. I scribble on my hand: *Pseudorhiza haeckelii* or Haeckel's jellyfish.

We post the photograph on the internet, on Redmap, among the other unusual sightings. Marine life spotted where they haven't been reported before, out of context, in unnavigated waters. An eclectic collection of aquatic pioneers. Or are they refugees? Survivors? There are many. I scroll down the images on my screen: loggerhead turtle, box jellyfish, rock cale, kingfish, the gloomy octopus, we've seen that one hiding in the kelp beds in the bay below our home. Alongside the buoyancy of the new – a weightier, more portentous feeling.

*

In our bay, the snorkelling season is lengthened and shortened by the colour of the water. When the rain falls in the mountains, this river-mouth cove turns blood-red, black with tannin. This year and the last we've swum later, the water warmer, still clear long into the autumn months. We linger on the beach with friends until bedtime, our naked children occupying the water's lapping edge. They build towers of wet sand, whelk farms, driftwood dragons. Our dogs skid in and out of the shallows, digging frantically into the crumbling foundations of castles and stick-drawn, dissolving maps. It is April, it is May, it is June and I am happy. Surely this is as perfect as life will ever be?

There is something on the sand and you are nudging it with your spade, the other children crouching around you. We are coast dwellers now, collectors of fragments – storm petrel feathers and urchin spines – we know to expect the unexpected. In the history of this sand there are cetacean bones, there are giant squid washed from the deep ocean trenches, and there are footprints of brown-skinned women who carried their babies, their piccaninny children on their backs.

I think of those women, the sails on the horizon, the ocean smooth as abalone pearl. The *Recherche*, the *Esperance*, their own apocalypse in the shape of distant frigates, of trinkets left in camps on the coast of Bruny Island – Lunnawanna-Alonnah, Mellukerdee. The people who left behind the middens on the point, where the orchids unfurl their sail-like petals faithfully each spring.

You are fascinated with the stories I tell you, with the rhythm of their words. You draw pictures on the tide-line – huts of bark, infant babies wrapped in pademelon skins. We follow long untrodden tracks through whispering she-oaks, through this scented, needle-red forest. We weave ourselves into the past of this place. 'You be the mother,' you say.

*

What am I afraid of? That your future will be stripped of magic? Devoid of

17

elemental beauty? There have been nights where we've huddled together on the balcony under a blanket, and watched the aurora's pale green light, swelling above the horizon. Our perfect, life-giving atmosphere protecting us from the solar wind. As we watch, you are shivering in my arms, full of questions, like those searching, incandescent beams – reaching out to somewhere beyond, something secret, unknowable, ancient. That molecular beauty that hovers over ice sheets, over earth, through the pale open forest of the hills behind our home, colouring the tannin-red river that spills into this warming, acidifying ocean. It is incorruptible, surely, that beauty? It will still be there, won't it? The colour of fire, the rhythm of waves, they will still be there?

*

This is your world: your father's laugh, his chest, his hands, our small house, this river of rainbows, the possibility of snow.

You want to see a thylacine – the shy, tiger-striped, bounty-doomed marsupial that once inhabited this island. I explain to you about extinction, about mistakes that were made. 'What is *shot*?' you ask, and I describe how I imagine a rifle must work, the trajectory of a bullet. You are just four years old, my daughter, and you are weeping in my arms. Humans do stupid things sometimes, but lessons were learned, I tell you. How long before you realise what we are doing to this world? How long before you ask me what it means that the seasons I have taught you, which sustain us, are failing?

I've tried to use words to make a difference but I've failed. So I will write the world for you, as it is now, as it was when I searched the sand for the surfboard skeletons of cuttlefish, as a child. I will try to weave a web of words around each vanishing species. Etch out in syllables the freckled constellations of a pardalote's weightless feathers, the silk fins of galaxias, the wild flower tundra, the ice bears of the frozen north. I will wrap the wings of the Ulysses butterfly and the goshawk in pages of silk, and try to keep them safe for you – but it will not be enough.

Susie Greenhill

Ngingali

my mother is a granite boulder
I can no longer climb
nor walk around

her weight is a constant
reminder of myself
I sit in her shadow

gulls nestle in her hair
their shadows her epitaph
I carry

a pebble of her in my pocket

Ali Cobby Eckerman

Memento mori

Jet is the bead for mourning,
black, pure and hard –

it is the shadowed forest, vibrant
with birds and leaves

and the death of forests –
long nights of rain sweeping

fallen branches, abraded
by river stones, to the sea.

A rich silt covers them,
seeps into grains and fissures,

the weight of time and waves
compressing the fibres to a dark

jewel, a lens to view the earth's
histories: the first expulsion,

the voyage on the swollen tide,
the siege of mud – each bead

is a bereavement: the empty crib,
eroded hills, fields of blood, the burial

of love. Add your own lament
to this inventory of loss. Catch

in the lustre of a stone whose colour
never fades, your mirrored breath.

Lyn Reeves

Fragmented elegy for my father: at the exact speed necessary

Who imagined it like this? A car
cartwheeling into a ditch at the exact
speed necessary to roll over and over
until punched to a stop by a culvert.
It was Monday the first day of summer.
It was a sunny day and the beribboned
wine basket in the trunk must have slammed
back and forth several times.
Its handle is broken but the three
bottles of wine are intact
still whole and
wholly silent.

My father is dead

waiting for the kettle to boil
I sink into grief the way
I might slide into a lake
from the end of a dock at twilight
the water silky
letting me in.

It's just another morning, papers everywhere, business as usual. Random
explosions of car horns, rain in the forecast, the unspoken with its back
turned haunting the windowsills. I'd like to think something's worming
to the surface, something good and enlightening like the day itself, but
I don't believe it. Only more of the same, more of the same.

Paper and confusion crumpling together. Words leak into each other,
meld, dissolve in static hum, off the highway and –

My father is dead.

O Alice adrift and drifting down, brace yourself for the thump of landing, for the switching of big with little, or little with big, for the fluidity of terrain and machines. In the garden no one paints the trees.

At St Peter's Abbey I sleep
the sleep of the dead, though not
like you, who *are* dead
and not sleeping

though you *were* sleeping
when the car left the road

I'd been afraid you might
one day drive past a stop sign
or fall asleep at the wheel

but you were not driving then
as you are not sleeping now

you died instantly, they said

you, who could sleep through anything,
did you think a single thought
before that instant fell on you
with the car's crushing frame?

Flying home it's all ocean above the clouds.
I feel the grip and resistance of air
like water against a boat's hull, the boat
bouncing or rolling on the surge,

and your death is a flare of light rising still
from that tumbling car as I rumble home
over fists of air pummelling the plane,
passing it from hand to hand.

I'm flying toward everything I don't know –
where your ashes might reside, what my life
is now, tossed and rocked by accident.
High over the prairies, I'm held by thin air

as clouds separate and light glazes
the land's lovely rumpled surface.
If the hands let go I might leave
the air the way you left the road. Undone,

weak with grief, I give in to the air's
turbulence. How did I not understand
we all travel on the planet's unsteady
breath? Anything can happen.

On Christmas Eve, we stand in front of the bodega at Epcot
like moons flung from orbit, half a year from your death

hearing voices emanate from the night market – carts filled with
giant paper chrysanthemums, cartoon sombreros, and a figure of Death.

We ride a boat into the vent between worlds, passing Aztec pyramids
and a painted street where papier-mâché puppets lean, among them Death –

a Day of the Dead *piñata*, blank-eyed skull blossoming from a trellis of ribs.
We buy two small ones so your granddaughters can gossip with Death.

I think of your name on the marble gravestone in the snow,
while the two girls sit on a chesterfield and dandle their paper deaths.

Where are you? The question ghosts in
as I look across the cemetery
its graves buried in snow.
Nothing answers.

The tops of the grey headstones
names half-erased by white,
stutter a rhyme above the drifts.
All these spent lives –

what for?
Outside the double hedge are snow-covered
gardens, bush, orchard, tall
spruce trees, and the dugout's frozen

reflections. It's eight months since your death
and I stand knee-deep in white.
A magpie floats past without calling.
From the bell tower a dome of sound

rings out beneath the sky's larger
dome. Light spears across snow
piercing my eyes, and the dead speak:
We're the earth you stand on.

Maureen Scott Harris

The mariner's funeral

I took the chilled seawater in the small cup of my hand. I dropped it on the warmed brown arch of your back as you slept. Your eyes opened far too wide. I knew I'd dragged you from a secret place. You were angry.

That's the last shot in a reel of unedited film that runs relentlessly through my head. Though there were months to prepare, death came too quickly. I can still feel the heat from my father's cigarette. I can smell the sea we left behind twenty years ago. Now, my head is a reluctant projectionist. This is another all-night screening. In the last dark minutes on the day of his funeral I sift through a collection of unrefined memories. *The water's too cold to swim. Just wait.* I feel the weight of his arms like barriers through a rough towel.

Somewhere outside, birds on naked twigs usher in daybreak. No room for song in this house. It's already too cluttered. The voices beyond the door chatter in excited sadness. There's much to be done. My family spent hours choosing a casket and picking out hymns. We drag these out on auspicious occasions and refer to books so we can mime in time with the organ. The older ones know them by rote. We drafted a shipshape eulogy and paid the undertaker with credit cards.

My brother arrived at Tullamarine, the first of a handful of airport pickups. I shopped for a new blouse and he got a haircut. He scooped up our basset, Mr Big, and assured him that everything would be all right. Mr Big has been out of sorts. My mother ordered cheese and asparagus sandwiches. Her home is festooned with floral arrangements and sympathy cards and the echo of long-distance phone calls. Her house is inhabited by stray relatives who bring their own towels because they don't want to be a bother.

Aunty Doris will arrive from Perth and God willing she will play Mendelssohn at the church. She's in her eighties and only does what God is willing to let her do. If he is willing, she'll play while we stare at the scentless roses on the casket. My uncle will read passages from the Bible in a trembling voice and all the time my father will be watching.

My dead father sees all. He'll watch Doris board the plane in her orthopaedic shoes, animal-print travel bag rattling with medication. She'll spill her sugarless cola on a neighbouring passenger and my father's death laugh will fill the cabin silently, inaudible to mortals because God loves a good mystery. My father will read in unison with my uncle and polish the fingerprints off his coffin. He might cling-wrap cheese and asparagus sandwiches. It's a long way to heaven. In heaven there's coffee and a comfortable reclining throne and, from here, he'll watch us stumble through mortal life. I hear death is just like stepping into another room but we are architecturally bereft. We cannot begin to appreciate its measurements and dimensions. My father is with Jesus. They have a private room. It overlooks the sea.

We will handle his corpse with care, slip it into his best suit, box it and drop it into darkness among the tree roots. He'll watch the whole thing. If it rains, it's OK; the parlour has umbrellas embossed with their company logo. They have fold-up chairs for the exhausted. As for the ascended, they never get wet. However, they are bathed in light, their heads giddy with rapturous joy, diaries crammed with reunions.

Mr Big is hiding under the kitchen table. My grandmother dries wine glasses. My mother applies her lipstick. It is Anthurium red but her clothes are black. Black prevails at funerals. We are all in the dark but my father found the light; just think how happy he must be. More flowers arrive wrapped in reams of crackling plastic. They are placed strategically between cards displaying clouds and crucifixes, lilacs and lambs. Surely the lambs are a mistake? A priest once told me that animals can't share heaven. They have no soul.

We dress till we're black and brown and grey. Long, shining cars arrive and perch in the driveway, certain they'll be fed. We crawl into their bellies and slide into place. 'Don't be sad,' my grandmother is rubbing my niece's hand. My grandmother's known God the longest. They are old allies. 'This is part of his plan. We just don't know what it is, yet.' God loves a good mystery. Our steely beasts rumble along the highway past auto repairers and bottle shops. I roll down the window and fill my chest with damp June air. My head throbs with the scent of freshly cleaned vinyl. My grandmother gazes into the bleak sky trusting that someone is watching. The stretch before the church is flat and clear of buildings. We eventually glimpse a stunted iron spire and catch the glare of glass walls. If I prayed now, I'd pray for trees.

We are greeted by the minister's receding hairline as he fake bows and embraces family members. He is a mumbler and a rambler. He saves souls as per his job description and is, in return, saved from poverty by a corporation which exports and imports the invisible. The minister likes to expose his palms to the mourners while tilting his head towards the sky. My father had a telescope that he pointed in the same direction and filled our head with moons and planets. The minister closes his eyes and whispers. He's been known to speak in tongues.

The church is warm with hushed talk and the breath of the grieving. *I am far away on a private beach. I share it with my father. My legs are heavy. Wet sand fills the long space between flesh and growing bones. He buries me meticulously and the sand is my well-built sarcophagus. It is patted and smoothed right up to my collarbones. My body revels in the temporary thrill of paralysis. I try not to breathe and crack the illusion. I am still encased when a cool breeze comes off the water and carries the smoke from the orange tip of his cigarette to my face. Sharp palm leaves shimmy as they slice what's left of the day into coloured ribbons. The sea dries in our hair. I have no wish to go home.*

The raised and unmistakeable voice of my aunt brings me back to my pew; it drifts shrill above the bent heads of a small gathering around the open coffin. There's panic and movement. The bereaved lean into the casket, close enough to smell death. Suddenly all eyes are on the melancholically perturbed. My aunt licks the corner of her handkerchief and dips it inside my father's expensive crate.

I join the panic and look inside. My father lived in this body once. He grew it and it was nurtured by my grandmother and nourished by my mother. Inside it he travelled a hundred countries, worked overtime and played college rugby. He took it to the races, the Christmas markets at the docks, and made it stand guard the day I broke my arm and was rushed to Emergency. Its dark crags and sharp angles pierced the bland white of the ward. His body was a lifeline that ceased to be of use the day he died. It lay distorted and unfathomably useless in a box. This is the body when all intent has departed.

The morticians scrubbed the smell of hospital from it but the unmistakeable scent of cheap chocolate now rises from the sharply pressed pocket of my father's best jacket. On closer inspection, I notice a small brown stain leaking through the pale blue fabric. I open his pocket and find a half-melted chocolate koala wrapped in torn plastic. Sweet cocoa flows in a tiny trickle but my aunt's constant dabbing has smeared it into a dirty swirl on my father's chest. I lift the koala from the casket and my hand brushes against my father's chin. It is as smooth and cold as an egg. The viewers weep as the lid is hoisted into place by those who are paid to look solemn. They are sending my father to God. He will spend eternity in a dirty suit.

My niece is crestfallen. She is on a lap in the middle of a crowded pew. Heads shake with disapproval. She is watched. God watches everything. The chocolate is her gesture. It's for his journey. Someone mentions ants. I think of the dead Egyptians in their pyramids, equipped with riches they'll never use. My niece twists a lank strip of her hair and sucks the tip of it. Chocolate for the afterlife; a child's way of making a dead man remember.

Mendelssohn starts. It's 'O, for the Wings of a Dove' and Doris's manicure is tapping an electronic keyboard. I rub my sticky hands in the mountain of tissues my mother thrusts at me. I leave fingerprints on hymn books and prayer books. He is watching; God of the giant spectacles. Then rambler takes to the pulpit surrounded by white candles and stained-glass angels. I hear that my father has been called home. Jesus is calling.

But there's a white weatherboard on the corner of Banksia Street;

nothing fancy. If you push your thumbnail against the planks on the eastern side, you make an indentation. That's OK; it can be fixed with filler, no need to replace the boards. Every summer there's talk of repainting but no one has the time. It's the season of no alarm clocks and beach days that spill into impromptu barbecues. It is an excellent house for dogs and grandmothers. It's full of open newspapers and ornamental geese, of curries in clean Tupperware and cassette tapes of Miles Davis. It is a house of sleep-ins, debate, conjecture, disappointment but never apathy.

In winter it's a house of fermented friends, ladies' handbags and even more jazz. They dance till late on scuffed linoleum, spilling red wine and talking about long ago. Outside there's the smell of cut grass and a giant lilly pilly. Its outstretched boughs nearly touch the kitchen window. On windy days café curtains billow like moored ghosts. He called it *home*.

Jesus is calling. Heaven is waiting. The sharp edge of a cash-filled envelope gouges my palm. It's for the salvation of a soul. It's for the minister. It's for the church. It's for beverages and light refreshments. It's a deposit on a home for a dead man, a gesture of faith and it's to be given with thanks. When it's all done we'll feel better. We'll know he's watching. The Americans call it closure.

I sit in the church hall nursing a cup of tea and an Order of Service imprinted with my father's face. I don't know why they chose this photo. He's practically naked without his glasses. My niece joins a rambunctious group of children playing hide-and-seek in the car park. Her dark head bobs in the distance like an escaped scarab beetle. It's a good turnout. The sandwiches slowly disappear and steam rises from chipped cups as people embrace and confide and comfort. They will not accept that loss is disorderly. The minister has talked them around. Ritual makes sense of chaos, even when it's led by men who take orders from invisible friends. In plain sight of the dead, I open the envelope and remove most of the cash. I'll put it towards house paint next summer. I press what's left over into the minister's sweaty hand. I squeeze his shoulder and wonder if he'll pray for us.

The sea is never quiet. It trickles into ears and eyes. It drops like tears off the rough tip of your chin. The sea is tiny and immense. Sometimes the films in my head run of their own volition. On the way home, I will stop at the empty beach. I will fill it. One last swim.

The sea is never lost.

Suzi Mezei

A room inside a high-care nursing home

Pop's hand tremors as he tries to get the spoon from the bowl to his mouth. Grains of rice and bits of mashed pumpkin spill onto the bedsheets. He has been eating his dinner for forty-five minutes, and has managed to get through almost a quarter of the portion. He finally gets the spoon to his mouth, but most of the food has already fallen off. He puts the spoon back down and sighs. It is late afternoon in St Michael's Nursing Home. Sunlight is slowly sinking into dusk. The cream-coloured fibro walls have a faint orange glow. Pop looks out the small window as a packed train shoots past and rattles the glass. On a chest of drawers beside the bed, packets of pills are stacked at the foot of a vase holding daffodils and chrysanthemums.

Every afternoon for the last six months, I have sat in this room and watched my grandfather become a breathing ghost. The only thing that keeps his flesh from turning into ash is his pride, and a pulse that grows slower by the day. He lies before me, bedridden, skin as frail as tissue paper, arms and legs whittled away to sinew and bone. His feet are pink and swollen and poke out the bottom of bed sheets permanently stained with the blood and pus that seep from his bedsores. The stench of stale faeces is imbedded in the fibro walls and in my nostrils. At ninety-five, Pop's mind is still sharp, but his organs act their age, so he is aware of every bowel mishap and every marathon meal. His mind is forced to bear front-row witness as his body splutters and trembles through each hour. It's a cruel binary. He cannot even hide in unawareness. He simply goes on, another breath after one more breath, sighs in place of tears, and a wan smile to mask a wince; all the trappings of irrational Australian manhood, right to the last pulse and the last dry blink. He is a wharfie from Port Melbourne. In my wallet I keep a black and white photo of him standing tall in his work clothes, cradling my mother in his arms.

Pop was born and raised in the industrial crucible of The Borough.

His body is adorned with the scars of the factory, the wharves, the football field. But his mind and manner are softened by the graces of fatherhood, lifelong friendships, and simple pleasures like holding his granddaughter's hand as she picked flowers in the park, or teaching his grandson how to kick a drop punt. Over these last few months, he has told me many stories. I have seen him as a skinny child, an athletic young man, a husband, and a grandfather. I have also seen his city: W-class trams rolling in Carlton or bluestone factories billowing smoke in Collingwood during the Depression. Pop has always told me stories, but now that I am older, I am aware of how people's lives ebb and flow through time and place.

When I think of Port Melbourne, I picture my grandfather as a boy, running barefoot through laneways to warn his dad and the other wharfies that the scabs were about to arrive at Prince's Pier. I walk down Swanston Street and see him on the day Whitlam was sacked: a middle-aged wharfie, sleeves rolled up, amidst a throng of people and placards. Memories woven through the streets of Melbourne, from days and dates that funnel down the decades to this day, this bed and this impossible present, where the only prospect is to perish, and the only hope, to do it with dignity.

'Where'd you go today?' he asks me.

'A few shops in Richmond. Bridge Road, Swan Street, and a new shopping centre near the skipping girl.'

This is enough for him to go on with. It will take him away from this room for a while. That's why I lie. I didn't really go to Richmond today, and I didn't really go to Preston yesterday. But it's a way of entertaining him without it seeming like I'm deliberately trying to distract him. Besides that, I like hearing his stories. It is true that I'm a courier driver, but I only ever go to the greater Dandenong area, or along the Mornington Peninsula. After Pop's first few weeks in St Michael's, he had exhausted his memories of places like Berwick and Rosebud, so I suddenly had a change in my delivery run, a wider itinerary that took me (and him) all across the city.

Pop takes the bait and tells a story from his days as a young foundry worker in Richmond. He sliced off part of his finger, and left it sitting in the sawdust because it was knock-off time and he had a date with my grandma. The scar is still there on his index finger. That abandoned piece of flesh, however, lies somewhere beneath the concrete foundations of Victoria Gardens shopping centre.

'Look for it next time you're there,' he says, and I laugh. 'You got soccer tomorrow?'

'Yep. At home…no, sorry, away…at Flemington, near the commission flats and the bypass.'

'Flemington?' He smiles. 'I saw Phar Lap the day he won the Melbourne Cup. My old man woke me up at the crack of dawn so we could get a good spot by the finishing post. We didn't move from there all day. I couldn't even go to the dunny. It was worth it, though. I saw him flash past, big shiny red coat. I could feel the thud of his hoofs shooting up my legs when he passed the post.' Pop looks down at his legs, which haven't worked for six months.

'So, we're playing the top team tomorrow, Pop. They're very strong, very tough. Got two big defenders who are hard to get through.'

'Well…maybe you and your mates are faster than they are.'

'Yeah, we're probably faster.'

'Well then, you go around them instead of through them. Everyone is good in certain ways. Some are quick, some are strong. Ian Stewart… now, he wasn't fast, but he was a strong mark for his size. So he'd focus on that. I remember walking past Punt Road one night, and I stopped to watch them train for a bit. Now, the other blokes were doing sprints, but Stewart was off with the trainers, getting them to kick high bombs to him so he could practice his leap. That kind of thing worked well for him. Triple Brownlow medallist.

'Bobby Skilton, too. He was the smallest bloke on the field, and he'd walk off the Lakeside Oval every week with two black eyes, but he could kick with both feet…just beautiful. Tony Shaw, there's another one. He was fat and slow but he went and got the ball, and he was a leader. Premiership captain. It's the same in anything, really, not just football. People do different things well. A lawyer could know the ins and outs of every law in the country, but he mightn't be able to fix his dunny. Us wharfies couldn't do our taxes, but we could stow three hundred boxes of fine china so they wouldn't move a centimetre from here to London. So, you do what you can. Whatever situation you're in, you do what you can.'

I nod. He picks up the spoon again and tries to manoeuvre some rice and pumpkin. He sighs. The conversation has worn him out. His hand is still shaking and the spoon rattles against the plastic bowl.

'Do you want me to just steady your hand for you, Pop, like Mum and Erin do? You hold the spoon and I'll just sort of wrap my hand around yours and...prop you up.'

'Nah, she's right. We'll get there. Is it cold out?' He has another go with the spoon.

'Ah...no, it's quite nice actually.' I suddenly realise that, since I was about ten, I have only ever touched his hand in handshakes. Even when I was a little kid, I only held his hand when crossing the road.

'Where do you go tomorrow?' he asks. More bits of rice and pumpkin spill onto his chest.

'I'm heading to Williamstown, Yarraville, around there...Footscray too.'

There's hardly any food left on the spoon as it rattles against his teeth. Little bits of pumpkin are smeared on his chin and lips. I hand him a serviette and pick up a few bits of food from the bed sheets. I begin adjusting the table so that the bowl is closer to his mouth.

'Yeah, we'll move it up a bit...thanks...that's better.'

I look at his swollen feet and notice that the left one is a little puffier than the right. I walk to the end of the bed to have a closer look. 'Did you get bitten here, Pop?'

'Oh...that.' He chuckles and then coughs. 'You need to speak to the Association of Steamship Owners about that one. And Bob Pratt.'

'Bob Pratt?' I sit back down and listen.

'First things first. I was working the hand crane at Williamstown, loading slings of wheat and sugar. Now, the metal twine was replaced every few months, but the pulleys were more expensive, so the shipowners would only fork out for them every year or so, and they'd rust after only a few weeks of winter.' He takes a breath. 'So we loaded the sling, tested the weight, and I heard a creaking sound. I looked up and, bang, down she comes, the whole load. The wheat bags tumbled into the hatch and whacked some poor blokes on the head. The pulley came down on my foot and crushed some of the nerves.'

I look at his foot again.

'I had to take three months off work and football. Then in my first game back, at Coburg, I was on Bob Pratt. I thought I was OK for the first ten minutes or so, then he stomped on my foot as he made a lead. It felt like a railway peg driven straight through my foot. I missed the rest of the season.'

We talk some more about sport and places around Melbourne. But he's tired, and the conversation gradually peters out. He begins to doze off.

'I'm just going to the toilet, Pop.'

He doesn't answer.

'Pop?' My heart beats quicker. 'Pop?'

'Wha'?' he says, drowsily.

I act like I'm not frightened. 'I'm just going to the toilet.'

'Oh…all right…listen…give us the bowl. I better finish this before they come to take it off me. Put the bed down a bit, I've got an idea.'

I lower the bed, so he's lying flatter.

He grimaces as he tucks his left arm high up towards his chin. 'Now wedge the bowl in there…that's it. Now give us the spoon…ta…I'll scrape it in.'

I leave Pop to grapple with his new theory.

I open the door and see the grinning face of Dimitri, a senile, incoherent man who wanders in and out of any door left open. His face is always set in a look of mild surprise, with his bushy grey eyebrows slightly raised. He gently grasps my collar and mumbles a mishmash of heavy breathing and Greek. I reach behind me and close the door.

'Your room's this way, Dimitri.'

We shuffle off down the hall. He is shaking, as always.

'Your room's this way...through here. *There* we go. That's the way. OK.'

I leave Dimitri standing in front of the mirror in his room. He stares, knees bent, trembling arms outstretched towards his reflection. He reminds me of a young child teetering on the edge of a diving board, contemplating the depth and coldness to come. I close the door and head to the toilet.

I return to Pop's room. I open the door and feel the squish of rice underneath my shoes. I look down. The plastic bowl is upturned behind the door and the spoon lies in a little mound of mashed pumpkin at my feet. Pop's mouth is agape, his eyes frozen wide open. His arm dangles by the side of the bed. A grain of rice clings to his index finger.

I stare at his hand. I stare at his mouth, his eyes. I don't know what to do. I look at the nurses' buzzer. I look at my feet. Then I turn to the window. Another packed train flashes past towards Dandenong and rattles the glass. And here, in this room that was never home, are two men: the man I am and the man I have always longed to be. And there's a spoon upon the floor, some flowers in a vase, and a hand to hold, now, till the warmth runs cold.

Liam Brooks

Longing for homeland

for Father

exiled to a patch of green
the cat and he till the same land
and every year at harvest
excitement follows unpeeled skins
when he could just as easy
buy them at the store
and spare himself the rake and hoe

his children stare unmoved at this longing
mystified by a bowl of new potatoes
they neither want nor eat

the story of this one small thing
beyond their hearts to understand
they see the loss in Janus eyes
and how he vacates some moment of pain
because of vegetable skins

like Columbus
he brings potatoes to a new world
waits in vain for their discovery

Lucy Czerwiec

With my father at Te Kopuru

A man may connect thus with his origins.
It is a form of musing, like falling asleep.
We stood at the gateposts, on the edge
of the overgrown paddock, in the warmth
of the afternoon sun. The gateposts
were all that remained of the old men's home
where my father spent his childhood.

The paddock ended in willows and a creek.
A cold wind blew, chasing the clouds across,
and we woke from his dream of a life
so long ago – the dead men, the crippled heroes,
his mother and father fighting and making love.
Somewhere, elsewhere, that creek ran on
and, where it came out, the sea ground on the land
beneath the shadow of a ruined jetty, as we drove away.

Stephen Smithyman

Submerging

The veins on Grandpa's legs protruded like thick tidal lines. Sam and Caleb scrambled to catch up, their toes vanishing and reappearing in the chalky sand as they trailed him homewards. Sam stared up at the island's cliff, its base gnawed away by the climbing ocean, leaving only a thin shelf. Other places were submerging too. The jetty where he had nearly caught that white sea snake was completely underwater. *I would have brought it in, jewelled skin glittering silver and white, if only they'd let me.*

*

Once home, Sam and Caleb sink into their beanbags and watch *Family Guy* as the aroma of stewing fish, breadfruit and coconut milk wafts out from Grandpa's kitchen.

This was the family; Dad did not count, not any more. He had nicked off to Brisbane. Their two aunts lived in New Zealand and never visited.

Sam remembered his Grandpa's words: 'Everyone runs away.'

Caleb will leave. All his brother spoke of was Queensland and the trip their dad had taken them on. Those adventure parks where the mad rides were higher than any dune they had ever run down; the flash cars that purred; the beach girls that came in every colour.

Tavloa is a paradise – it just needs some care. It was their place and their island and their ocean.

'Sam! Caleb!' hollered Grandpa. 'Set the table.'

The boys placed cutlery and bowls on the small pine table that still managed to saturate the kitchen space.

'Groper today, boys.' Grandpa ladled the steaming stew out before them and clasped his ocean-scarred hands together. 'Thank you, Christ our Lord, for our dinner, and take care of our ancestors.'

They crossed themselves and dug into the large fish, which was good, soft and flaky-white. A change too – usually they used those finicky finer nets to catch the tiny ones, like baitfish.

'Just got to adapt, I guess,' Grandpa would say. 'Lil'uns are tasty. But years ago there was big fish everywhere.' He gestured, as did all fisherman, spreading his arms to indicate size. 'Those ships way out've scooped 'em up and the lil'uns have grown crazy with fewer big'uns to eat 'em.'

Ordinarily, Sam could not wait for Sunday. Tomorrow was when everyone gathered outside the town hall after church. They would gorge themselves on pigs off the spit, crunching on the salty crackling and then tearing into the white meat beneath as the juice and fat dribbled down their lips and over their fingers.

But tomorrow was the dance.

Sam stared at his plate.

'You'll get it one day, Sam,' said Grandpa. 'Just be strong, be patient.'

Caleb laughed. Sam jabbed his brother in the rib.

'Hey! I didn't mean nothin'.'

Sam gripped his fork and stabbed down at some pale flesh on his plate. *It isn't right. My arms slap the wrong places.* He often hid away behind the rusted goat shed and practised until his feet felt heavier than iron but his body did not respond like the other boys'. Disobedient knees buckled when he spread them; his shoulders slid when they should tremble.

They washed the dishes then sat at the table as Grandpa warmed some goats' milk on the stove.

He unwrapped a bowl next to him, revealing two mangrove crabs already painted red by boiling water, and brought them to the table. 'We'll eat 'em tomorrow night.'

Caleb grabbed a claw and pretended to cut his wrist off.

'We only had one or two of these ever when I was a boy,' continued Grandpa. 'Didn't really have a mangrove swamp back then. Caught six today, gave two away and sold the other couple.'

'They're massive,' said Sam.

'You boys be careful down 'em mangroves. Could really snap your hand off there, Caleb.'

Sam picked one up, rapped the hard shell and gingerly touched the spikes near the joints.

'Remember to take a long stick to test for bogs around the 'groves. Some of that mud sinks dangerously. You'll do your part to grow that swamp on the east side and plant 'em mangrove trees to keep the ocean back.'

Grandpa's talk of the mangroves and combating the ocean was an echo the boys heard time and time again.

While they sipped their milk, Grandpa told a tale of an ancestor who called turtles to the boat. It was said he would feed the entire village in a single outing. 'One day, however,' his voice hushed, 'he called too many, and turtles of all kinds: leatherbacks, greens, browns, leapt from the water onto the craft. Their shells cut into calves and feet. Others yelled at him to stop, eventually pushin' 'im down and wrappin' their hands round his mouth, but it was too late, they kept leapin' on board until the craft sunk, drownin' the Turtle Caller and all the crew. Some say they're still on that ocean bed and if you fish that spot you'll know 'cause you can still hear his ghost callin' for 'em turtles.'

The boys shared the mattress, feet to head.

'You'll be OK tomorrow,' said Caleb. 'It's just a dance.'

'Yeah,' Sam said as he lay there, sleeplessly awaiting the grey light of dawn.

*

A throng of people gathered around the three pigs smoking on spits in the foyer of the whitewashed hall. The boys formed two lines with gaps so that everyone could see. It would be better if the girls weren't watching; their brown eyes swallowed him. Grandpa, with an encouraging smile, stood behind Seth the instructor. Sam imagined Seth as his grandpa's younger reflection. Muscular, able.

Caleb turned round in front of him with a wink that said, *It'll be fine*. When they began the chant, Sam felt OK as his first knee bent but then the smoke from the spits floated over, almost choking him. He lost rhythm.

Seth called a halt. 'Sam, hit that leg, let your knee tremble and your body will follow.'

'It's the smoke,' his voice quavered.

'Don't blame the smoke. Watch.' And Seth shifted from one bent knee to the other, his chest shaking in response. 'See?'

Sam gulped some phlegm and fought to hold back tears. There was too much shame in crying.

They started again. In the background, fat dripped onto the coals, striking it in sharp sizzles. The air was heavy, leaden with the heat. Once more, he missed the step. Everything buzzed. Sounds blurred and amplified: the laughter, the hissing and crackling, the dull thud of their feet on the pavement. He hung his head. His eyes watered a little, surely from the smoke. He was not some crybaby.

He pushed past one dancer, then another and another. Girls pointed at him; the crowd pointed too as he shoved his way clear through them all.

'Sam!' Grandpa called.

Grandpa wouldn't catch him. Sam's toes hit the ground as he sprinted through the village. Past the few tiny shops joined together by common walls. Past the sole asphalt road and the fenceless homes with overgrown beach shrubs. His mind emptied as the wind cooled his face and his heart drove blood to all parts of his body. He held his head straight and pumped his muscles, even when his calves ached and his thighs trembled.

Once out of the village he kept running, now more measured. One, two. One, two. As his pace slowed he began to think of isolated places. The caves? Too damp. Too dark. The beaches? Too open. He decided on the mangroves. *This is my island. No one can steal it from me. Not the dance, not the rising ocean, not my father in Brisbane, and not the people drawn to the mainland that blinds them.*

One, two, one, two. Across the island he ran. Around the small brackish lake that had held fresh water in his grandpa's youth. Past the scrubland and the crumbling house of some former English governor. He ran until his breath wheezed and all that could move him were the numbers: one, two, one, two, one, two. He reached the swamp's outskirts, jogged for a while before entering the shallows. As the foggy water sprayed his ankles, he did not feel the midges and sandflies or see the mudskippers hop away or notice the crabs retreating with pincers raised.

The wind between the swamp trees sounded like the faint singing of old ladies who knew all the hymns. Soon he was in a world of shadow, mangrove branches above him, occasional blades of light piercing gaps between the trees. Standing cormorants, their prehistoric wings held out to dry, flew from his approach.

He'd go deeper, out to where the bogs stopped and you could swim if you were gutsy enough. But his feet sank, plunging up to his calves in mud. He made to move and it swept up higher. Again he stirred and this time it climbed to his knees. *Be still. That way it'll take longer to sink. Move and no one will arrive in time.*

He yelled, a wordless noise. If anyone were searching for him, they would be a while yet.

To stem his breathing rate, he counted the air in and out.

His thoughts fled briefly to hopes of a vague future. To finding a wife who wanted to stay on the island; to becoming a fisherman like Grandpa and a better family man than his dad.

The mud rose slightly, concealing his knees. He yelled once more. This time his mind sank into the past as if the mud laid claim to him. Sam remembered fragments from as far back as four. His mother, with eyes like warm coals and hair that fell in waves like the night ocean. He remembered when they all slept together, sandwiched on that same bed with Grandpa sleeping alone in the other room.

He remembered the UN men who came with countless sandbags, instructing the islanders on where and how to lay them to keep the ocean back. Sam could recall their words but only one face, a Welsh UN officer, John, with a mop of red curls and a moustache that flamed down his face to his chin. 'Nice place,' John said and his lagoon-like eyes gazed at Sam's mother. Sam, even then, knew something was askew, and grabbed his mother's hand to lead her away. But their eyes stuck like the eyes of competitors. Who knew where they disappeared to on the island? His mother abandoned them all for Wales soon after. He wanted more from her than farewell, more than tears.

The mud gradually crept up to his thighs. By the time Sam was five, his father, defeated, no longer fished with Grandpa. He became flabby like a seal. It was Grandpa who allowed Dad to leave. When they came into the house that afternoon, it had reeked of that overly-sweet stench of coconut left to rot. Dad had not cleaned at all but sat by the tinny radio, listening to the stories of others. Grandpa switched the machine off. Dad stood up, swung at Grandpa and missed. Another side of Grandpa unveiled itself as the old man's hand snaked out and grabbed his son's throat. Dad's cheeks turned the colour of a bruise as Grandpa spoke. 'Don't let this hurt swallow your life.'

The mud climbed, tickling Sam's testicles.

'Help!' he screamed as loud as his lungs permitted.

He recalled his obsession with his teacher, Miss Rodanui, in Year Three. Drawing attention to himself by leaping onto a desk in class and reciting the opening of Roald Dahl's *Revolting Rhymes*. He remembered those stinking hot days. Sandy-coloured grass, no breeze, giant hornets terrifying them. He trailed her around the tyre swings in the dirt playground just to hear her voice and glimpse her face.

Muck seeped up to his nipples.

He remembered rafting with Caleb, way out past the breakers. The wind turned, slapping the raft, stirring the water. Shadowy clouds jostled overhead. They toppled and were caught in the white foam, twirling. Sam's arms thrashed until he found the raft's edge. He clambered up in a splutter and heaved Caleb – who was gripping the raft – back on board. Blood streamed from a gash in his brother's head into the ocean. It stained parts of the water a powdery red.

Mud neared his shoulders.

Just offshore. Sampson, the sea lion that mauled everyone's catch but they loved him regardless. Stingrays, which they handfed in the shallows, moving like dark ponds over the ocean-bed. The white sea snake that he wanted to bring in off the guano-stained jetty but they'd cut his line. 'Let me bring it in,' he'd called out as others around him laughed, making him feel red.

'Let me bring it in.' Those words recurred in his mind over and over as the mud reached his barely developed Adam's apple. Briny rivulets fled from his eyes, he lifted his head and shouted – or sobbed – repeatedly. 'Let me bring it in. Let me bring it in.'

There were voices in the distance. Sam looked over, his throat raw, his body ensnared.

Grandpa and Caleb lumbered through sludge on the far side of the bog. *Is there time?* Perhaps if there were, even with the jetty long since drowned, he would bring that ivory serpent in.

Anthony Panegyres

Born with no homeland

Write of your country's beauty, your lands, your rivers, your trees, she says.

My cells tremble,
a volcano sears my heart,
a storm is in my mind –
but silence controls me.

Dust, wars, dead bodies, weapons,
women with no power, children seeking water,
fill my mind.

Others extol their homelands
speak feelings of belonging,
great achievements,
spectacular views,
but nothing beautiful visits my mind –
not even a smile on a child's face.

People like me
can't say a word.

We were born with no homeland.

People like me
can't recall beautiful scenery.
We were too busy burying dead bodies.

We were born
with no skies, no stars, no moons.

The sun was there
but not for us.

We were born
with no relatives, no neighbours, no childhoods.

Air was there
but only contaminated air was ours.

People like us don't need pity.
We are strong enough.
We are still alive.

Ahlam Mohamed

Nostos

There are signs

Middens.

My big sister leads us out past the sandhills to the Island. It's not really an island. We're only allowed to go there as long as we stay away from the river, which is deep and dangerous. Children would drown in a minute.

The undertow is fierce where the river meets the ocean. We watched Dad swim across once and we thought he wasn't going to make it. The river got hold of him and pushed him right along towards the surf beach. My sister started to cry, *Daddy's drowning!* Dad got further and further away and smaller and smaller. Mum was scared, too, but she said, *He'll be all right. Dad's a strong swimmer.* We were glad when he climbed back up onto the bank on our side of the river. *Don't ever let me catch any of you going near that river*, he told us, *or I'll have the hides off you.*

So we steer clear of it, even though it holds a deadly fascination. But this day we pass it with hardly a glance. We are on an expedition. We're archaeologists. *Looking for artefacts*, my sister says. We march along in a line behind her, singing a French song she's been teaching us: *Sur le pont d'Avignon l'on y danse, oh l'on y danse.* The little ones can't get the words right and then they get puffed out and we have to wait for them. When my sister finds the right place we start to dig in the bank, scuffling out handfuls of sand, crumbled oyster and mussel shells and the roots of grasses and scrabbly bushes. We show her the shells and chipped stones we find and she decides whether they are artefacts or just bits of rubbish.

Then we get tired of digging and begin to skip the shells across the water, go paddling and look for pipis and soldier crabs. *This is where the Aborigines lived*, my sister says. *They made fires and cooked oysters. They didn't eat ordinary fish, only oysters and mussels and limpets and pipis and crayfish.* I wonder why. I ask her. She doesn't know. *Nobody does. They just stopped eating fish, that's all.*[1]

I try to imagine not eating fish, but I can't. We go floundering all the time, and netting in the surf for mullet and whiting and flathead. It's scary in the surf with the waves breaking about our ears, and Dad shouting not to let go of the end of the net, even when things flap around your legs, but it's exciting too. Floundering's better, though. You have to walk quietly, in the dark, with just the lantern to see by, and keep out of the way of the spear. It's hard to see the flounder on the bottom, in the mud, then whoosh, the spear hits and the fish tries to wriggle away. Later, eating them, straight out of the frying pan, all crisp and juicy, sucking the bones, licking your fingers. It's the best.

We spread out along the beach. *Stay where I can see you,* my sister calls. I go searching in the wind among the rocks on the seashore and under the wind-racked bushes. That's where I see them, far along the beach, on the waterline, the silent ones. They're playing in the little wavelets that frond and froth up onto the beach. The mothers and grandmothers digging pipis and dropping them into their string bags, the children soundlessly calling to one another, laughing silently as they wave and dance at the sea's edge. When I call back, only the sea answers and the wind and the squalling seagulls.

Language

She travels to Navajo, to a vast, high, wind-racked stone and grass place where the map-makers have chopped the land into four and called it New Mexico, Arizona, Utah and California. Oódtà is a quiet language which doesn't impose itself but seems to emerge from its surroundings. Lots of the words resemble the sound of branches bending and rubbing, grasses rustling, dry leaves and twigs cracking underfoot. Does language, she wonders, grow out of the place where it is born? Reflect the country of its origin, and shape the people who use it? And what of languages that are no longer spoken by anybody? Do they go back into the earth from which they grew? Are they still there somewhere?

Dead languages

Like Latin and ancient Greek. *Latin is a language as dead as dead can be, first it killed the Romans and now it's killing me.* But the books are still there, the statues, the temples. The evidence. They are real. Everybody knows Latin and ancient Greek are real. That they helped create English.

A Pakeha historian comes to Tasmania from New Zealand to speak at a writers' festival. He talks about the resurrection of lapsed tongues – dead languages – languages that have no longer any living speakers. *Are these resurrected languages authentic?* he asks the audience. No one answers. He poses another question: *If we discovered the score of a Beethoven sonata that had lain unseen, unknown, unplayed for more than two centuries, and gave it to an orchestra, so that it was played in public once again, would we consider it to be an authentic Beethoven sonata or not?*

This historian has just published a history of the Moriori, at their request. *The Moriori,* he explains, *are the Indigenous people of Aotearoa, New Zealand. They occupied the land long before the colonising Maoris arrived in their canoes and massacred most of the Moriori. They enslaved the rest. New Zealand history states that the last Moriori died in 1948. Therefore the Moriori are extinct. As you can imagine, the Moriori people are not all that impressed with that version of their history. That's why they asked me to write another side to that story. I imagine some of you in the audience would appreciate the Tasmanian parallels.*

Languages with no words

I am walking on the mountain with my newly-adult son. We are talking about life, religion, history, art, politics, loss and grief as we walk up the track. I bemoan the loss of the Palawa languages, the old lore, the knowledge of the ancestors. He listens for a while, then, quite suddenly, dives into an icy-cold mountain pool and comes up with a slab of wet rock, embedded with fossils. He gives it to me with a grin: *Here you are, Mum, a history book. Learn to read it and stop whingeing.*

Mount Strzelecki, Flinders Island

I buy a second-hand grammar in Christopher's shop. Take it with me to Flinders Island. Read the word lists while I walk the coastline, pushed and pulled by the wind. Wonder about the Tasmanians who were brought to this island by Augustus Robinson to be 'civilised'. To learn to read and write English, to work, and to live in houses. How quickly they died, scouring the horizon for a glimpse of home.

One day she climbs a mountain, her senses keen, searching for footsteps, her ears straining for…

A few words and phrases begin to jostle together to form a poem. Palawa-kani and English juxtaposed. She speaks this poem on a deserted headland, to the air and the churning sea and the sky, to the wind-whipped marram grass. She listens for their response.

Mena legata I will tell you
how I climbed the rock-peaked mountain
the *poymalangta.*
I found a track made by the one-toed –
rialuganna – no *pugaluganna,*
black man's footprints,
on this hill.
Niripa crawled below me
her white waves curling
lukagana leapt among the gum trees
blowflies drank my sweat
Palla-nubra-na – the sun was high
but still I trembled –
mienni tyack –
for this *poymalangta* holds *warrawina,*
spirits of the dead.

Before she leaves the island, she reads the poem, red-faced and anxious, to one of the aunties. The old lady smiles. *Not too bad,* she says. *You must have patience and they will teach you.*

She sends the Pakeha historian a rock crusted with fossils. He writes back, *I received your history book yesterday. Thank you so much. Write and tell me what else you know.* Then he and his wife are killed in a road accident.

The losses mount.

Terry Whitebeach

1. A common misconception that still holds currency is that the only seafood the Palawa ate was shellfish.

The trees of Antarctica

I can sing a true song about myself,
tell of my travels, how in days of tribulation
I often endured a time of hardship,
how I have harboured bitter sorrow in my heart
and often learned that ships were homes of sadness.
> From 'The Seafarer', Anglo-Saxon poem,
> author unknown, c. AD 900

It was late in the afternoon when we finally left Hobart. After only a couple of hours, we were well and truly out to sea. Nothing but sea and sky and the occasional bird. It was close to the longest day of the year. The sun set late.

I spent as long as I could on deck. I didn't want to meet my cabin mates – I resented having to share with anyone.

This is what I longed for – emptiness.

*

I tell Sue that my strongest memory of that trip is the sense of lightness, of evaporating, while standing on deck, staring at the sea. She is visiting me in Hobart twelve years later.

We sit close together on my lounge, looking at photos, or watching slides projected on the living room wall.

Sue made a film with her super-8 camera of the mosses and lichen beds near Casey Station. She called it *The Trees of Antarctica*. I remember when Sue showed me the film about a year after the trip, I felt like I was flying over a forest. Sue says that she had forgotten about the film. It's been sitting in a box at her place in Melbourne.

She tells me that her strongest memory is of coming into the cabin a couple of days into the voyage, and finding me sobbing on my bunk. And of me telling her about Rory. He'd died in the snow about eighteen months before, on a bushwalking trip in the Adirondack mountains, New York State. I was with him.

Sue told me then that her friend, Tibb, died of cancer not long before the trip. His death was expected; she spent a lot of time with him while he was sick – and dying.

*

I got to know every inch of the *Icebird*'s outer deck, the parts where we were allowed to be. The green-painted floor, the crisp walls, the top half white, the bottom part grey, the orange lifebuoys and boats, the huge ropes, all became very familiar. It was all so clean, so bright, so comforting in a steely kind of way. I even loved the smell of the paint. The greasy mix of diesel and cooking fumes at the back of the ship didn't put me off. I felt at home.

The sea was calm – it was the calmest trip the *Icebird* crew had ever experienced. I was grateful. I get seasick on the Derwent. Some people wished for stormy weather, but not me. I wandered around the deck and gazed at the sea.

*

Sue tells me that a huge albatross followed the ship for much of the trip south. It used to hover in the wake of the ship. She says she got to know it quite well, as it was often there when she went out the back to smoke a joint.

I vaguely remember a white bird, but I can't remember an albatross following the ship.

*

I had been cocooned by my friends' love and support since Rory's death, friends I had not known for long. I'd even had a visit from my mother, a big effort for her. Recently, the gloss of my grief had worn off, at least for others – I felt that they were growing weary of my need.

I'd bought a house not long before the voyage, and was trying to cope by myself. It wasn't working.

*

The first iceberg was sighted about three days into the trip; fairly far north, someone said. It was a momentous occasion – much clicking and whirring of cameras by those of us who hadn't been south before. Of course those who had, gave us knowing looks and told us that we would see much more impressive icebergs later. We were excited and took the photos anyway.

After the first iceberg sighting, we were given iceberg-watching duties. We had two-hour shifts. Sue and I were on together. We laughed hysterically during our efforts to work out how to use the iceberg-measuring instrument – a sextant? – and hoped that the records weren't being relied on for serious research.

Sue has a picture of herself, holding the implement – upside-down, she now knows. She says that we chose a late iceberg watch – 10 p.m. to midnight – in the hope that we would see an aurora. We didn't – maybe there was too much light. She tells me about the intense blues and greens of the ice and the sea at sunset.

*

The word went out – whales! Everyone raced to the side of the ship to look at them. A pod of sleek dark creatures, too large for dolphins, swam close to the ship. There were quite a few of them, pilot whales we were told. I was a bit disappointed that the first whales I had ever seen were so small.

*

The days were getting longer. There was less and less night, more and more light. The engines thrummed beneath me, the sea gently rocked me, but I couldn't sleep. I'd been sleeping badly since long before we left Hobart. Now it was even worse. Sue's snoring didn't help.

Sue and her colleague, Ted, were on the trip doing a multi-media education project. It made no sense to me, what they were doing, but then I was completely uninterested in anything generated by a computer, other than words. I was even having trouble stringing those together on this trip.

*

We took to lying on our bunks, Sue and I, sipping port bought from the ship's shop, watching icebergs drift by. We were accompanied by Bob Marley, on Sue's portable CD player. Ted joined us sometimes.

We were on a South Seas cruise. There was nothing else, but the sea, with its mushy ice and icebergs of all shapes and sizes, and the sky, and the ship. Bergy bits, which had broken off decaying icebergs, scraped the sides of the ship. The icebergs had an intense blue at their core.

*

We travelled further south, the days drifted into each other – there was no division between night and day any more, only a few minutes of twilight as the sun dipped below the horizon. At 'night', there were videos in the mess, and there was the bar, The Freezer, which was on the lower deck. I spent most of my time out on deck, unless there was a special occasion. We had the captain's birthday party. We danced to 60s and 70s music, someone played their guitar, some people sang. People got very drunk. I danced with Ted.

*

After our iceberg watch, Sue tells me, she would stay up until four or five in the morning and sleep in until lunch. Our body clocks stopped working. I remember lying on my bunk, a top one, only half asleep. Only a few others and I were usually up for breakfast.

Sue says I was in a daze during that trip. Maybe that's why my memories are so sketchy. She reminds me that we shared the voyage with some glaciologists. One of them, she says, had a beautiful image of an ice crystal on his T-shirt. I can't remember it.

The glaciologists were studying ice cores, taken from deep in the ice cap. They studied the composition of ancient ice, to detect signs of climate change, including changes to the vegetation that covered the Antarctic land mass eons ago.

*

As we got closer to the continent, we reached the pack ice. Huge clunking noises resounded throughout the ship. I spent hours at the bow watching the ice, dark fractures forming as the ship forced its way through. Occasionally we saw crab-eater seals resting on the ice. There were more birds as well; we even saw a couple of emperor penguins, standing in their stately fashion on ice floes.

*

On Christmas Day, we had reindeer races in the bar, organised by the army contingent. The reindeer were perfectly formed little black cardboard cut-outs that stood up on a hexagonal 'track', marked out on the floor with black tape. We formed teams; each team owned a reindeer. The reindeer raced around the track according to dice throw; our reindeer was knocked out early on.

There was more drinking, and more dancing. I hadn't danced like this since the parties Rory and I used to have in Hobart.

On Boxing Day we were close to Casey. We were in the pack ice, and there were icebergs everywhere. It was overpoweringly beautiful.

*

Arriving at Casey was a shock. After a week at sea, in our own dimension, surrounded by the sea and the sky and the ice, we stared in disbelief at its ugliness. It was what I imagined a mining camp to be: dirt roads, vehicles and box-like metal buildings. The shipping container seemed to be the design model here. There were a few patches of dirty snow marked with vehicle tracks.

There was no time to be indignant. To disembark, we had to climb down a rope ladder over the side of the ship into a waiting LARC (an amphibious vehicle). It was an alarming thought that we had to entrust our safety to the army men we were drinking with the night before.

Much of our time at Casey is a blur. Sue, Ted and I slept on mattresses on the floor of the gym in the Red Shed – the living quarters. We were lucky to be able to stay ashore, some of the other round-trippers from the ship had to sleep on board.

There was a radio station operated by the expeditioners, Sue tells me. She says that whoever was on 'slushy' duty in the kitchen got to choose the music. I remember someone kept playing 'Achey Breaky Heart'. It was like a ski lodge gone wrong.

*

Sue also remembers a tour of the medical quarters, seeing a stainless steel bath chamber which was used for reviving hypothermia patients, and thinking, *this is what Rory needed.* She worried about the effect this sight might have on me. I vaguely recall the medical quarters but not the hypothermia chamber.

*

When Rory was dying, in the snow, we were a long way from any help. He had been weakened by an illness he'd picked up in Nepal a few months before and succumbed quickly to hypothermia. I cursed my lack of first-aid skills – I had no idea what to do. My fumblings with sleeping bag, tent and hot soup were of no use. At thirty-three, Rory was too young to die.

When I knew all hope was gone, I had to take the tent and leave Rory lying there in the snow. I needed to find a flat place to camp before dark.

The sound of early morning thunder always takes me back to the morning after Rory's death. Lying, alone, in our tent in the snow, thunder rumbling in the distance, desolate, stunned. I packed up. I had to walk past where I had left Rory the day before. In my mind's eye I had a picture of him – sitting up in the snow waiting for me, impish smile on his lovely face. I can still summon that image. But he was lying where I'd left him, sodden sleeping bag uselessly covering him.

That day I walked for seven hours through the snow. I noticed everything, marvelled at pale patterns on birch trunks, delicate pointy larch fronds, icicles hanging from small frozen waterfalls. I broke into a ranger's hut by smashing a window with a snow shovel. I put on dry clothes, cooked food, spread out my tent, sleeping bag and clothes to dry. I wondered whether I could just stay there. It was warm and comfortable, but sense prevailed and I radioed for help. I inspected my numb, frost-nipped fingers, toes and legs.

A helicopter arrived – I was delivered safely to the senior ranger's house. The kindness of that family broke my trance.

*

The round-trippers were taken on a tour to Shirley Island, a small island about a kilometre from the station; we walked across the sea-ice to get there. The air was thick with the voices and droppings of thousands of Adélie penguins. Adélies are classic, small, dinner-suited penguins, with triangular heads.

We had never before been so confronted with the reality of life for wild animals. A skua landed, its great brown and white wings flapping to earth. Skuas were waiting near penguins on their nests – a wrong move could mean the end for an egg or chick. Blood stained the ice.

*

One of my jobs for the Antarctic Division was to inspect the condition of the protected area at Bailey Peninsula, near the station. It is special for the plants which grow there – mosses and lichens.

Sue went with me. She didn't have a permit, so as an 'inspector', I should have arrested her. Instead, we looked at the fascinating shapes and colours of the mosses and lichens, which were so remarkable in this landscape dominated by ice. Sue filmed the plants, close-up, with her super-8 camera.

*

A few of us were taken to Robinson's Ridge by Arthur, a winterer; he was glad to take us as this was his last field trip. Robbo's is a two-hour, twenty-kilometre trip from Casey. It is a world away.

The sheer snow slope beckoned to me – I could fall into it, become part of it. Sue and I had been reprimanded the day before by the station leader for trying to sneak off, unauthorised, with skis. We realised now that we couldn't have skied anyway, the snow was icy and ended in a drop over a cliff.

Sue wrote a letter to her husband Michael and four-year-old son, Simmy, when we returned to Casey and posted it there with an Antarctic stamp (though it went back to Hobart with us on the *Icebird*):

We went for a long walk down on the snow. We walked along an ice-cliff overlooking the beautiful bay. There was an island in the bay with a penguin rookery. We could hear thousands of penguins, all talking to each other from across the water. A few penguins swam across the water and came quacking towards us, waving their wings like little arms. They were not scared of us at all. During the night we heard loud booming and crashing sounds – it was the ice crashing into the sea from the cliffs where we had been walking.

I stayed outside the hut as much as I could – it was very cosy in there, but the weather was clear outside. I had never been in such a beautiful place. I saw a snow petrel nesting in a nook in some rocks. I watched the sun setting over the slope behind the hut; everything – the hut, the tall triangular tent next to it, the snow, the rocks – was glowing orange-pink.

*

When I'm thinking about that luminous landscape, I want to be back there, alone, on the cliffs, looking out to sea.

*

The station held a barbecue to mark the departure of the *Icebird*. Our return voyage was taking back the Casey winterers, some of whom, including Arthur, had spent well over a year at the station. It was a difficult time for them, though they handled it as brashly as everything else.

*

It was New Year's Eve, and as a special treat, the captain steered a course through 'Iceberg Alley' or Peterson's Bank, with its rows of spectacular icebergs. A pod of killer whales accompanied us for a while. It was good to be back on the ship.

We saw in the New Year with a party, in the mess, out on deck, in the bar.

*

The return voyage is even more hazy than the trip down. After that first night, the atmosphere on board was more subdued, reflecting the mood of the returning winterers. I found an empty cabin where I could try to sleep in peace.

As we approached Hobart, after more than a week at sea, we could feel the tension in the air. The winterers were very quiet. I can't pretend to know what was going through their minds.

About a day out from Hobart, Tasmania was enveloped in the scent of eucalyptus. It must have been an overwhelming sensation for the winterers, if it was strong even to those of us who had been at sea and on the ice for only three weeks.

*

The ship was bagpiped to the wharf by the army chap, fully kilted, who, I now remember, had piped our other arrivals and departures. The winterers, especially, were hanging over the side of the ship looking out for family and friends. There were lots of people waiting on the wharf, waving, excited.

I waited on the ship for as long as I could; I couldn't see any of my friends on the wharf. Sue and I were the last passengers to say goodbye.

I felt as if I had been cut adrift.

I returned to my empty house in South Hobart. I was greeted at the doorstep by Rory's old shoes, flowers growing in them.

Sharon Moore

Frog forest

among the trees
frogs call and call

shoes on the boardwalk
stamp where the green light shows

faces lean over info boards
staring at misty photos

reading sparse words
on former habitats

former lives
then move on

flicking the occasional eye
toward the water below

still and clear
with only a dead leaf   floating

casting ghost shadows
and still the frogs call

from their microchipped throats
for the ears gliding by

repeating their songs
from the belly
of the archives

Duncan Richardson

Subdivision

Surveyor pegs section the land
sloping down
to our secret beach –

A gravel scar slashes
bracken and brown pasture
haunted with lanolin scent
and the scattered vertebrae,
whiter than surf crest,
of last year's early lambs.

At the twisted eucalypt
the dozers didn't fell,
a family of iridescent wrens
flickers in thin shade,

while a white-breasted sea eagle
carves its orbit across a winter-blue sky
and four black cockatoos, with harsh *kee-ows*,
wing low above their shadows.

Soon, the sealed roads and water pipes,
gardens fenced and flowering,
window-glass seared by the flame
of new dawns, domestic cats stalking
the shy bandicoot and potoroo

as the gauze of a snake's sloughed skin
crumbles to a whisper
and the midden on the outcrop by the shore
dissolves into wind-borne sand.

Lyn Reeves

Climate change

I painted this room green
silky sage green
but days were hot
the paint dried too fast.

I placed Auntie Louise's
Jarra Jarra country painting
against the long wall
golden and grey   cooling.

I sat at the window
pink laminex on its side
looked out to the vegie garden
willow   empty pond.

I smiled at a blue wren
picking at dried-out crab apples
cried   as other birds fell gasping
from the sky.

Janet Galbraith

Ocean of sacrifice

We search for a place
of rest
where our whole self can stay
and calmly abide
while restless waves sleep.

In our land, there is no place to remain.
Cruel hills and steep cliffs push down,
allowing no rest,
pushing all to the lowlands.

Forced out of our native realm
for a foreign land
we rub earthly dust onto our chests,
leave our own place, weeping,
weeping, exhausted in this ocean of sacrifice

for no end, for nothing at all.

Kumar

After the fires, Kinglake (2)

she is keeping the bricked veranda
she sweeps it clear of leaves
these grey stains
are where the window-glass melted
onto the bricks
she is keeping it clear of leaves

nature is cheerful here
the trees thronging back
head-high already
after less than two years
bright leaves dress the black trunks
and the small creek is singing its stones again

it is all that is left of the house

she unfolds a chair on the bricks
above the valley hazed with burnt trees
and the air resounds
with his heartbeat, his loss

she is sweeping the brick veranda
she is keeping it clear of leaves

Pam Schindler

Staying on

Everybody who comes to Salty Beach says the same thing at one time or another. They sniff, go on about the clean air, put on their parkas and scarves and can't get enough wind in their hair. They think the locals are all pleasant.

And then reality sets in and you can see them thinking, *Oh, there's no cinema for nearly two hours* and *Is that really the best coffee in town?* They spend half a Friday night in the pub – the better half, mind you – and their seaside fantasy pops. The breeze becomes a howling wind and they can never keep their hair in place. They put the house up for sale then and the next delusional mug comes along and says, 'What a steal' and it starts all over again.

But Juice was different. He turned up in February 1986. I know because it was the day after the wife died and I was staring out to sea trying to find something to grab onto – a gull, a ship, anything, and there was this bloke in a suit and tie, no shoes, strolling along the tideline, stopping regularly to examine last night's leavings. Suit and tie, but no shoes. I'll be buggered. Well, it was something to grab onto, that was certain.

It was hot even though it was only nine in the morning and it would've been hotter out on the sand. We'd had a run of days over 30° and no one could sleep. At three a.m. you'd see lights flick on, smell snags cooking on barbies, hear young ones skylarking in the water and worry if they were going to be all right. Wish Gracie hadn't had to put up with it. Those last few days I couldn't keep her cool, no matter what I did. Well, we had a fan in the bedroom but it made her shiver and then we'd cover her with a sheet but it hurt. A sheet hurt her – that's how ill she was. It was a nasty business and I wouldn't say this to anyone else, but I found it hard to watch. Very hard. Would rather it had been me, except then she'd be the one left behind.

I must've been watching the sea for an hour or more before Juice came along and I don't mind admitting I'd been crying most of the time. The nurse said it was mainly fatigue, but I'd been far more tired plenty of times.

I was sitting on a treated-pine pole far enough from a picnic table so anyone could use it if they had a mind, but close enough so I could still use the shade. The year before, the council had put in a path along the dunes for people who wanted to walk *by the beach* not *on the beach*. Complete waste of taxpayer money, I remember saying, and yet plenty of people use it.

About half a dozen people had gone past before Juice and nodded, 'Hello, Mathew.' Would've seen tears and snot and bloodshot eyes but they didn't bother to stop. Just an arm around the shoulder or the offer to drop round next week might've been nice, but then I'd never asked anybody for anything so they probably thought I'd handle it on my own.

Juice marched two laps of the beach – about two clicks each way – then he stopped, and started stripping off. Had a waistcoat underneath his suit jacket so he must've been boiling. He took that off and his trousers, undid his tie and unbuttoned his shirt and then ran flat out at the water in his underpants. Lily-white, he was, but he had a torso that looked like he did something physical for a living.

When he dived in I thought, *Mind your neck!* It's a shallow bay and plenty before him had come out different to the way they'd gone in. To start with, he must've been scraping his hands along the bottom but pretty soon he was kicking out.

He could swim, that's for certain. I was relieved. Because if they don't cause damage in the shallows, they get in trouble in the deep, and I didn't want any more death that week. If anyone had asked, 'How're you going, Mathew?' I'd have said, 'I don't want any more death. Not this week.'

Juice swam and swam. He swam straight out from the beach as though he was heading for Burnie, Tasmania, one arm then the other, over and over in even pasty circles. He swam until I couldn't see him, and that's not because my eyes are crook, either. At sixty-eight, I've still got all my faculties, including my marbles, and that bloke Juice swam like a man possessed. Made me want to strip down to my underpants and head out too. Just for a bit of purpose, like. Straight out, he went.

I got uneasy then. Wondered if I was watching something I didn't want to see. A deliberate act of getting lost. I'd never fathomed that sort of thing. Though that day, my first day without Gracie for thirty-two years, I had a fleeting glimpse. Not that I'd tell anyone. No, people don't like talk of topping yourself. Over the years I've noticed it's the best way to keep folk away. Henry Villani talked morose and loose about his head problems after he came back from a stint in that city clinic until he was the only one sitting at the front bar – and that was saying something. Rudi Zahle was another. He'd corner women, probably because they tend to listen better than men…well, at least they nod and shake their heads and make funny little noises at the right times, but after a while even the nicest women turned their backs when he came in. And Dorothy Price was a woman herself who ran out of friends long before she took her last bow. There's a cliff at the eastern end of Salty Beach that people throw themselves off. It works. No one's survived so far. Remembering those who'd made quick work of it while no one was admiring the view from the lookout just ten metres away, reminded me that I still couldn't see Juice.

Kids and teens and parents started to spring onto the beach. It was after ten o'clock and getting too hot for the kiddies and their soft skin, but who am I to judge? We never did have kiddies ourselves. Just as I was considering raising the alarm to search for a determined swimmer, there he was. A pale flash and then another and before long I could see both arms winding round and round towards the shore, just as strong as before. I sat back down. Must've stood up to see what I could see. But my bottom was stiff from all that sitting. I punched the cheeks to get the blood going, heard a car pull in behind me and stopped punching, waved at the tinted window, though I didn't recognise the SUV, and started the warm walk back up Ozone Lane to No. 37.

The next time I saw Juice was when he moved into No. 44. A posh, long-term rental with views for miles, though I've always said that a view of the water is a view of the water. There's no need to spend the extra money going higher up the hill if all you're getting is more water. It's a rip-off. No one agrees with me but I'm holding to it.

I was out watering the front garden and pulling a few weeds. It wasn't seven o'clock yet after a dampish night, as though autumn wasn't too far round the corner. The automatic watering system I'd put in years ago was split somewhere and I simply couldn't find the energy to fix it. Everyone would've said, 'That's not like you, Mathew', so I didn't say anything. It was the day before Gracie's funeral so nobody came round the whole day anyway. If you'd asked them, they'd have told you they were letting me be alone in my grief, which I suppose was true. But I think they were just plain scared and it was just convenient to Leave Mathew Alone.

Obviously Juice didn't know because when he saw me he swanned down the steps of No. 44 and strode directly over, a cup in his hand. I thought, *Here we go. The old meet the neighbour by pretending you need a cup of sugar, flour, water, or whatever.* But, no. Turns out it was just his empty coffee cup and he was a self-described clean freak, so didn't want to leave it unwashed on the balcony railing.

'Hello, neighbour.' He thrust his hand out. The shake wasn't so firm as the thrust or his stride or his swimming, for that matter. He had a young face, younger than his stoop suggested.

'I'm Mathew,' I said. 'I'm on my own now.'

I felt the waterworks coming on and when it rains it bloody pours… I tried squeezing my eyes and holding my belly in and swallowing the lumps down the back of my throat. After about ten seconds of no one saying anything, my face was covered in tears and when I tried to get rid of them I smeared dirt right across it.

Juice said, 'I think your mascara's running, Mathew.' That's what he said. Didn't know me from Adam and started taking the mickey.

'Here,' he said, 'this'll fix it,' and went to grab the hose out of my hand.

But I was too quick – not dead yet – and I squirted it myself instead. Gave me a hell of a fright. Got it in my gob and up my nose. Everywhere.

I spluttered, and then he was laughing and I was laughing as though it was the funniest damn pickle we'd ever been in. Had me gasping for breath.

'I'm Juice,' he said, shaking my hand again as though starting over.

I don't know how long that handshake lasted but it might have been four minutes of Juice putting his other hand on my elbow holding me there. Gently, like, but I wouldn't have been able to get way if I'd wanted to.

I finally gathered myself enough to say, 'What sort of a name is Juice?'

'The real name's Bruce,' he said, and went on to explain that as a kid he just loved oranges – was raised in Wentworth, near Mildura, in among the orange orchards – and used to squeeze and squeeze them to make juice. When his right hand got tired, he learnt to swap to his left. Got just as good on the left, which was pretty handy for a lot of things, he said with a wink and a little smirk and that was the second time I'd laughed since Gracie passed. So young Juice tried setting up a little stall on the side of the road to tempt the workers driving back from Mildura with an ice-cold juice. Generous serves for only a dollar. Every evening he sold the lot and every night he'd have to steal out and collect produce for the next day. He'd made $467.50 by the time Joe Granada from next door came round and asked where he might be getting his oranges from.

Juice and his mother rented a small block trimmed off the original farm. He had to admit their two scraggly orange trees didn't fully meet supply. Joe said tomorrow ought to be his last day; enough time to make a new sign, NO MORE JUICE, and tell all his customers he was closing up shop.

'You still like it?' I said, noticing his shoulders were already getting burnt.

'What, juice?'

'Yeah.'

'I love it!'

'Still squeeze your own?'

'When I can.' He flipped his sunglasses on top of his head and revealed a long light scar beneath his left eye. Old, but it would've been vicious at the time. It was the only line around his eyes. He was younger than I thought.

'You like the organic bought stuff?'

'I do.'

I reckon he could tell what I was getting at because he was playing along.

'Want some? I got some in the fridge. The container's almost full. Got more orange juice than I know what to do with.'

'Don't you like it?'

'I like it, but it doesn't like me. I can have about half a glass every other day, but more than that and my bottom…oh, you don't want to know…'

'No, you're right, I don't. But I'm the same with beans. Borlotti, kidney, adzuki…oh, man. Not good.'

'You want to come in for a juice then? Your shoulders are pretty red.'

He followed me without agreeing or disagreeing. I veered to turn off the tap and he hovered, waiting.

'I went for a swim the other day,' he said, from the shade of the carport. 'Got pretty burnt.'

'Saw that. You swam for miles. Wasn't sure if you were coming back.'

'*I* wasn't sure if I was coming back.'

As we walked into the kitchen, I could tell by how he said it that he meant what he'd said. I'd known him less than twenty minutes and already I knew that in important matters he didn't play with the truth.

'Glad you did,' I said, pouring the juice and handing him the glass.

We clinked them together out of habit. 'Probably don't feel like celebrating,' I said, just checking.

I pulled out a seat at the kitchen table and sat down at the other end. The laminate tabletop was cool against the flesh of my forearms so I kept them there for a while.

'Today's a better day.' He drank thirstily. 'That's great juice, isn't it? It's the only bought stuff that tastes like the real thing. The others are just orange flavouring or preservatives or watered-down vaguely citrus. No, these guys have got it right.' He drank again, held it in his mouth before swallowing. 'Yes, today's a better day, Mathew. Got left at the altar on Saturday.' A weighty out-breath followed the pause. 'Well, it wasn't actually an altar. Got left at our favourite beach standing barefoot in a penguin suit with about seventy guests looking on.'

He caught my eye and held it. Had a way of doing it that didn't threaten and didn't appeal. It seemed as though he was just making sure that what he'd said had come through clear.

'Not my best moment.' He paused then, ready to throw back the last of the drink but seemed to realise this would empty the glass and stopped.

I refilled it then returned his gaze.

'It's bitter to say it, I know, but I'd had reservations myself.' Juice held the glass close to his lips. 'Wouldn't tell anyone that. They wouldn't believe me and what would it prove? Look, she did the right thing. It's just her timing was about sixteen months too late.'

I had nothing to say. I was scanning to find something because the silence was about as easy as a turtle on its back but I figured it was my turn so I took it like a man, and drank my juice.

Next thing, he was standing up and looking through the photos on the fridge door. A real estate agent's magnet half-covered a photo of Gracie and me taken the week before she died. I'd put her lippy on and a bit of blusher on her cheeks. She wasn't vain, but she knew she was close and wanted to dress up for what might be her last time. We played a couple of our old favourites, 'As Time Goes By' and 'They Can't Take That Away From Me'. Me, holding back tears the whole time because she was being so brave as we waltzed – her sitting in the chair holding my hand and me standing with my hand on her shoulder doing the steps. One. Two. Three. Little did we know we were counting her last breaths.

'Is that your wife?' Juice lifted the photo off the fridge and held it to the sliver of light coming through the kitchen curtains.

'Yes.'

'She's a looker, Mathew.'

'She is, yes.'

After that, with his back to me, I couldn't really tell what he said, but it was something like 'Still, looks aren't everything.' For a while it seemed Juice wasn't seeing anything at all and then he jerked himself back into focus. 'When was it taken?

'Last week.'

'What? When did she die?'

'Three days ago.'

'Oh, mate, I'm sorry. That's not long.'

'It's not. No.' I poured him more juice. I'd had my fill. 'This is her juice. Even on the day she died, she drank a tiny bit, through a straw, like.'

'I don't know what to say.'

'Come to the funeral?' It was out before I'd even thought the thought. And yet I didn't withdraw it. Not straight away.

I said goodbye to him about ten minutes later, closed the door and went to my room. I lay on my side of our bed and howled. I didn't stop until it got dark and then, the morning of the funeral, I went up to No. 44 and said, 'Juice, you don't have to come. It was silly of me to say it. Not right in the head.' And then I realised he was wearing his suit again. 'Off for another walk or a swim?'

'A funeral,' he said. 'Anything I can do?'

'You can wear some shoes.' I patted him on the shoulder and turned to walk back to my place.

Ann Bolch

Geese

for Ron Barnes SJ

In ribbons of sound all afternoon, geese,
their straggling formations
over mud-flats filled with spring rain.

In the cemetery below, a plain stone
with your name, a date of birth, death,
and the year of entry to the Order –

nothing else. I walk back to the house;
a priest in overalls is raking last year's leaves
that have lain black under the snow

all winter; a mulch for these beds
of lettuce, green-beans, red bell peppers.
On a shelf by the kitchen window –

which faces south to catch the sun –
the brothers grow mint and basil, chives
and coriander; a pair of binoculars

left handy to observe the birds.
The geese I thought returning,
never leave, I'm told.

Rosemary Blake

Legally dead

One ordinary Sunday morning long ago, my grandfather, a tall man, stooped early in life, an eccentric inventor with sad eyes, went out walking. Wearing shirt sleeves and braces, he closed the front gate and walked up the road. He left his jacket and third wife behind and kept walking. We never saw him again.

> my grandfather
> born 1885
> vanished 1954

In the sheaf of police missing person files, only one clue. A description of a tall man with no jacket, seen sitting by the road outside a gun club. After seven years he was declared legally dead. His third wife, a Scots woman with blue hair, never spoke of him again.

> my grandfather
> left two letters
> for his sons

Mardi May

Expiry, a last breath

I push the Medicare card across the counter towards the post office official. Bank detail verification. I don't need to look at the card. I know her name is still there. First on the list, first in my heart. Not that it matters when collecting your 100 points. They don't care about name ordering, don't care that one of the people on the card is dead. Well, they might if they asked. If I said.

That would be my loss.

We had such fun that day. We hadn't planned to get a joint Medicare card. Somehow it just came about. Unintentional, accidental card creation. I rack my brains. Trawling through the vagueness, recalling details. Trying to pin down nebulous, evasive memories, skipping, rushing through my being. Did it happen then? Straight away? When we moved in together, that November? A measure of our love and joint life together. Unlikely. We were so cautious at first. So risk-averse. Both holding onto financial independence, a semblance of separateness. Defying bodily connection.

Hence the surprise. The joy. I can take you to the exact place where I felt the rush of excitement fly through my body. The flush of realisation. The Medicare clerk just asking a simple procedural question. Whether we wanted both names on the same card. So innocently, so unknowingly. Us, just standing there, giving a quick look, a smile, a slight nod. Hand in hand, leaning up against the counter. Inadvertent joining of lives. Bureaucratic connection.

Now this card has taken on its own symbolic representation.

*

I look across at the post office official holding this very same card, peering at the numbers, typing them into the computer. Always the same guy. Always ready to help when I come to pick up parcels, registered letters.

Show identification. A small man, rings on his fingers, speaking with an effeminate voice. I like him. I like his efficiency. The way he arranges his body, moves his limbs, the way his hands engage with the keyboard, with numbers, with me.

I can sense the queue behind me as I wait patiently, watching him methodically go about the job of checking my credentials. The university post office is always busy. Run-down, it has seen better days, tucked away as it is at the back of the newsagent. Almost a relic, with its forgotten task of sending letters. Times past. Shelves packed with papers, folders, details. Spilling out onto the floor, covering benches. Information pinned onto walls, giving parcel options, registered or not, sea or air, large or small. Information passed across counters. Authorisations, verifications. Driver's licences, passports, Medicare cards handed across.

Cards with names of dead people.

Body shifting, tension held in abeyance, I imagine the process of eventually getting her name removed from this card of ours. Visualise me, for a moment, standing in a different queue, waiting for an electronic instruction to go to the next available Medicare counter. Certified death certificate in hand, removed from the filing cabinet that morning. Taken from her hanging file, the one called *Mary's bits and pieces*. Picture me standing at the counter, trying to get my voice to speak, working up the courage to formulate the words, even though I'd practised them many times before. Feeling the tears, sensing the tell-tale catch at the back of the throat. Words that won't be formed, words that won't emerge, words that don't want to be said. See them lean forward across the counter in order to hear a quiet request. They won't know how much time I spent throwing around different words: remove, erase, delete, take off. Wondering how to best formulate this activity of name removal. Will there be tenderness in their voices as they realise what they are being asked to do?

Administrative clerks, under time pressure, expected to deal with a set number of customers per hour. How to respond when faced with the unexpected. I'm sure this situation isn't included in their 'how to' manual.

Confronted by death, by sadness, by a woman crying in public. Will they mumble, fumble, avoid eye contact, before calling the supervisor? Their pay isn't high enough to manage this sort of dilemma. Plus, it's not easy to remove a life from this bureaucratic world. You need confirmation of a life lived before allowing a life to be removed.

*

Name deletion. Elimination of being. You'd think everything would happen at once, the day she died. A last breath, a final look. Transitioning from a conscious being to someone who is no more. Closing down a life. But it's not that simple. Tidying up loose ends is a long slow process. Loose names casually left on cards, accounts, email addresses.

Gas and electricity were hard. Unforeseen, unanticipated. Bills in her name, so soon after the event. Of her death. I was still getting used to being just me, sleeping alone, cooking for one. Still trying to understand what had happened only a few weeks before. Standing there by the mailbox, turning letters over, letters in her name. Trying to breathe, to understand. Letters addressed to the woman I loved. Followed by a slow realisation that I can't just retreat into myself, alone. I can't continue to close off the outside world. Things have to be done. Bills have to be paid, even if they are not in my name.

Dying is not a simple business after all.

Getting her name removed from the internet account was the hardest. Close to impossible. They wouldn't even allow me to pay the bill because I wasn't her. Such a small amount too. Thirty dollars a month. They wouldn't remove her name either. Eventually, under special dispensation, they allowed me to pay the monthly account until it was sorted out. It took months of phone calls, emails, discussions. In the end there was a file. I could avoid having to say the words *She's dead* by just referring them to a specially created reference number. I could feel myself waiting patiently on the phone while they read through pages of information, details of problems.

Do you think this happens every time someone dies? It seems hard to believe. Eventually they would come back on the line, voice lowered in commiseration, gentle, considerate. Slowly taking me through the next step of the process. There was always something more that needed to be done. Before finally, five months later, at an arranged time and place we turned off the life support. Me sitting in the study, cold in the middle of winter, shut off from the warmth of the rest of the house; the IT guy sitting in his office at work. Step by step re-configuring of an internet connection. Remove her name; delete her email account; fix up the modem that no longer worked without her; change the internet plan; start afresh. Plug blue into this; test red with that; now take this out of that. Is the modem light flickering now? The IT guy held my hand down the phone-line, as I sobbed silently through it all.

There are no manuals for name removals.

Then sometimes it's surprisingly simple. When putting in the car for its regular service, they just took her name off. Just like that. I'd been standing there, watching the mechanic search for our car on his list of names. Then it struck me. Maybe it's under her name. I quietly suggested to the grease-covered, frantically-shuffling mechanic to try a different name. Her name. I choked up, tears in my throat, pain in my heart. Forcing my tongue to formulate the syllables of her name. He found it, easily. Straightforward matching of letter to alphabetic list.

Then in a quiet, still, remembering voice, I said, 'Can we take her name off? You see, she's passed away.'

Without blinking an eyelid, not a word, a glance, a hesitation, the young man says, 'Yeah, sure' drawing a line through a name.

Oh, too quick, I internally gasp.

Losses piling up on top of one another.

*

The bank was difficult. An investment property had to be remortgaged before the inevitable removal of a name from our joint account. I delayed this one. Too hard. Too many details. Too many decisions. In my still foggy state. Eventually, though, one day, as I was cycling past the bank,

I dropped in. Just like that. Told the story, slowly, softly, into a bank teller's ear. They responded in kind. Gave me calm advice. Paved the way to move forward, if removing a loved one's name can be seen as a step forward.

I still feel the internal struggle. More than a year later. Viscerally, physiologically. Sense it rushing through my body, through my veins, clogging up my heart. Blend of resistance, tied up with sadness, leading (maybe, possibly, inevitably) to acceptance. Here now, as I write, the feelings rise up again. Feelings of loss, contradictory feelings of needing to move on, knowing it will mean I'm leaving someone behind. Removing her from my life. I observe, as if from afar, how these feelings take over my being.

*

At last, as I stand there, the post office official hands back the familiar green card. I hold it in my hand as I lean against the counter. Feeling her through the card (if that's at all possible) sensing her there with me, wondering what she would think about me standing here, getting on with the ordinariness of life.

I force myself to peer more closely at the worn plastic card now resting in my hand. Testing my resolve. Searching faded numbers for an expiry date. Making the linguistic connection between *expire* and *a last breath*. Is this what will happen? Are we moving towards the last breath? How much longer have we got, together, on this green card?

Knowing I'm not quite ready to let go. Still wanting, needing, desiring, to carry her with me. Name on a card. Carrying a loss, her loss, my loss. For a little longer at least.

Johanna Rendle-Short

Beach wedding

I am about to have a wedding and I am dying. Not today; no, I am alive today, and I am dressed in ochre silk. It's an odd colour choice, I know. But I saw it there in the op shop and it was all I'd imagined I'd be married in. It was aged-photograph brown, hanging there amongst all the taffeta and tulle, and I knew I would have it. I would rinse it in yellow dye and come here; my final resting place. The bodice is ruched and there are clam shells gathered high at the neck, a tiny fringe grazing my skin. The trimming might have bothered me in the past, but chemo forges a strong resolve. You can endure anything after chemo; especially a scratchy ochre wedding dress.

My husband – we've been married before – is shifting my hairpiece into place. It's glossy brown and fashioned into a plaited knot. I bought it that way, and it is real hair. The strands are fine like a child's. I wonder if I wear a collection of young Thai women, woven and bound at my crown. I think of them: they who cropped their hair for a pittance and gave it away so that a sick Western woman could wear a wig while renewing her vows. It's a luxury; a strange first-world custom. My own hair would be grey, if I had any. Now it looks as it did when Bernard and I first married, though the style is modern, stolen straight from a glossy magazine and customised in a Thai warehouse.

Bernard rests his hands at my hips and kisses my cheek. 'Beautiful,' he says, though I'm drawn; a praying mantis, long-limbed and reedy. He caresses my back in circles, the way he did in the hospital.

I shrug him off; I'm here, not there, and this day will not be about sickness. 'Go on,' I say, 'go and get yourself sorted and I'll see you out there. Tell Lily she can come in.' I take a miniature Scotch from the bureau and have a swig.

Bernard raises an eyebrow and looks like he might say something, but shakes his head and leaves instead.

*

83

The wedding invitation was a fine offer, written in elegant italic script: *All expenses paid trip to Thailand*, it read. Lily baulked when I told her that my life insurance would not fund her next gap year (she'd enjoyed three, where I thought the idea was to take one), but she grew quiet when I explained. Of course, it's not the done thing to tell a dying woman how to spend her money, even if she's your mother. That's not to say that she made no noise.

Lily ranted. She rolled her eyes and carried on. 'You don't invite people you haven't seen in twenty-five years to your second wedding, Mum. Especially not…under the circumstances…'

'Those are precisely the people you invite. You don't understand, Lil. You don't have children…or a career. Life gets busy and you leave people behind. You leave some of the best ones behind.'

Lily didn't listen. She spoke to me (her dying mother) in clipped tones and one-word answers for the rest of the day. I thought about throwing her invitation in the bin.

*

I skived off from chemo; bypassed the grey and apricot cubicle curtains in a moment of defiance and instead walked the nearby streets. I held a spiky seed pod and looked skywards, marvelling at the Japanese maples, the way the light touched the leaves. I grew lost in the shades of green and the sun-shot fluorescent yellow. Loosening the turban from my head (an affectation; it was never me), I let the breeze cool my clammy neck. I wound the scarf around my wrist and shoved it into my handbag. People averted their eyes; began to smile their pitiful smiles.

I stopped in at the local shopping centre to find the perfect notebook, and in the end it was plain: spiral-bound with a black cover, only $2.96. I bought a new pen, and set myself up on the veranda with a cup of tea, the scent of jasmine spilling softly from the side gate.

Laurel Styles was the first name on my list. Golden-haired Laurel, the girl who had moved to Esperance in the ninth grade; she who had been my pen pal for fifteen years, before I became too busy at the hospital and forgot to write back. We both trained as nurses, so I thought she would understand: the hours, the stress, motherhood. I still have her letters, bundled together in a puffy patchwork box. But a little bit of research revealed that I was too late: Laurel went in a car crash in 2004. She died, a mother of two small children, at thirty-three years old. I can only imagine her as a blonde, fourteen-year-old waif.

Second was Nigel, the primary school friend who shared his secret with me first. Mum used to look after him on the weekends when his mother worked. She would pop her head in and say 'Go to sleep, you two!' She never once told me to get into my own bed, because of course, she knew. Ten years later, and Mum confirmed, 'Your father and I knew he was a homosexual by the time he was thirteen.'

Nigel had moved on to bigger and better things, and by the time I found him, I had to write 'New York City' on his envelope. I didn't think he'd come, but there he is with the rest of them. He's chubby now, but attractive, and he's holding hands with a much taller lanky fellow. Nigel's fingernails are squared and recently polished. They shine like pearly shells. He meets my gaze and smiles the same tooth-gapped smile and it feels like I'm back there; I'm a girl again and he's endearingly calling me his 'hag'. I give him a tiny wave and step behind a large potted fern.

My daughter frowns at me like the embarrassed mother of a wayward child. 'Don't peer around and let them see you yet! Wait for the music. For goodness sake!'

Lily's wearing an expensive cocktail dress. I know it's expensive because I told her I'd foot the bill. Said she could choose what she liked. But it's too simple; like smart office wear; black, and definitely not a bridesmaid's frock. She'd grudgingly let me take her shopping and then turned up her nose at everything I suggested. No, she didn't upturn her nose; she scowled, she smirked and pretended to retch.

Lily rolled her eyes at me thirteen times that day – I was counting. Then I asked her if she'd prefer to walk in front of me; the wiry woman shaped like a Sikh man.

And Lily said, 'Maybe I just might,' before strutting ahead.

*

I scowl at my daughter and shift a frond so that I can see my old history teacher peering over her shoulder. Ursula Matrioni is nibbling the ends of her nicotine-stained fingers. I was stunned when I received her RSVP; I thought they'd have to redirect her invitation to the afterlife. Her hair is still dyed mulberry-wine red, and fits like a helmet, framing her old face; the same, but lined and marked with deep brown patches.

My elderly aunt is up front, and my mother's hand is at her shoulder. Aunty Sue is crying already. The chairs are white with yellow satin sashes. I see my father; he's leaning forward, shiny head in hands, and Mum begins to rub his back, though they've been divorced twenty years.

'Go and do something,' I say to Lily, gesturing towards them. 'I wrote it in the invitation: *Please politely excuse yourself if you start to feel like you are at my wake. Thank you.*'

Lily starts to speak, but Debussy begins to tinkle on the sound system and she pivots, draws her frangipani bouquet to her navel as she begins to walk. I wait until she has reached her father and younger brother. Steven is sixteen and handsome and awkward; he hides his hands in the pockets of the hire suit, keeps his gaze firmly fixed on the floor. Bernard holds Lily for a while and when he releases her it is time for me to move. My daughter is weeping and I begin to roll my eyes, but then I see them as a group. There are ten people here; ten indispensable people. Ten invitations sent on the wind into ten different geographical locations. They are all here.

*

I don't drink the champagne or eat the tapas. I rotate around the table like I'm partnered in a progressive dance. I ask them to tell me their stories, but first I apologise for leaving them behind. I remember details of my youth long-forgotten; the neural pathways firing like flints.

Mrs Matrioni tells me to try a hippy retreat and a sweat tent to rid my body of its assailants. I realise she's gone mad when she tells me, 'It's intense – in tents – get it?' and then cackles like a crazy witch. She eats all the chorizo before anyone else can, and then makes for the haloumi.

Bernard throws me a hiked-eyebrow glance and I laugh like I haven't laughed in a year.

Nigel tells me that he and his younger partner, Phil, have left their twin girls at home with a nanny. They show me a picture of two pretty Indian children and begin the sweet banter of men in love.

Phil turns to me. 'I've heard everything, Xanthe. Nige has told me about all the shenanigans when you were kids. Truth or dare at the…'

I cover my eyes and laugh, '…the youth group camp. Oh dear. Nigel, you beast.'

My old friend laughs and squeezes my hand, 'I'm sorry I haven't stayed in touch.'

I shake my head and kiss his cheek, 'No, *I'm* sorry.'

'How long, Xanthe?' Nigel whispers.

I grasp his forearms, 'Not for discussion today, dear friend.'

The hotel wedding planner opens the wide bifolds onto the beach because the afternoon thunderstorm has passed. I toss my shoes aside and head for the surf. The others follow, in various stages of undress – I prescribed swimsuits in the invitation. I reach the tideline and wave Bernard over. He unzips my dress at the back and it falls around my feet. I slip into the waves in my new yellow two-piece. As I make to dive under, Bernard launches himself at me, yanking the shiny hairpiece off just as I edge below. The water is perfect against my itching scalp and I stay submerged, just beneath the surface. When I come up, the guests are lined up along the water's edge, clapping. Bernard is beside me, and we're floating, feet in the air, toes splayed in the mauve water.

I urge the others to come in and they begin to peel off their cheesecloth shirts and beach dresses; then they're circling us. Lily plucks the frangipanis from her posy and throws them over us, her parents. Steven is kneeling in the water, shirtless and thin; still boyish. Bernard takes my hand beneath the water and squeezes because I am crying. I pull him towards me, into the circles of orange sunset. We turn towards the horizon and watch the light fall away.

Kristen Levitzke

You can't do that

leave me here in the emptiness
even a cat knows to climb the walls
rub up against the furniture

nothing seems different
but nothing is the same
nothing has been moved

but there's more space
no one lights
the lamp by your chair

there's no set of footsteps
on the staircase
no tea in your cup

something's not starting at its usual time
something doesn't happen as it should
someone was always, always here

then suddenly disappeared
stayed disappeared
refuses to be found

if you can do that
so can I
just help me disappear

to you

Elizabeth Goodsir

Guidelines for mourning

Don't buy too much fruit
or too many capsicums. They slump
and turn grey underneath.
Open windows to allow the air
free passage and keep the mould
from shoes. Watch the bag
that holds the poise of having
just been put down.
Keep the house tidy
as though somebody lives here.
Don't cook too much pasta, and
if you do, refrigerate.
Leave the radio on when you go out
even if the voice upon return is strange.
Careful with solitaire…
the imperatives of chance are
an illusion – it is all written,
all improvised.

Get out a bit and always say
you're keeping busy.
Be prudent with visitors,
those that ask, *And what have you been
doing with yourself?* while you sway
upon a rope bridge in Nepal.

At intervals strike a bell and hear
how that sound, rather than diminish,
just gets further away
beyond apprehension.

Fruit, shoes, vacuuming, the days travel past
your windows. The weather
stays inside.

Tim Bass

After, there are the birds

He sends me photos
of the singular crimson rosella
who observes him through the kitchen window
as he cooks dinner for one.

He sends me boxes of her best clothes:
designer jackets, silk shirts, tailored trousers.
Asks me to share them among family
even though she was the size of a wren
and we're all currawongs.

He sends me photo after poignant photo
of white-breasted sea eagles,
    soaring   roosting   gliding.
Years before, knowing death might swoop,
she signed emails: 'from the White-Breasted Sea Eagle',
or sometimes, when energy was low: 'WBSE'.

He sends me photos of her grave
in a paddock so close to the ocean
sea eagles patrolling there
sense the running of rabbits and fish.

He sends me photos of the funeral,
me bearing her coffin with his three sisters,
my face bleak as a cliff
as we lay her in that space –
best bird's-eye view of the ocean
and she –
without eyes.

He sends me news of the satin bowerbird
drowned in the liquid compost.
He retrieves the corpse, places it on an ants' nest.

Later, he sends the clean, exquisite skeleton
to an artist friend who draws skulls,
so frail, so strong.

There are no photos to send,
there can be no speaking of
how our sea eagle is composting now,   drowning
in the rich soil of her ocean paddock.
These, our desolate imaginings in that birdless hour,
round three in the morning…
          we simply cannot fly there together.

He sends me the last days' photos,
her three sisters and a niece bundled
beside the aluminium bed
we all knew so well   at the end.
We look so bonny and robin-round
beside her wren-bone frail.
She, still railing strong against
the determined flocks of starlings
roosting in her spine, liver, lungs.

He sends me copies of *Australian Birdlife*,
we speak of the plight of the orange-bellied parrot,
as the wind-farms of loss
slice across his sky
as he attempts to migrate
from   *mated for life*
to   *flying solo.*

After my sister dies,
her husband says,   'Now,
there is the company of birds.'

Gina Mercer

Parting

Part my legs, part my lips. Wait.

Eyelid resting on eyelid, smooth line of protecting skin. Eye opens.

You withdraw. Your skin under my nails. Your distant breath. The spiral of your double crown, a sign.

I put the phone down and your voice is cut off. You left your tears on my cheek. You left your fingerprints on my thigh.

I talk to you in the bath, anticipate what you will say, put my head under the water. I talk to you when I can't sleep. I dream and you are here. I see you in the street, but it isn't you. I hear your voice in your letters. You and you and you.

I talk to the dead. They never leave me, their conversations low in the corner. They follow, and we hang the washing on the line and notice the new growth, the bud, the colour of the flowers. I sip my coffee and talk, and their replies are so predictable. I want their smell, their touch. I have made them change.

You are always about to go. Calling out from the car, driving off, waving at the corner, the last lunch, the last kiss, is it the last, will we meet when we are old, will you still be alive, will I?

I must be going now too. Getting out of bed, leaving the room, the house, the country, leaving my mind. We steal ourselves from each other. We sleep and are gone, animal bodies loose in bed, touching, our dreams are with others. I wake you up to say goodbye.

Your lips part, telling me the words of the music, then they close. Opening the curtains I brush past you accidentally. You flinch.

I strip the bed, hack the foliage from my door, take out the garbage. I have cut myself open, right down the middle. My heart is falling out and I only just catch it, hide it, stuff it under my clothes, clutch it as I walk around.

Whose bed is this, whose body? Skin separates us. I read the signs, a hair, a smudge, a spot of blood. Objects moved and removed. Is that you? Did you close the door? Did you lock it? I hold myself together, folded in the sheets, contained. Only me here.

Sarah St Vincent Welch

Sis

You wrote that note, sis, like you did, in your diary, that note, a sigh, a cry, left in a drawer, that note about a part of you we never knew, you lying on your bed against the wall, lying on the bed, your arms open, red from your arms on the wall, face speckled like the wall, and rain falling soft outside, light fading at the window, rain falling on the window, running down, like red from your arms, pooling on the carpet, warm for a while, then cooling, like it did, sis, like you, ebbing away on the bed, without a sigh, not a cry, just a note, a page, a cry in your diary, like it was just a day, another day, another queer day, like it was, sis, your fingers cold, white, you on your bed against the wall, carpet knife on the floor, your hand open, arms open, running as they did, you whispering silent, your mouth moving without a sound, you in your room, sis, upstairs, cold, you upstairs and me downstairs, downstairs with mum, listening to rain soft on the window and hearing your silence, like it was wrong, like it was, sis, and us running up the stairs, seeing red on the wall by the stairs and wondering, wondering what it could be, as you lay there, like you did, sis, cold, white, speckled, not sighing, and us wondering why, wondering how, how it could be true, like it was, and us not knowing the note in your diary, not knowing what you wrote, and rain still soft on the window, telling us it was true, us not hearing a sigh, your cry, that part of you we never knew, and rain running down and light fading at the window, a queer light fading, saying it was wrong, like it was wrong, like it was, sis.

David Francis

Lacrimosa

Scene One

The beach, waves crashing, darkened house, roller shutters down. No dog barks. No cat meows. No baby cries. No one is at home.

Rush, run, dash to suburban emergency department.
Drive carefully.
Turn your mobile off, the nurses shout at me.
I can't. I have to text. I have to call everyone so they know. I need to let them know.
Grief-gorged eyes.
Mine or yours?
Don't take me to the hospital, my mother pleads without words as she looks up at me from her trolley. Not that hospital. They stick you with needles and kids treat you like a slab of meat. I don't want to be an experiment. That beautiful androgynous man with the Transylvanian accent. He'll be the death of me.
There is no music in this episode.
Resounding silence.

Whatever happens.
There is no need for guilt.
Red light.

Scene Two

The city. Emergency department. Waiting room.
I sit next to a man with a beetroot face.
I've been here for five hours, he says. Heart aches.
I ignore him.
You look angry. No one likes an angry woman.
Go away.
I'm sick.
Then stay.
Are you sick?

No.

Your mother?

Yes.

Very sick.

Yes.

This will be the worst day of your life, I know. I've been there.

I know.

Scene Three

Pink curtains. Eight beds in the ward. The morning after.

Restless night.

I'm going to lunch, I'll be back soon. You need your rest.

Don't go.

I'm hungry.

I call up a friend and we eat sushi. I talk about everything else.

She will get better soon. It's happened before. Brain haemorrhages are a part of life. A team of rehabilitation staff. Doctors. Soon I will wake up at home and hear her laboured breathing. Just like the last time this happened.

Back at the hospital.

Roll of eyes. Weakened.

Face flattened.

No control over facial muscles. Any muscles.

Pale.

Pink.

Cold leg.

Pale, pink, cold leg. Urinary incontinence. 111 beats per minute. Her heart is going 111 beats per minute. My heart is usually at 72 beats per minute but I don't feel it right now.

She tries to speak.

130 beats per minute.

Groan.

Her tongue is unable to move.

140 beats per minute.

Don't worry, I tell her.

I know she wants to ask me where my brother is.

Boys are far less complicated, she always said.

Travelling in Spain, Santiago de Compostella, Allicante, Madrid. Somewhere Spanish. Maybe he's in Mexico. He doesn't have a mobile phone, but he checks his mail every second day. He is sleeping through his final peaceful night.

Scene Four

Chinatown. Uncle Billy's Restaurant.

I'm allergic to MSG but I feel closer to her when I eat here. It's been almost twenty-four hours since she last ate, since her last meal. I've just met a man who I know will one day be my husband, and even now, I am thinking about him and trying to figure out how or when I will ask him out. Now is as good a time as any, but fledgling love is discordant with dying. The plastic bowls are cheap and burnt. I have no appetite, anti-inflammatory pills eating through my stomach lining. I look at my broken wrist but it doesn't hurt any more. I order salty fish porridge, her favourite.

I never took my mother here, nor anywhere, for dinner. We weren't really friends. I think about the gambler in the waiting room. If she pulls through she will be a vegetable for the rest of her life, and I will have to quit my job and be a full-time carer. If she doesn't pull through, what will I write in the eulogy? We weren't really friends. I hardly knew her because she was at work all the time. The only real conversation we had was when I stole a porn magazine from the newsagency and took it to school to show my friends. Breasts, I warned my friends, and hairs in strange places. This is our destiny…

Mum was called in to the headmistress, mortified. She is a puritan. Afterwards she kept asking me why I did it.

Just because, I said.

Scene Five

Hospital car-park. Full parking lot. Anxious wait.

I have driven my neighbour here to say goodbye to my mother.

We wait for an obese couple to finish eating Subway.

Are you leaving?

Yes.

Twenty minutes later. The woman steps out of the car, throws her wrapper in the bin and squeezes back into her seat.

They leave. We prepare for a reverse park. Brown car passes.

Red car takes our spot.

Didn't you see us waiting there?

No.

This was our parking spot.

They ignore us.

Two short Italian women with big hair in bright red cardigans.

It crosses my mind that this could be my future husband's relatives.

This was our fucking parking spot.

Don't you swear at me.

Shit.

Don't you swear at me.

We've been waiting for a long time.

Maybe your mother is dying too, but right now my pain is more than yours, and so is my guilt.

Don't you swear at me.

I shout at them. The coarsest word in the English dictionary, rhymes with hunt. I've had a bad day.

My friend, our gentle Vietnamese neighbour charges out of the car and thumps their car window.

I'll call the police, the woman says.

Call the police, my gentle friend shouts.

Yes, I will call, the woman's friend screams.

I'm going to call too, I say, and take out my mobile and pretend to read out the number plate.

They drive away, far away, from the gentle Vietnamese woman and the potty-mouth Chinese girl.

Scene Six

Interior. She is alone in the room. Dying is a private affair.
Chest infection. Bed sores.
Both are common in the elderly and the dying, but the dead only have the latter.
She knows what is going on.
Limited speech. They try to give her jelly food. The therapist asks me if she is socially isolated.
We hadn't spoken for months.

Scene Seven

Entering the house of Adams.
Morticia on pot. Condescending schizo.
What do you mean no op no op no op?, she gnaws.
She is my mother's long-lost sister.
Palliative care, I say. I don't know what the word for that is in Chinese, or Arabic for that matter.
Why do you only tell me now? she chews.
Uncle Fester is at work.
Why are you alive? I wonder. Because your mother had sex with your father…that's why.

*

There is no eighth scene, nor ninth, nor tenth.
It ends after a week. She dies on a red sky morning and I walk over to the cathedral across the road. I don't enter because I'm not sure if He

wants me in His house. I've never really considered Him until now, so I sit on the doorsteps and wail. A nurse walks past and tells me that it does get easier. She lost her son ten years ago in a motorcycle accident. That's life, she says and gives me a hug.

The sky turns orange and she tells me it's because my mother is in heaven knitting me a multicoloured scarf.

I am allergic to wool.

On the Monday she was still fighting.

She knew she needed to pee but didn't want to pee in nappies in front of her daughter.

She could understand me and signal her needs to me.

On Tuesday I thought she'd make it.

She was hungry on Wednesday and asked me for food. The IV was still in her arm so I pointed to it, explaining that it would keep her alive and well nourished.

On Wednesday my brother returned and I called my aunt anything I could come up with in every language I knew. My brother spent all of Wednesday night with her and in the morning they took out the IV. The nurses wet her lips with some water. She's rotting from the inside and starving to death like the hungry black children she used to see on the nightly news.

On Thursday and Friday she hung in there and I said I wanted to spend the night there too, but she shooed me away with a pained look in her grief-gorged eyes. They injected her with morphine not long after that.

Coda

I wander around cathedrals on cold mornings waiting for the sky to change colour, but it only ever transitions from pale blue to dark grey. Soon, I run out of churches. I quit my job, my life. Use my savings, my housing deposit, to wander, aimlessly. I try not to think about the dead or the dying. I go to France where there are old cathedrals in every town, but I never step within the doors. Not even of Notre Dame in Paris.

Then one day I find myself inside St Cecile's, the red-brick Gothic cathedral of Albi. I'm only there because the owner of the *pensione* I'm staying at has given me her ticket to a performance of Mozart's *Requiem*. She tells me that I'll enjoy it because I've told her that I used to play the violin in an orchestra. It is Mozart's mass for the dead, his last composition, written as he lay on his death-bed.

Despair, grief and yearning from two hundred years ago fill the cathedral, weave through the pews; between the crypts, candles, along the aisles and in and out of the confession box and bounce off the even older stained-glass windows. Up until this stage in my life, I have only ever attended concerts in halls where the seating, panels, doors and even the ventilation has been designed to replicate a studio sound-recording.

The Requiem is the first piece of music I have sat down to listen to since my mother died, and I begin to understand why people have for hundreds of years gone to worship their God in these skyscrapers. I weep silently in my seat, and realise that my recent desire to collect words in all different languages is a poor man's substitute for music, and a distraction from what I cannot bring myself to recall.

Emily J. Sun

Like someone who is leaving

this morning I catch myself putting things away
like someone who is leaving
like someone who will never use dishes again

a thousand miles to the south, your sons
feel for the slot behind the rose bushes,
let themselves in with the spare key,
find the shoes, side by side,
the half-worn shirts, soft with your shape,
the sheets quiet on your bed, all
forgetful now

that for a while they clothed
your kindling smile
and those thin hands I loved

and I have slipped back too
from dishes and work and shoes
to follow you a little way

as far as yearning will take me
toward wherever you have gone

Pam Schindler

Your Fibonacci

in memoriam D G S

Death
is
never
the way you
think it will be – last
words, memorable and profound.

Felled
by
a stroke,
damaged, you
turned your head away,
withdrew your hand, said, *Let me go.*

Five
day
vigil,
tears frozen,
we count every breath.
Silence, then someone says, *He's gone.*

Doves
fuss
beyond
the window
near your bed, intone
their doleful lie: *Untrue, untrue…*

Bound
by
futile
conventions,
generosities
of love, we arrange your last rites.

*

Time
and
again
you showed us
delicate patterns
spiralling round sunflower heads,

the
way
seedlings
put out growth
one, then another,
three shoots, five, eight, thirteen – growing

spear-
straight
towards
the light. Now
we walk the dunes, find
empty shells, weeping she-oak cones,

trace
the
spirals
and count spikes,
recall your talk of
Fibonacci. We speak of you,

your
love
of birds
visiting
your tree ferns, birdbath,
blue wrens daily on our sundeck,

we
read
again
your writings,
peruse your paintings
hoping perhaps to find you there –

wide
skies,
moonrise
from the deck,
lighting a pathway
across the quiet estuary.

Megan Schaffner

The great silence

It is best heard with the radio on in the background
or the surf breathing a kilometre away.
It can be strong in supermarkets
or in dinner conversation with five.

It isn't like tinnitus
except that it too is a parallel presence
behind and alongside what you expect to hear.
It is incurable (for those wishing to find a therapy).

The great silence inhabits the house upon return
it envelops as you leave,
it is loudest when the moon rakes fast clouds
or when the first sun-shaft wakens you to morning.

A brass bell at the front door
I ring to shape the silence
I turn up the car sound system
to appease its appetite.

The silence is the pause before utterance.
The silence is the listening for a sound –
a footstep, a door shutting,
a tap running, a saucepan lid.

After years, one gets to know it
a silence only you hear,
that speaks only to you,
speaks only from absence.

Tim Bass

I don't remember when I first began to call her friend

I wrote letters to Mary for nineteen years. I bought writing paper for her whenever I went on an overseas trip. Her round neat handwriting (and her particular world view) filled those pages bordered with elephants and henna palm prints. Every year I sent her notepaper. Every year she complimented me on my good taste in stationery and said she would love to travel to Mumbai and Jaipur with me as her guide.

I met her only once. In 2006. By that stage we had been writing to each other for twelve years and knew those quirky things about each other that best friends know. She liked her garden overgrown and it drove her batty that her beloved John clipped everything to 'within an inch of its life'. She grew river red gums and Cootamundra wattles and crab-apples and lilacs wherever she lived, then regretted the necessary 'amputations' required after a good year of rain. When I complained about annual rose pruning adventures in my own garden she said tartly I was fortunate I didn't have a chainsaw-toting hubby who wiped out everything before it had a chance to flower. She told me I would never rid my garden of onion weed so I may as well learn to live with it. She was right.

She warned me that my cat would Make Me Pay when I returned to Perth after two years away; citing the example of her own cat who shredded curtains and peed on her scarves whenever Mary went away. Her cat was called Lamb. She sent me a photo of this large ginger tom she could barely hold in her arms. Years later, when both our elderly cats had passed on she wrote to me about the 'large holes these beloved pets leave in our lives'

She sensed trouble brewing in my first marriage before I did and instructed me to send her my scribblings 'for safekeeping'. A few years later, when I was settled in a new home and a new relationship she mailed the manuscript of my first novel back to me because she knew I was going to be all right. We applauded each other's attempts to be published, sharing small triumphs – a poem, a short story, a rant to the editor – along with long meditations on the sorry state of 'what passes for literature these days'.

She never forgot my birthday or my age because she had been married for as long as I had been alive. When I was in tears about the trouble I was having with a colleague at work, she offered to put a hex on the co-worker and told me I was a good person and of course it wasn't my fault. This, before she met me.

I saw the South Australian landscape through her eyes before I ever went there. She described the Flinders Rangers and the sheep stations of her early married life, her short-lived career as a nurse, the boarding schools 'in the city' her children went to and her fondness for French novels at the end of a hard day at the station.

In 1999, when she and her husband retired and went to live in a small town near Adelaide, she said she couldn't understand why she resisted joining the local writers' group. 'Perhaps,' she wrote, 'writing is too important to be sidetracked into a pleasurable activity.' And in 2010, she told me sternly to keep writing – 'Just because my creative gene has pensioned itself off, don't you let yours do the same.'

When she was diagnosed with non-Hodgkin's lymphoma in 2007, she told me not to worry. 'It kills the young ones,' she said, 'not us tough oldies.' She wrote her funniest letters during this period, describing her scattiness, her lethargy, her oncologists, her surprise at the fussiness of her adult children and her own concern for John, whose knees and heart weren't as good as they used to be. She wrote that someone she knew had named their baby Morve Violet and it cracked her up. 'Morve is French for snot,' she said, 'purple snot – why burden a child like that?'

Our letters to each other dwindled to three times a year; both our birthdays and at Christmas. And sometimes these were delayed on account of travel, health, family and all those urgent little things that life requires we attend to in the moment. As long as we wrote to each other, it was enough. We told each other we could always collect and publish our letters if nothing ever came of our attempts at writing fiction. 'Has to be done posthumously,' she said, 'because no one we know would ever speak to us if they knew what we really thought of them.'

She wrote immediately after I sent a card for her birthday last year, telling me she had found the box in which she'd kept all my letters and occasional poems and that photograph of our single meeting. Us standing in her spring garden where the irises and daffodils and bluebells had enchanted her with their unrestrained gallop across the flower beds after unusual rain. 'Dearest Rashida,' she said, 'it was a joy to have found the box and all that you've regaled me with over the years. I've always loved them to bits.' I wrote back briefly, promising a longer letter later.

Later on in the year, I didn't get a birthday card from Mary. I quelled the alarm and waited. She was visiting the son in NSW, no doubt, or the grandchildren in Canberra, or the sister in South Africa. She was with her beloved granddaughter in Adelaide. I sent a Christmas card, early. In January I got a card in an unfamiliar hand from that familiar address informing me that my friend had succumbed to the cancer she had admitted only last year would kill her.

I am adjusting to life without Mary. It's a peculiar adjustment because it is a solitary one. I cannot gather friends and family here to celebrate her life because no one I know knew her. I cannot write or call anyone who knew her because they don't know me. She was my friend and I will miss her. And of course, Mary is the name I knew her by, the name she preferred – but that wasn't the name she was given at birth. We were separated by a generation, physical distance, an ethnicity she was frankly curious about. We had nothing much in common except our connection as writers.

I read her letters and know myself better through her words. I make a promise to myself to plant a crab apple in the cooler months. And maybe a lilac. And definitely jonquils and daffodils. And listen to Handel's *Messiah* in an old church. But never a saxophone. Because it was the worst noise she ever heard.

Rashida Murphy

This essay was written in January 2014 in response to news of my friend's death. Mary was my friend for more than half my immigrant life in Australia. My experience of my adopted country is richer for having known her.

124-LUV

for Terry Windred, 1951–2012

Don't even think about spending more than two seconds
bleating about your broken heart in her salon
because she'll tell ya straight –
men are only good for one thing.
After a hair appointment with Terry
you leave feeling like you've danced all night at a disco
'steada having the dead cells on top of your head tizzed up.
Every time you book in, she's redecorated
and is swirling around in a weird teenage outfit
running a hand through the latest colour in her hair
or the tinsel wig she wears after the chemo.
Hates it when she can't work any more.
Drives her husband nuts as she runs up her Bankcard
on huge mirrors and rows of lights across the living room ceiling.
I see this jazz when I come to stay the night.
She's wearing slinky black pants and a sexy pink T-shirt
and I'm in my fake leopard fur to help her believe
we're drinking cocktails and not spending the evening
lounging on the double bed she can hardly leave
now her bones have started to shatter.
Darl, she tells her husband, *you gotta get me to the hospital*
for a decent shot of morphine.
The poor bugger's so sleep-deprived he can hardly dial the ambos.
When they realise she has multiple myeloma they know she's in trouble
but she chirps away as if they're two spunks tempting her
into the back of their panel van to zoom her to a midnight beach
instead of the Emergency Department.
Haven't I seen you guys somewhere before! That naked ambos calendar?
They laugh back, *Lady, you should be on TV.*

And before they close the ambo doors
her husband calls,
Darl, you won't believe the number plate, it's 124-LUV
and she says, *I'd like to give these spunks 124 love.*
They ease her away like she's celebrity cargo
while we stand in the empty driveway
and punch the air
and cry 124-LUV –
as if we've discovered
the meaning of life.

Lesley Synge

The cancer end of town

Naturally, the trees are melancholy at the cancer end of town. This is how I read them in their gold, their brown. I carry my life back through the factory doors to the ceaseless workers. Beneath me the drains and furnaces, hot with rescues. The clock ticks. Headscarves and bones. The waiting room smells of terror wrapped in hope. I know that smell, shut in my diary in a deep drawer, but my body has resumed itself. A healed breast, I am come to report a happy ending. Oh, there is no ending. The doctor is too slight, too young. How can he carry the drowning through the waves, and may he yet have need to carry me? I open the notebook in my head, write I do not know what my cells are doing. Go home. Bathe in the quiet waters.

Debi Hamilton

A guest for dinner

Arthur tidies and cleans the entire flat, but spends the most time preparing his bedroom. He washes the glass doors to the balcony so that tonight's guest can admire the ocean view without getting distracted by cobwebs and bird shit. Next, he sweeps the balcony in case his guest might wish to breathe the cold salty air before turning to him with a smile, with open arms. Well, Arthur is hoping for a little romance anyway. He leans over to collect the pile of leaves. Pitching, he drops the dustpan and brush, and sprawls across the tiles.

A moment of panic, then Arthur tells himself to breathe, relax. A few days ago at his six-week check-up, his surgeon, Dr Connor, assured him that the dizzy spells were nothing, a reaction to the strain of the operation. Arthur has tried to believe her, but fears that he has suddenly become an old man. Before the operation, he could pass for fifty. In fact, the last man he dated just two months ago had assumed that Arthur was aged in his late forties but then, Arthur remembers, the lighting in that particular bar was dim and the man turned out to be lonely.

When the dizzy spell passes, Arthur gathers the leaves from the balcony and drops them into the kitchen bin. He returns to his room, strips the mattress of its fusty sheets and makes the bed using his best linen: the cream sheet set of combed Egyptian cotton. He puts new candles in the candelabra and a selection of jazz CDs next to the CD player. When he looks around to admire the ambience, a thread of nerves jitters along his ribs. He holds out his hands to see if he's trembling but instead notices how the bones now show through the loose skin.

He's lost too much weight. Hopefully Jeff, his first guest since the operation, won't notice or won't mind. But Arthur spelled it all out, didn't he? Was upfront on the dating website about his age and his condition, and Jeff, a forty-five-year-old IT specialist who breeds tropical fish, was still keen, wasn't he?

Arthur hurries to the flat's second bedroom, set up as his study. The computer is already on. He scrolls back through his email exchanges with Jeff to reread what he has read many times over: 'I'd be honoured. Don't worry, a few years ago, one of my friends had surgery for prostate cancer so I know about the side effects.'

Arthur sits back in his chair. *Prostate cancer.* It still strikes him as ridiculous, even though he expected something in his body to go wrong eventually. He used to fear HIV and AIDS, but after turning sixty he'd begun to ponder his other options: a heart attack, perhaps a stroke. When his urine stream slowed to an exhausting, exasperating dribble, he assumed it was nothing to worry about. Even when his GP referred him to the urologist, Arthur was sure despite the X-rays, ultrasounds, the blood and urine tests that he would need nothing more drastic than a course of antibiotics.

Every wall in Dr Connor's consulting room was covered in posters showing cross-sections of male anatomy in vivid primary colours. What made Arthur smile was the incongruity of a single framed Monet print.

'*Nymphéas bleus*,' he said.

Dr Connor, rifling through paperwork with a frown as if she needed glasses, looked up. 'I'm sorry?'

'Blue water lilies,' Arthur said, and inclined his head towards the print. 'It's a bit lost amongst all the dicks, balls, bladders and bums, isn't it?'

'Yes, I suppose it is,' she said, and smiled, briefly. 'Mr Ryland, what do you do for a living?'

'Please, call me Arthur.'

'Arthur, does your workplace owe you any leave?'

A prickle of alarm nettled him for the first time since these silly tests began. He said, 'I'm actually a college professor. I teach English and American literature. I have twelve weeks off a year, and the usual sick leave entitlements on top of that. Why? What's wrong with me?'

That night, he rang his brother to tell him the news. Arthur stops himself from recalling their conversation. *It's best not to think about that, too painful to remember.* In fact, compared with that terrible phone call, the operation itself, two days later, was nothing. They wheeled him on a gurney into a white room with bright lights and stuck a needle in his arm and when he woke up, groggy and confused, it was already over.

He spent six nights on the ward. In the beginning, time passed in a pleasant fog of morphine dreams. Then, as staff switched his medication to codeine and anti-inflammatory drugs, he began to re-enter the world. First to register was the hospital stink of bleach, cabbage, and musty refrigerant from the air conditioning system. The bed sheets were so starched they rustled like paper. Plenty of Arthur's friends, colleagues and students came by with hearty smiles and offerings of balloons, fruit baskets or flowers, but he came to realise that there was no one to haunt his bedside, no one to hold his hand and weep. Arthur's last significant relationship had ended twelve years ago, at his partner's instigation.

On his fifth day in hospital, Dr Connor visited him in the morning as usual, but she was dressed in jeans and a jacket rather than her white coat, and this time she took a seat. It made Arthur uneasy.

He said, 'Not operating today?'

'It's Sunday.'

'Already? I'm losing track of time in this place. What are you doing here?'

'Checking up on you. How are you feeling?'

'I'm not sure,' he said, and braced himself. 'Am I going to die?'

'Probably not. Try not to worry, I think I got it all. Now let's have a look at the wound.'

Arthur flipped back the sheet. A square of gauze the size of a handkerchief covered his abdomen, with a feathered bloodstain along the dressing's midline. Dr Connor lifted the surgical tape and opened the dressing like a book cover. A snarl of black stitches wove through a raw clotted slash that ran from Arthur's navel to the root of his penis. The skin along both sides of the cut was buckled and puckered as if the sutures had been pulled too tight in places. Arthur felt sick to look at it.

'Terrific, no sign of infection, that's great.' She closed the dressing, tucked the sheet around him, then laid her hand on his. 'Are you doing your pelvic floor exercises?'

'As best as I can. How long before I can stop wearing a nappy?'

'If you keep up your exercises and do them every day, you'll have bladder control in about three or four months.' She patted his hand. 'No one likes wearing the incontinence pads, but it's only temporary.'

'Unlike the other issue.'

She nodded, gave his hand a squeeze. 'Have you spoken to the hospital's social worker about that? She can arrange some counselling for you, put you in touch with a support group in your area.'

Arthur set his teeth. 'I don't want to talk about my dead dick, and I certainly don't want to sit around and play woe is me with others in the same predicament.'

'It's not dead, Arthur.'

'A dick that can't get hard is as good as dead.'

'We had to cut the nerves that control erection but the sensory nerves are intact. You'll still feel pleasure, you'll still be able to climax.' She paused, searching his face. 'Please consider seeing the social worker. OK? Don't try to get through this alone.'

'Why not? I've got through everything else that way and I'm pretty bloody good at it by now.'

But for the first few weeks at home, he was an old man and it frightened him. His spine was a column of broken bricks, his insides a bucket of broken glass. The drugs Dr Connor had given him were only pharmacy-strength ibuprofen and he watched the clock, waiting for every dose. Reading was too much effort so he lay on the couch with the television on and allowed whole days to pass in a blur. Friends dropped in from time to time with casseroles and soups. When he could be bothered, he ate the donated meals cold from the fridge. *This is what dying must feel like*, he would think, nothing momentous or grand in any of it, just pain and humiliation, an unmanning of oneself.

Arthur shoves back the chair from the computer desk and stands up, panting. For a moment, he is lost. Then he remembers Jeff. He checks the clock. Just after five. Jeff will be here in less than two hours. Arthur heads to the kitchen.

According to his profile on the dating website, Jeff likes Italian food, so Arthur has opted to cook fettuccine carbonara. He chops the bacon and onion, and refrigerates them under plastic wrap. He washes and dries the rocket leaves and mixes olive oil and balsamic vinegar in a jar. He takes the store-bought mud cake from the fridge so that it can come to room temperature over the next few hours. He tidies the kitchen and wipes down the benches. He sets the table in the lounge room with his best napery and puts out wineglasses, silver cutlery, the cruet set. He places a posy of cream ranunculus on the table, and steps back to admire the effect. Dizziness washes over him again.

By the phone in the kitchen is Dr Connor's business card. On the back of the card is her handwritten mobile number. Arthur picks up the phone. *Where do I go from here?* he wants to ask, but that's a stupid facile question for a Saturday evening when Dr Connor is probably out with her husband and children, maybe enjoying a movie, an early dinner. He puts the phone back on its cradle.

He thinks of calling his brother, but the impulse is fleeting, nothing but a sad hangover from another time. Their last conversation, the phone call Arthur made on the day of his diagnosis, was more than Arthur could take and he has nothing left for another try. He doesn't want to think about it but the memory is insistent this time and comes back anyway.

'I'm sorry this has happened to you,' his brother said, 'but I can't say I'm surprised.'

'I know,' Arthur said. 'I shouldn't be either at my age. Something was bound to crop up.'

'No, that's not what I meant. Our choices have consequences, Art, and when we make the wrong choice, a choice against nature, we have to pay for it.'

A singing of blood started up in Arthur's head. 'I don't follow.'

'No, really? You're going to make me spell it out?'

'Yes. Yes, I think you'd better.'

There was a long pause. Finally, his brother said, 'You don't see the significance of getting cancer in your cock, of all places? Come on, Art, it's obvious, isn't it? It's time to pay the piper.'

'Oh, Jesus,' Arthur said, his heart banging and flopping against his ribs, 'you can't be serious. You're not serious, are you? I could be dying.'

'Maybe you should've thought of that in the first place.'

And in a rush of awful comprehension, Arthur's relationship with his younger brother suddenly made sense. For years, Arthur had found out after the event about parties, school concerts and graduations. *My brother has his wife and kids; they're busy*, he would say, defending them against the accusations and suspicions of his friends. *I'm always overseas, I'm a difficult man to catch*. But privately, Arthur was baffled by his exclusion. It had made him try harder. He'd never forgotten a birthday and had always hosted them regularly for brunches, Sunday roasts or barbecues, despite the lack of return invitations. Now he understood, truly, what their silences had meant.

'You rotten bastard,' Arthur said and hung up.

His brother never called back. Neither did his sister-in-law or his teenage nieces. It was like he'd already died. The sensation of being dead killed his appetite and broke his sleep, left him sitting in an armchair staring at nothing, peeled his skin and made him cry at unexpected moments.

He passes a hand over his face and notices that he's sweating. He checks the clock. Only an hour until Jeff arrives.

Arthur shaves first. He rinses the stubble down the bathroom sink and regards the mirror. He smiles, mouths a few words of greeting, nods, waits as if listening, all the while studying himself in the glass. The normalcy of his face is curiously reassuring. Sometimes he stares at his reflection but doesn't know what it is that he's looking for. A way back, perhaps.

Arthur strips off his tracksuit. Six weeks on, the scar is a thin rosy line and the pubic hair has grown back into its familiar grey frizz. But then there is his dick. Arthur touches himself, tentatively, fingering the softness, and remembers the dream from a couple of weeks ago. He dreamt that he was sitting on the toilet when he glanced into the bowl and saw his severed dick and balls, waxy and bloodless, floating like seaweed in the water. He woke up and switched on the bedside lamp to chase away the shadows and slow his heart but it wasn't enough.

Out on the balcony, the frigid night air hit him like a train. For a while, it soothed him to imagine the breeze having travelled from the caps of Antarctica, skipping across waves, phosphorescence, ships and breaching whales, to finally include him in its icy breath before moving on to sweep over other balconies, other faces. Then he opened his eyes. The front yard's evergreen alder shook its knotty arms at him. Illusions of the dark, he saw ravens in the branches, witches' claws in the leaves.

While towelling off after his shower, Arthur decides that if Jeff changes his mind, there'll be no hard feelings. Arthur steps into his underpants and affixes a fresh incontinence pad along the gusset. He puts on his favourite linen trousers, a white shirt, and a cotton jumper that matches the green of his eyes. With fifteen minutes to go, he pours himself a Merlot, sits in his armchair and contemplates the flowers on the dining table at the other end of the room. Whatever happens tonight is an experiment, an intellectual exercise. The ticking of the mantel clock hushes him.

The intercom buzzes. Arthur crosses the room, hesitates, and presses the button to unlock the building's front entryway. There is the faint clang of the security gate as it shuts. The shuffle of footsteps carries up the stairwell. The knock at his door is a jaunty shave-and-a-haircut kind of knock, which makes Arthur smile. He takes a breath and opens the door.

'Jeff! Good to see you in person at last.'

'Same here. Thanks for the invite.'

They shake hands. Jeff has dark wavy hair, big eyes behind wire-rimmed glasses, and a dimple in his chin. He's shorter than Arthur and stands heavy and round-shouldered with something of the teddy bear about him. He's even wearing a fuzzy brown jumper and brown corduroy trousers.

119

'Please, come in.'

'I brought you this,' Jeff says, and holds out the wine bottle. 'It's Tempranillo, from Spain. Have you tried it before?'

'No, my experience of Spanish wine begins and ends with sangria.'

'Then you're in for a treat.' Jeff puts his hands on his hips and surveys the room. 'Great flat. And what a location. You're practically on the beach. Any balconies?'

'Only one, in my bedroom. Would you care to go out on it? It's quite cold, I'm afraid, with the sea breeze.'

Cars whoosh back and forth on the road below. The wind brings the chill and the sound of the ocean breaking against the sand. Above the black horizon is the glow from a solitary ship.

Jeff, leaning his elbows on the railing, says, 'That wind is coming straight off Antarctica, right?'

'Why, yes. It's funny you should say that. I think about Antarctica every time I'm out here. How I'm sharing the same air with penguins.'

'And whales too, don't forget.'

'Yes,' Arthur says, and smiles. 'And whales too.'

The alder tree sways and rattles its branches but Arthur keeps his gaze on Jeff's profile. The breeze sifts through Jeff's hair and for a time there is nothing else.

Jeff turns to him. 'Hey, you're shivering. Come on, let's go in and have some Tempranillo. I hope you like strawberries and plums because that's what it tastes like.'

'Really? I can't wait to try.'

Jeff holds out his hand. Arthur takes it, and allows Jeff to lead him back into the warmth.

Deborah Sheldon

Double mastectomy

After the surgery
she touches herself shyly
the way he might
if he ever touches her again.

She remembers reading
amputees feel aches and itches
in phantom limbs,
thinks about the memories

her body holds, wonders
if, when she hears a baby cry,
she'll feel lost nipples prick
with engorgement's almost-pain

and then the sweet release
as the milk lets down.

Robyn Mathison

Prosthesis

She stands on her bed, eyes in the mirror
holding the fabric just so,
eight inches above the ankles
where an over-muscled leg
and a withered one almost match.
She dreams of the day she'll be old enough
to wear her skirt that long,
born too early for the blue-jean craze
that would make her look like everyone else.

When miniskirts become the fad
she gets a zip-on mould, skin-toned.
Covered by tights it looks just like her big leg.
The spongy form gives her a reprieve
from *the look*,
the one guys give her
the first time they notice
and turn off.

Dianne Hicks Morrow

Before they fall

And in this dream I'm going grey
If you can't take your friends with you
you can take them a long way
before they fall
into the madness or the grave[1]

Lightfoot lads[2]

In 1972, my sixteen-year-old brother had a scrap of handwritten Hindi
script taped up on his sleep-out wall. A budding linguist, he had asked
the new boy in class to write down something in his own language.
Translated into English the text read 'Mohan fell down from the roof'.
The choice struck my brother as delightfully odd. Multiculturalism
and flat, terraced roofs were unknown in our working-class Australian
suburb. My brother and the new boy, whose family started the first local
Indian restaurant, became friends.

I have a habit of inheriting other people's friends and this lad was
one of them. To begin with, he wasn't all that different. In those years
all of us were a little crazy. Late adolescence is a time when everyone
is tumbled up and experimenting and it's hard to predict trajectories.
After a while, though, it became clear that – in defiance of McMurphy's
maxim – this young man actually was a little crazier than the 'average
asshole out walkin' around on the streets'.[3] He was still loosely connected
with a circle of friends but you could see people starting to withdraw,
to recoil at his strangeness. It was worse with those meeting him for the
first time. Their automatic equation of mental illness with murderous-
maniac was compounded by the fact that he was a giant of a man. And
I understood that he could appear scary. The thing is I knew he had no
harm in him, that he would do no willing damage physical or moral to
any other living being. I can't tell you how I knew this. I just did. And
in the decades of friendship that ensued I never had cause to go back
on that original instinct.

The one that got away

In my late twenties, suffering from deep depression over the loss of a long-term relationship, I spent two weeks in a psychiatric ward. Even at that time, buried under a ton of neurosis and grief, I must have possessed an internal recording device: Graham Greene's 'splinter of ice in the writer's heart'.[4] All my life I have valued seeing how things operate backstage of normality. My friend knew of my brief sojourn on D Ward and it created a certain *esprit de corps*. It was a matter of constant fascination to him how I managed to be the one that got away. He would speak of it more with awe than envy – thrilled by my escape, and rueful about his own inability to elude the clutches of lifelong mental health care. Recourse to the DSM would provide no genuine response to this puzzle. His questions were, at heart, philosophical. Neither of us had good answers. I don't know why he had such a tough and lonely life. I don't know what could have been done differently or by whom. I've no doubt his psychiatrists were equally stuck. Heavy drugs, some with hideous side-effects, were often all they had in their repertoire.

The brook too broad for leaping

If medicine was grossly inadequate, neither did education help. Perhaps he's been in your classroom. I know his kin have been in mine. Have I been kind enough? Year after year my friend enrolled for diploma and certificate courses. He had a mental illness. He was not stupid. Both culturally and personally he was wired to see education as the royal road to the dream. He laid siege to this citadel for most of his adult life. He'd pace by the broad moat outside the castle walls. He was convinced that the sure-fire strategy was qualifications plus employment equals eligibility and therefore marriage and family. He tried to storm the battlements again and again. It just didn't work for him, although once or twice he captured a certificate that could be framed and hung on his wall. No surprise that when his illness was florid he awarded himself all kinds of extra titles and qualifications, particularly the one with most currency in his world: *Doctor*. If courage, persistence and life experience were worth credit points, he'd earned the right.

The gentle art of conversation

For the most part, our friendship was conducted via the telephone. He would call me perhaps two or three times as frequently as I would call him. He did not call too often. There are no edicts on the etiquette of conversing with people who are mentally ill, so we figured it out as we went. This mutual and organic building of boundaries worked, which is fair evidence of the health of our connection. For my part, I cleaved to the principle that his mental state was not the sum of his identity. I am no post-Laing Pollyanna – his illness and its markers were undeniable. I entertained no fantasies that unlike psychiatry or education, my friendship could 'save him'. It's just that I strived to avoid reducing him to that ill-labelled thing called schizophrenia.

It's true that the topics of conversation would sometimes get a little weird, in the vein of people-speaking-through-the-TV and claims of having lived for three thousand years. My first gambit was always to ignore this stuff in the hopes that it would go away soon, which half the time it did. If it persisted, he could sometimes be deflected with gentle teasing. He had a wonderful sense of the ludicrous. Every so often his deep sexual frustration would manifest in talk about details I really didn't wish to hear. And I would tell him so in just about those words. And he would desist.

Unless you, too, have a friend like this you may be wondering about duty of care. Surely someone whose speech is delusional should be reported to the er – um – *authorities*? So that they can be placed in the right *care setting*? Of course, if I had ever had reason to believe his life or another's was threatened, then I would have fought to have him hospitalised. Even though I'm quite aware that such placements can be damn hard to come by. As it was I knew that he was in community care – medicated and seeing his psychiatrist regularly. By this stage, as far I could ascertain, practically everybody else in his life was interacting with him from the position of concerned professional. His mother had died years ago; his father remarried and moved interstate. Other friendships had withered. I was glad he had professional care, but I didn't want to be his caretaker. What are a few delusions between friends?

The hunger

Rarely I would receive a letter – always with the full allotment of honorifics and qualifications accorded to both the addressee (actual) and the sender (a mixture of actual and imagined). These letters were heartfelt and highly literate. Some were filled with haikus of loneliness so raw, so honest they bypassed my literary scruples and pierced my heart. One such letter arrived out of a long silence to tell me that he was being kept in Graylands Hospital and suffering dreadfully from hunger. Would I please bring food? Now I cannot attest to whether or not the food in Graylands is unappetising, but I've yet to see any kind of hospital food that would cause me to rejoice. Still, I wasn't going to give the gothic free rein and imagine that he was literally being starved in some Victorian House of Horrors. I did think that perhaps some new drug regimen was increasing his hunger – and that he was being fed lightly to keep his weight under control. The institution was neither demon, nor saint. But my friend was hungry and he had written to ask for food.

The airlock

By this stage, my husband had also inherited my inherited friend. We packed a basket with fruit and chocolate, bread and cheese. It was early evening when we arrived at Graylands which, at least architecturally, was a reasonable facsimile of a Victorian House of Horrors. The grounds were deserted and no central reception was evident – no easy way to discover which of the many buildings housed our friend. It was hard to even find someone to ask but we were eventually directed to the right place and, after being questioned with some suspicion, invited to wait.

I guess if you visit someone in prison, then it's an unpleasant fact of life that you will be viewed as a criminal associate, the purveyor of drugs or other contraband. But it took me by surprise that such guilt by association is also a hazard for those visiting the mentally ill. We were invited to sit in the airlock of a dismal waiting room, where the light was deeply unflattering and the furniture drab. An orderly locked the door from the outside.

Inside was bedlam. We could not see, but heard a loud voice over a PA system summoning one or another of the inmates to the nurses' station at frequent intervals. It was not conducive to serenity. We waited, wondering if we were under surveillance, until the key clicked. As an attendant ushered him in, I giggled nervously, hoping he hadn't made any grandiose pronouncements about his friend, *the Doctor*. I could see only too clearly how this might seal my fate as a fabulist, a potential denizen of the wrong side of the door, exactly the sort who might smuggle cigarettes or razors. Once the door was locked behind him, we unpacked the basket and he ate. Then it was just the three of us and we were OK in the neutral zone between here and there, the shared territory of our friendship. We set up the camera on the table and took several pictures of us together on the couch. The sort of casual snapshots people post on Facebook. It could have been an airport lounge anywhere.

The Larson dogs drive home

On rare occasions when he was relatively well, my friend would drive down and visit us at home, sometimes seeking assistance with an assignment. In recent years, it was more likely that we would visit him in his small flat. I never knew for sure, but I think the whole block was Church-run as supported accommodation. Although basic, his home could have been made pleasant. It was on the ground floor and had wide windows overlooking a park. Housekeeping was never his forté, though. The place was always cluttered and grubby but nothing we minded. Just shove a bit of stuff off the couch, sit down and have a cup of tea. The water had been boiled after all.

Harder to take was the incessant chain of cigarettes. We'd sit there like kippers being slowly smoked until one or other of us could stand it no longer. We'd drive home with our heads hanging out the car window worshipping the slipstream like Larson dogs. Maybe we should have said something, suggested we all go and sit in the park. I guess we could have tried. But at what cost? He would not have felt comfortable in the park. I witnessed him lit up with the ordinary joy of friends dropping in for a cup of tea. Such a thin filament this connection – I did not have the heart to snap it over smoke.

The Chinese vase

Mine was a late marriage, one made after many years of single life. Again, the gentle character of my friend can be seen by the fact that it was enthusiasm not envy that dominated his response to this change in my life. He and I had both known loneliness and he was thrilled at this turn of fortune, adamant that my husband and I should get on with it and produce a houseful of kids. And even though in that regard I'd left my run too late, he was glad of my luck in finding love. Happy, too, that the marriage had doubled the sum total of his friends.

It's a wired and multicultural socioverse we live in today. Maybe, given time, social networking might have provided him with a way to be more engaged with a wider world. Or maybe, like so many others, he might have fallen prey to the porn lords of cyberspace. No way of knowing. None of us were born digital natives. We had our beginnings in a different era. Beyond this, he also retained something of the slightly old-fashioned graciousness of his Anglo-Indian heritage. Being caught between so many cultures, he knew how to treasure the small courtesies. I learned from him that birthday and Christmas cards could be more than just a meaningless surrender to retail culture. Without fail the first Christmas card of the year was always from him.

He appreciated a good ritual, so it was sad that his illness prevented him from attending our wedding. He'd felt unable to deal with so many strangers. We'd wanted him to come – he would have been so welcome – but we understood that he couldn't face it. This led to a delicate situation because we were acutely aware of the slender resources provided by a disability pension, and the difficulties attendant on him moving beyond the very circumscribed boundaries of his world.

I tried suggesting that a card would be lovely, but a present completely over the top, as he was not actually coming to the wedding. He would not have a bar of it, was quite offended and utterly determined that we should have a present from him. And so he sourced and wrapped a large Chinese vase. Other friends thought we 'put on a good show' waxing enthusiastic when we unwrapped this particular gift. But it wasn't show. We knew its true cost. It was priceless.

Shadow line

Joseph Conrad[5] talks of crossing the shadow line, a particular passage known to sailors. It's his metaphor for those invisible points at which life subtly and irrevocably changes. My friend was turning fifty. A birthday card would not suffice. A fuss would be made. We rang up and said we were taking him out to lunch at his choice of venue. He nominated Hungry Jacks. We turned up with presents, card, balloons and the most over-the-top chocolate cake we could find. He bounded out of his flat and across the grass beaming like a huge shaggy bear being offered honey in spring. I had dressed up. He noticed and was touched. We made an odd trio. The young girl behind the counter looked a little unsure. Modestly, my friend ordered a very small meal. My husband leaned across and whispered. 'It's your birthday, have two if you want!' And he did. I do not frequent fast food joints but this was a happy meal for sure.

We returned to the flat for cake. We toasted with tea the fact that we had all survived to the age of fifty. On this day my vision lengthened and I began to see the wins as well as the losses. My friend had shelter, food, stability, independence. Too often people with similar illnesses are homeless, so many die young. The social contract was threadbare, but it held.

The following October we chose an all-you-can-eat Indian buffet – another winner. In the third year we had several phone conversations where he talked with relish of biryani feasts; we tried to track down a restaurant he had heard about on the radio. It was all arranged, but when the time arrived he could not bring himself to leave the flat, so we simply visited with him instead. We never saw him again.

No Christmas card came that year, early or late. We sent one to him that was never returned. It was the silly season. We were busy. I rang from time to time and only got the answering machine. I began to think he was back in hospital for a season, something that had happened regularly over the years. More time passed. I tried for information. I rang ARAFMI. I had no official status. Confidentiality could not be breached. But eventually a social worker took pity and told me over the phone that my friend had died in hospital from a physical illness three weeks after his last birthday.

With rue my heart is laden

I thought long and hard before writing this. I doubt it's possible to know for sure whether my wish to venerate a friendship violates instead. In the end, though, all of us are 'being what we could not help but be'.[6] He could not help being ill; I could not help writing. When I heard of his death I was compelled to talk to anyone I could think of who might have a passing remembrance of him from our shared youth. I was haunted by the anonymity of his death. Angry that the social net had in the end failed, that we did not visit him to offer comfort during his last days in hospital, that we had not been able to attend his funeral. Who had? Perhaps his few remaining family members; perhaps his psychiatrist; perhaps his overloaded caseworker. Did they all make the same assumption – that he had no friends at all? The sane can do you in as easily as the insane.

Like the fictitious Mohan, my friend fell. Suspend time; suspend suspicion of difference. Before he hits the ground, hold the whole arc of his life to the light. In sickness or in health, this was a good man, a golden friend.

Remember him for me.

Liana Joy Christensen

1. Erik Christensen, 'Personal Radio', unpublished song, quoted with permission.
2. This and other phrases throughout taken from A.E. Housman, 'With Rue My Heart is Laden', *The Norton Anthology of Poetry*, revised, W.W. Norton and Co, 1975.
3. Ken Kesey, *One Flew Over the Cuckoo's Nest*, Macmillan,1973.
4. Graham Greene, *A Sort of Life*, Simon and Schuster, 1971.
5. Joseph Conrad, *The Shadow-Line: A Confession*, Oxford University Press, 2002.
6. Judith Wright, 'The Poet', *Australian Poets: Judith Wright*, Angus and Robertson, 1963.

Journeying to lithium

A drunken night in Austria.
Black whisky sky. Stars
skewered by mountains.

You at the inn, propped in a corner, head
drooping on your outstretched arms. Being
Jesus. Toothpicks for your crown of thorns.

Me, playing Mary, sprinkling
pub salt on your bared feet.

Sacrificial Lamb meets Woman of Sorrows.

Baptised a Catholic, yet Jewish in name and nose,
your mania found expression in religious dilemmas.
Marriage crucified you on the altar
of an incurable disorder.

Lithium dulled your genius.
You preferred to soar and crash.

Me, shepherding the children
to sanctuary in your father's house.

You in the lady chapel cracking the midnight
with fractured psalms, kissing black Mary.
Your bleeding palms. Her carved breasts.

Gill Goater

Serengeti refugee

Politely smiling
she hides in the wilderness
behind her eyes.
Rooms can smile too
and gardens.

Or weep.

Cruel how soft the snow
beating against stark trees
the black and the white
pale fingers and dark bones
the pink fragility of flesh.

Behind the armchair
mullioned windows
and the green spears of snowdrops.
She has buried the grey baby
beneath the beech tree
where it can hear
the chatter in the afternoons
the plastic clatter of teaspoons.

Crouching behind the armchair
which she has stuffed
full of secrets she dreams
of the Serengeti
and the bulk
of elephants.

Gill Goater

It's called anencephaly

I wait amongst a sea of pregnant women,
wonder how I'm going to make a decision.
The nurse fills out forms,
asks me questions.

I ask if the malaria tablets I took
have caused harm to the foetus.
The doctor doesn't think there'll be a problem.
I would like an ultrasound.

Sometimes I imagine the baby
without a face. No eyes.
Hard to even say the words – *my child*.
It may not be true.

I like the smooth ultrasound appliance
moving over my stomach on thick cold blue gel.
The woman in a white coat
is a little awkward with all my questions.

The genetics counsellor sits squarely in front of me,
nothing between us,
she reminds me of what they could be looking for.
She mentions one – its name I never remember.
She is beautiful, and looks sad.
I want to hold her, comfort her but I am frozen
without feeling cold. Just suddenness.
Thick iron doors slam closed on my chest.

She calls it a freak of nature,
says it can happen in first pregnancies.
The baby may be born, but will not survive.
People in white coats hold my hand or touch me,
say they are sorry.

I speak as if I am telling somebody else's news:
She's not going ahead with the pregnancy.
There are complications; she'll be going into hospital.

It is gone now.
My breasts are sore and will soon deflate.
My stomach aches, soft with emptiness.

Like in a cave today.
Dark, empty.
Because I don't really know
what or how it happened.
I fumble through dark, empty caves,
pre-history of these days,
home that was once womb.
Lining of the soul, spread like green.

I am thinking of the earth.
Dark, rich mulch.
Thick with wet leaves and manure, composted.
Beauty decomposed.
The moist, heavy smell.
How soft it feels when light and dry,
by the end of summer, how fine.
How ready to receive the breakdown
of dry grass and old leaves. Spent twigs.

I am thinking about hard clay ground
strewn with quartz, held together by cold slate,
blue-grey and fragile.
How quickly it all turns from dust to mud, mud to dust.
Today I remember what I learned from the earth.
The way I could tell when the rains would come
and when they didn't, how to save.
Knowing how much each plant needed.
What made them grow a certain shape or height.
The taste of them.
How to shelter the weak and display the strong.
How to mend the broken.

Katherine E. Seppings

The Tao of loss

Even an abstract mindset
won't hold the canvas still.
I finally caught up with her
eating grapes outside the supermarket.
It's four months since the child died.
In typically comic mode, she says
nursing that kid was the hardest thing
she's ever done. She throws the
grape seeds into the ether as we talk.

The artist leans wildly into the work
looking for meaning.
She told me of the trip from
death's threshold in the Whittle Ward
direct to Myer because T-shirts were
on special and the kid wanted
to do her shopping since it now
looked like she'd see Christmas.

Beyond the horizon float watermelon
dreams and coloured stars.
I could see six years of exhaustion
in her face. She had the flu –
time at last to be sick.
She misses the child, she says,
but dislikes having the grave.
Wants to know where she really is.
Grape pips fly over her shoulder.
Her former belief system's crap now, she says.

Blended memories tumble in
and blow restless across the landscape.
Our paths have diverged since the early days.
She's still the consummate eccentric.
Laughing was always what we did best.
Even in grief she has life on a string.
Her agony is elusive and intangible,
dim and shadowy,
with almost an oriental flavour.
It reminds me of the time she came to a party
wearing chopsticks in her hair.

Fran Graham

Calving

My daughter appears from behind a mountain of salt to sing for the child. There is a small lake behind the mountain; from where I am sitting I can only see its edge. Algae has turned the water light pink. Rachel's dress is the same colour as the water. It looks as though she has risen from the lake to be sculpted by the salt into human form, an underwater goddess sent to name newborns.

She walks towards us. Her limbs seem heavy, minerals in the landscape pouring into her blood. The dress accentuates the roundness of her belly; she cradles it briefly with her hand as she walks. The woman sitting next to me, a family friend, notices the gesture. She raises her eyebrows and turns to me with a smile.

I shake my head and turn away.

My wife has explained to me that the event is called a naming ceremony. 'It's a sort of christening for people who aren't religious.' The parents are colleagues of our daughter. I suppose they're what people these days call foodies. They host regular dinners out here on the salt plain, showcasing local produce and wine. The tables have been set out in a row along solid ground. Crystals of different colours and textures decorate the tablecloths, forming swirls around the cutlery. Today's lunch is celebrating the naming of the couple's little boy. The child is seated on his mother's lap down the other end. He is tracing patterns in the salt. Rachel will perform the ceremony, singing a special composition. Normally I'm a bit bemused by these new-age celebrations – a christening should be a christening – but I'm touched by the idea of my daughter performing for this little boy, as though she is going to sing him into being.

As we wait for Rachel to reach the table, I sprinkle salt onto my plate. I dip my bread into olive oil. I am about to dip my bread into the salt.

My wife is gesturing to me from a few seats down. 'Darling, it's…'

I put my hand behind my ear. 'What?'

She points to my plate. 'It's sugar. Sugar.'

I look down. I have chosen the one bowl in this whole landscape that contains something other than salt. Neighbours have turned to look at me.

My wife looks around for a way to save me from this social gaffe, as she always does. She rolls her eyes, grinning. 'He can't help himself – he's a sweet-tooth!'

My neighbours laugh, turning back to watch Rachel. I try to focus my mind. I try not to think about this afternoon. We will be driving Rachel to the hospital straight after the ceremony. She has refused to cancel. Waiters around me have started serving up a new wine sorbet. I can't help wincing each time they scoop up a red mound.

'You won't know yourself,' Rachel's doctor has said to her. The doctor has been telling her to focus on the positives – she will have less pain, more energy. 'Honestly, you won't know yourself.'

I wonder if the doctor realises the prophecy in this statement. When Rachel wakes up after the operation she probably *won't* know herself; she will have to get used to the new person she has become. I wonder if my daughter is afraid of invisibility. It is a concept I read about in a women's magazine in the waiting room. Afraid that men's eyes will no longer rest on her as she walks past, that she will no longer be in the possession of something chemical, primal. I wonder if she will feel loss. If she will feel lighter.

Rachel picks up the boy. He rests in her arms. They look into each other's eyes. For a second I think I see another figure emerge from behind the salt mountain. It looks like a man with arms outstretched, about to embrace them both. I blink. The figure is the shadow from a piece of machinery. I raise my hand to shade my eyes. My elbow knocks over a bottle of wine. The liquid moves down the table. It is heading straight for Rachel and the boy. I jump up from my seat. For some reason, I think I have to stop the liquid from reaching my daughter. I am running with the wine as it soaks up the crystals, staining everything in its path. I reach the last table and put out my hand to stem the flow.

Last week, my colleagues forgot to invite me to lunch. I came back from a meeting to an empty office. My anxiety levels rose as I did laps of the floor, trying to work out if there was somewhere else I was meant to be.

The receptionist found me staring at a cartoon on a colleague's pinboard. 'I'm so sorry!' She is young; she wears very tight trousers and always touches my arm when she talks. 'I think I must have used an invitation list you once sent me. Because the email came from you – you weren't on the list!'

She had obviously practised the explanation with the other girls over coffee; when they realised I wasn't there, I imagined them putting their hands over their mouths, making the same sounds they make when they see kitten photos. By that stage I didn't mind – I was relieved to see everyone. While they were gone, I had noticed that all the clocks on the floor show slightly different times. I had taken the route from my pod past the kitchen, around to the sales team. Each clock I passed was a few minutes faster than the one before. I walked slowly, stopping to look at colleague's photos. As I walked, I saw my reflection in the glass windows of meeting rooms. When I reached the other side, the clock told me that time had stood still. I felt as though I had departed the world quietly, without anybody noticing – including me.

That night, I heard a strange noise in my sleep. It sounded like a howl of mourning, the dirge of a wild creature. I woke. The noise continued. My first instinct was to reach for my wife. She was there, soft and breathing. The noise was coming from Rachel's room out the back of the house. She was staying with us for a few weeks before and after the operation. I raced out the kitchen door across the garden, dew on the grass soaking into my feet. When I reached her room, she was slumped over in a chair. At first I thought someone was grabbing her head, pulling her down. My eyes focused. I saw she was wearing headphones, bending over her keyboard. She looked up with mild curiosity.

'Sorry, Dad.' She took off the headphones. 'I thought I'd made the room soundproof.'

I calmed down. She explained that she was trying to create a new sound with her voice. I am always fascinated by these experiments, even though I prefer her more conventional tunes. She has become well known for interpreting landscapes in her music. Fans line up to hear her singing rock formations, trees, sand dunes.

'I'm trying to capture the sound of calving.'

'Oh, right.'

She turned off her recorder to give me her full attention. I am no longer shocked by her ideas. Her most crazy thoughts always turn out to be the most successful. Experience has taught me to give feedback at these moments. 'Interesting. It does sound quite...bovine.'

She stared at me. Her nostrils quivered. It was a sign. She was about to collapse with laughter. I seem to be the one person who is able to do this to her; usually, I might add, when I'm not trying to be funny. It starts in her nostrils, moves to her stomach then takes over her whole body, as if a cheeky imp is shaking her. Eventually her frame can no longer contain the humour; she is forced to cross her arms, slumping forward with her forehead on her hands. I think it is when I love her best.

'You dag.' She pulled herself upright, wiping her eyes. 'An *iceberg* calving. I mean the sound an iceberg makes when it splits from a glacier.'

It was a sound she heard during an artist's residency in Alaska. She showed me a video on YouTube. It showed a massive glacier, turrets of ice rising up like a castle. The landscape was still. Suddenly, without warning, a crack appeared and a small turret of ice cleaved away. It fell, as though a magician's hand had ordered it to disappear. It splintered into hundreds of small islands drifting on the water.

'It was the most amazing sound. There was a crack. A low roar became louder and louder.' We watched the video again. 'It had this incredible... energy. As though it was crying out a warrior call – a protest – before it fractured in the water.' She smiled up at me. 'If I can create that sound, I think I will have pushed my voice as far as it can go.'

There was no doubt she would succeed. I said nothing. She responds best to a challenge. I patted her head (she still lets me do this every now and then) and went back to the bedroom. I heard the sound again as I was getting back into bed. Even though I didn't like the sound – I didn't really understand it – I loved listening to her voice. She would work long into the night. A thought occurred to me as I pulled the doona up to my chin. Perhaps the noise was not all practice.

*

The wine seeps into my hand as though I've been marked.

My wife touches my shoulder. The little boy's mother smiles up at me.

'Well done, you stopped it getting on anyone's clothes. And the one thing that gets a wine stain out of a tablecloth is salt – there's certainly no shortage!' My wife leads me back to my seat.

In the last year or so, people have started treating me very kindly. I wonder if this is some sort of sign.

Rachel sings to the boy. She is transformed. The young man opposite me sits up straighter, seeing my daughter for the first time. It is something I have witnessed often. The notes peel back an invisible veil to reveal her true self – all the beauty, passion and strength that usually stay locked away behind her shyness. The song is perfect. There is a certain quality in her voice – I can only think of it as saltiness – as though she has drawn up the whole landscape through her feet into her heart, pouring it into the eyes of this lucky child who is being welcomed to the world. I have never heard her sing like this before. She is drawing on something new.

'There is something inside me, it's just not human.' Rachel was on the phone to a girlfriend last night. 'And hey, at least it's not cancer! Still. It's like mother nature's punishing me – giving me all the symptoms of childbirth without the child.'

She laughed. It was a brave laugh. The woman on the end of the phone was laughing with her. I am surprised when I hear people talk about the lack of support between women, the malice women supposedly show each other. Rachel's girlfriends have helped her through all the difficult times in her life. Never more so than now. They turn up with a sort of holy trinity of healing – DVDs, chocolate and tissues. The strength she gains from her friends is different to the support she receives from family. Even her brother, usually so supportive, has been absent this time. 'I'll be there when she's out of hospital but I can't talk to her about it,' Mark said when I gently reproached him. 'It's too hard.'

On the other end of the phone, the woman must have asked Rachel why she feels she is being punished. I leaned in.

'Not sure. Forgetting I'm a woman, perhaps. For drifting.'

I was surprised. For someone so driven, so focused, I couldn't understand how she could describe herself this way. I have listened to her practising one sound, over and over again, for weeks on end. There is still a whole universe inside my daughter that I will never see. I stayed awake for hours. I remembered something my wife had said to Rachel a few years ago, not long after our daughter's thirtieth birthday. 'You're not a nurturer. You never have been.'

I saw the shock of rejection in our daughter's eyes, as though she had been called a failure, cast out into the desert. My wife was trying to compliment Rachel on her ability to pursue an artistic life. Those two almost enjoy misunderstanding each other. No mother has ever been more full of love for her children than my wife; it flows out of her, on and on, like a waterfall. Because of this love – not despite it – my wife has always been slightly afraid of Rachel. 'It's that sliver.' We once heard a writer talking about his theory; all artists, he believed, have a sliver of ice in their hearts, a certain callousness. It helps them to detach from their strongest emotions; it allows the painter who has walked into the suicide of a friend to file away the scene for the next picture. 'She's had that sliver since primary school.'

I think I know what my wife means – it comes through as a hardness in Rachel's eyes. I have always seen it as something quite different. One day, when Rachel was very young, I saw her future. There was nothing airy-fairy or spiritual about it – I saw very clearly how she would interact with the world when she was a woman.

This moment happens to all parents, I'm sure. I was picking her up from school. A group of children were playing a marching band game with invisible instruments. The ringleader, a boy, was giving the other little girls roles in the drama; this one was to play the flute, that one the trombone. The game started. The boy had forgotten Rachel. He wasn't being malicious or bullying – he had simply not noticed her. There was no instrument he could equate her with, so he didn't see her. I saw the hurt in my daughter's eyes. I watched, fascinated, as she transformed it into something else. She hung her head then literally drew herself up, looking excited. She picked up the lid of a rubbish bin and began playing it like a drum. It was what the game needed. Before the drumming, the game was vague. The ringleader didn't have the skill to bring his little band to life. With the drumming, the marching began. The game worked.

As Rachel watched her reflection in the lid I saw that she too, at some unconscious level, was seeing her own future. We were both seeing the possibility of loneliness. From that moment, I think we both understood that she could not count on the idea of partnership; there might not ever be a mate who would hear her particular call. Men would respect her, admire her, listen to her. They would not necessarily choose her. Because she couldn't rely on anyone to take care of her, she would have to nurture herself. We enrolled her in music lessons the next day. I was determined. No matter how many times she had to bow her head, she must always be able to draw herself upright again.

'I think it's wonderful the way you encourage Rachel's singing and her intellect,' a teacher said soon afterwards. 'Not all fathers do, you know.'

As she started to become a singer, as her independence grew, so too (and this is one piece of advice which the women's magazines get right) did her desirability to the opposite sex. Her independence started creating its own energy. In doing so it pushed her even further away from the world of romance; like Frankenstein creating the very monster who punishes him for the act of creation. The men who had thought she was not worthy of attention now began to think they were not worthy of her.

It has been this way ever since. She is too timid in a crowd, too mythical on stage. The poor man sitting opposite me now is only one of many. He doesn't understand how to approach her. He will think about Rachel at dinner tonight; he will not ask her to join him.

Perhaps I should have taught her about men, desirability, the rules of attraction. Of course, I couldn't. I don't understand them myself.

*

My fingernails are digging into my palm as Rachel sings. I'm not sure why. She nears the end. I realise I am worried about that strange noise I heard a few nights ago – the calving sound. If she uses it now it will be so wrong, inappropriate. She reaches the last phrase. I needn't have worried. The sound was not for this song. How could I have doubted her?

She finishes. The final note is offered up. She kisses the boy on the forehead. The audience is still. Nobody claps. We wait, suspended in this magical moment. The boy closes his eyes. I suddenly see something very clearly. Rachel has not chosen this life, it has chosen her. She did not discover the sounds in the salt plain, they discovered her. She was called here today for a purpose. To bless a child, then give him back.

The parents take their boy. Rachel bows her head slightly. She turns to disappear behind the mountain, this desert iceberg. I don't want her to go. I leave my seat to take her hand. She is a salt sculpture; when she walks back into the lake, she will dissolve. She will dissolve.

'It's OK, Dad.' She kisses my hand. 'I need to get changed.'

When she reappears, she is wearing everyday clothes. Her outfit is strange. It looks like a patchwork quilt, a jumble of colours and patterns with no relation to each other. It makes me think of a picture of ancient earth with all the tectonic plates outlined before they shift. She has tied a scarf around her neck in a large knot. The scarf is holding all the separate pieces together, supporting her chin. She nods. 'I'm ready.'

We settle Rachel into her hospital room. She is in for observation overnight. The operation will take place the next day. Her brother is on his way from interstate. Mark will arrive for all the practical tasks such as carrying bags and helping her up stairs. She has taken a sleeping pill.

My wife leaves to find some water, returning empty-handed. Rachel smiles at us. She is almost asleep. We try to think of something to say.

An orderly enters the room with the glass of water for my wife. We turn, distracted. There is a bucket of ice by the bed. The orderly picks up an ice cube with tongs to drop into the glass. Rachel speaks behind us. We turn back. My wife bends down, trying to decipher what our daughter has said.

'Something about her brother?' She leans in closer then looks up at me. 'I think she's asking for Mark.' She strokes Rachel's forehead. 'He'll be here soon, darling.'

I squeeze my wife's shoulder. I have kept few secrets from her – this one will remain with me until the end. If Rachel had wanted her brother, she would have called for him by name. I know what my daughter has said as she slips into unconsciousness. It is something I have waited for since she was born – an insight into the heart of this mysterious creature we brought into the world and will never fully know. The words rise up from the bed as she goes under.

I could have been a good mother.

There is a crack – it could be the ice cube as the orderly drops it into water – and a low roar. It gathers energy as it reaches my ears. I'm not sure if it is coming from the bed or my wife or a machine or my imagination but as it fills my head I finally understand the sound my daughter has been trying to capture. I hear it now.

Georgina Luck

Vacant seats

I

I can see my friend is uncomfortable
explaining to me why I haven't seen her much lately
telling me about her morning sickness,
how she's been tired and nauseous in the evenings,
usually in bed by eight-thirty –
'…but anyway, what have you been up to?' she quickly asks,
too aware
of her belly's warm bump
facing my enduring flatness.

II

Have you ever noticed
how many cute babies there are
in airports?

As we wait at our gate,
I watch the ones around me.

A toddler in the row facing me
wears a mock miniskirt
attached to a blue stripy top.
The outfit hovers above pudgy legs.
She stands, wobbling, on the seat,
grips the backrest,
gurgles back at the adoring adults around her.

On the plane
I chew envy-salted peanuts,
jealous even of the parents
wrestling
the screaming baby up the back.

III

Despite what you might think,
the day the blood starts flowing
is not the worst day of the cycle.
It is bitter, yes,
but it is also a momentary resolution,
an answer to the unbearable uncertainty,
the what's-going-on-with-my-body preoccupation.
No matter where I am, what I'm doing,
my body is there too, teasing me
with food cravings, mood swings,
abdominal pains and strange sensations...
yes, the usual pre-period signs too,
but impossible not to get my hopes up each time
despite the foolishness of it...
so when the blood starts flowing, there is relief,
sadness
and sometimes despair
but at least there is an understanding again
between me and my body
and for a while there is nothing to do
but bleed.

IV

My french-fry-feeding fingers
leave oily fingerprints on my wine glass.
I savour the aroma
of a finely-balanced Tasmanian Sauvignon Blanc.

It's not good for the budget, this pregnancy game –
every bottle bought could be my last
so each month, at the bottle-shop,
I splash out on quality.

I secretly enjoy the fact
that I can take an expensive bottle
to dinner with pregnant friends
and know that it is all mine,
a crisp, clean, citrus-tinged
condolence.

V

Maybe my eggs have heard the scientist's predictions
of arctic ice melt, climate disaster –
taken the compassionate option
and bailed out.

VI

The board-game *Articulate*.
She holds the playing card over her pregnant belly,
gives clues excitedly as the sand funnels through the egg timer…
A woman who can't have children!
Like a desert where nothing grows!
Barren! another friend chimes, her two-year-old curled up in her lap.
Yes, that's it! Smiles, quickly moves on to the next clue.
I sit there, a sudden ache in my abdomen.
That's me you're talking about,
a desert where nothing grows?

VII

I drive around for a few days
with a baby capsule and a toddler's car seat in the back,
running errands before my sister and her kids
arrive for our wedding.

These seats should be for our children, my partner says,
as we ferry the flowers and vases to the wedding venue,
and I nod, admitting I have felt a bit uncomfortable
knowing they are behind me
wherever I go,
those empty seats
occupied by the could've, should've beens,
the ghosts of our desire.

Susan Austin

Sailing the sabot

You lie on your back, lashes bruising your cheeks,
shuttering the dark, so deeply asleep

you are marble, except for the faint snore
that is baby animal, all paws

and whiskers; your stillness shocks –
wriggles and twitches absent – my heart stops,

sound registers slowly, then my blood hammers.
That afternoon, clumsy with my cells' new clamour,

I'd pushed you off, your grandfather at the helm
and the boat luffed; you were in a separate realm,

tiny in the orange bow – Thumbelina adrift
on a water lily leaf. All I saw, was you swept

or swallowed by the waves, the horizon, the world;
I would have parted seas for you, kicked and called

with your brother dipping inside of me, his limbs
already swimming; water-winged.

I stood in the shallows, watched the wind whisk you
to submerged shadows, I cried to the steel-blue

to release its hold, the wind to blow you back
to my arms so that I could wrap

you like a flower, take you home
and anchor you, asleep in your room,

where the walls are a shifting-ocean blue,
fathoms deep as my need of you.

Adrienne Eberhard

Echo location

No lights are on inside. The headlights show the path to the door but she must turn them off. The six steps to the landing fade. She will find the car door open tomorrow. She will not remember not closing it. She trips on the bottom step and grazes the heel of her hand, the firm, padded part where the lifeline begins, or ends, she doesn't know which.

She runs her bloodied hand along the wall until it meets wood. Her keys are still in her other hand. One more lock and she will be home. She has to walk back to the top of the steps to choose the right key by starlight. No lights on inside, no light on the landing, no moon. She is usually home, cooking, curled up in front of the television, reading, waiting, by this time. She has forgotten about darkness.

Her back is between the starlight and the lock when she finds the door again. The key will not find the lock. Again and again it scrapes against metal. She leans her forehead against the cool of the wood to still her shaking. *Trembling hands*, she thinks, words, part of a melody that cannot soothe. A car hums down the road, brakes at the corner. A swoop of wings leaves the jacaranda out front. It can't be a bird. Not in the dark. She closes her eyes, blind, and lifts the key. It fits instantly and turns and cracks open the door. Bats find their way by echo location, she is using the echo of memories.

She clicks on every switch she passes. Light streams in her wake. The water is cold and hard as it washes her blood into the kitchen sink; the tea-towel is rough and hot as she pats the skin on her palm dry. She doesn't know what to do. Now she is home. That's all she wanted to do: get home. She will find her keys in the kitchen sink amongst the dirty teaspoons tomorrow. She is not drunk, that is no explanation.

She needs a drink. There is nothing in the pantry. The fridge light turns on to add to the illumination of rooms and corners and hallways and ornamental niches. Beer, cold, sits by the milk, but she does not like it and it is not hers. She goes back to the pantry and unscrews the lid of the vanilla essence. The lid sits like a yellow lolly in her good hand, and the small bottle knocks against the graze on the other. She takes a swig. Thirty-five per cent alcohol. Her gasp is the only noise in the house to compete with the drone of the fridge. She takes another swig. The dark liquid is burning the inside of her nostrils as much as her throat. The third gulp is better. Then it makes sense to finish the bottle.

Having someone wonder where you are when you don't come home at night is a very old human need. Something Margaret Mead wrote. She wonders why she cannot think in her own words but must borrow from others. Or perhaps this was simply a stray thought that had her name on it, ready to be picked up when she needed it, when there was no one there to worry why she was home late. Why there'd been no lights on. Why the darkness had got in.

There are stray thoughts and wild thoughts and she knows the feral ones are out there for when she turns the lights out again. They'd been there waiting at the hospital, they'd been there in the car. She puts the empty vanilla essence bottle back in the pantry between the cinnamon and thyme and the tin box holding birthday candles and matches. She closes the pantry door then closes her eyes again to find herself in the memories before the echoes fade to nothing.

After she's vomited up the vanilla essence and the salty chips from the vending machine in the corridor at the hospital, she needs to clean her teeth. She stands in front of the mirror and does not see herself. There is a very old woman there. Her jaw is indistinct and her eyes are at the bottom of black depressions. When old women like this lose their husbands, they are widows. When they lose their mother and then their father, they are orphans. Where is the word for when they lose a child?

No, she cannot find one. No word. It is not there in the mirror or in the pool of light splashing on the bathroom porcelain. It is not there in any of her memories. Eyes closed, eyes open. After nineteen years of being a mother, she thought she would have come across it. Learnt it. By heart. In her heart.

She is tired in a way she's only felt once before. Pregnancy-tired. A tiredness that fills her head and leaks out to fill the bathroom. She looks down at the two toothbrushes in the daisy-painted cup. A blue one and an orange one, both with stubbly grips and soft, worn heads. She stares at them. She cannot remember which is hers. There is no one to ask.

Jane Downing

He's only sleeping

My belly is a china cabinet
for you,
my Lithopedian child.

I have softly rocked you
calcified in your cradle
for forty-six years.

Your fingers are old ivy
seeking the door
of my womb.

Now the surgeon comes
with his starry hook
wanting to open your shell.

Roll your stone dreams into me,
preserve us, my natural pearl.

I'll tell the surgeon
you are only sleeping.

Karen Knight

Zahra Aboutalib defied odds of 600,000,000 to 1 when a baby boy grew to
full-term between her stomach and womb, died and remained there, fossilised,
for forty-six years. At the age of eighty-one, she had him surgically removed.

This too will pass

Water slaps at their bare brown ankles, maroon and saffron robes caught-in at the waist away from the splashing of tiny waves in the shallows. Dying rays of the sun glint on their smooth, shaven heads and the droplets of water flying around their feet. They scoop the wet sand in their hands and let it fall. The water washes back, dragging the sand with it. The occasional murmured chant mingles with the cry of seabirds and the endless rushing of waves.

A tiny body slides into the bare white and cold steel glare, wailing at the discomfort and unfamiliarity of this new world. They wrap him firmly in white and pass him to me. I feel my heart explode with joy.

The days pass by in a dreamy haze, punctuated by frequent visits from friends cooing and marvelling at this new life brought forth from my own body.

They crouch on their knees with smooth heads bent low to the task. Steady hands hold tiny tubes from which they tap coloured sands onto the floor, following the lines and curves of the circular pattern drawn there. Beginning at the centre, they work outward. Tirelessly, meticulously, heeding the tiny detail of the lotus petal, the cloud, the many-armed deity emerging beneath their hands. Onlookers chant like long horns sounding from the Gompa while night creeps softly to darken their windows.

I carefully set about making our lives comfortable, ordered. There is a purpose. I see it taking shape now. It no longer matters whether I see the pyramids or climb Mount Everest or take a balloon ride over Uluru. These desires are insubstantial. They are things of fancy, lacking the lines and curves of solid reality. He is what is real. And here is the greatest challenge. I put aside all other whims to build the solid blocks of his life.

The rustle of robes, the scuff of sandalled feet on the floor, give life to an otherwise silent hall. Their backs ache with the strain of crouching, but they

continue on doggedly. Each grain is a gem, each line, each curve, a mystery
to be lived. A secret.

The house is big and old. The weatherboards let in too much air, cold air. I'm more aware of it now that I spend long moments half-awake in the middle of the night.

I hear the rain patter on the tin roof, dripping onto the broad-leafed plant outside my window. He's asleep now. I place him carefully back in the cot.

The rain drips and I hear the sea outside in the distance, a muted roar endlessly eating at the shoreline. I fancy that I hear new shoots of grass pushing their way through wet earth, to the surface and up. Up and outward toward the planets hanging in the silent void of space. A spider spins a web in a corner of my room, I hear her reeling out the thread. It's May and the nights are cold. I pull the quilt up to my chin and hear him breathing.

I know I've slept because I'm aware of waking some time later. It's still dark, still cold, and he's crying to be fed. I stroke his smooth, warm head and listen again to the hum, the foreverness that beckons and gathers me in.

The deep guttural chanting reverberates through the high-roofed hall. A spider in the rafters has a birds-eye view of the circular pattern unfolding far below. The hunched backs, the hands tapping out the sands of the intricate embossment. The sun emerges from behind a cloud and sudden light washes the sand mandala revealing the tiny jewels hidden within its borders. They work now to complete the final rim, the curve closes the circle.

Something is wrong. I can't put my finger on it but I feel ill-at-ease. I don't want to go out, but we do anyway. We eat, we drink, we talk, we laugh. He sleeps, but I want to keep holding him. I want to go home. Something is not right. There's a small tear somewhere, a fraying of the fabric around us. Shadowy fingers pull the cloth apart. I struggle to avert my mind from the void I sense beyond.

We rush to the car in the drizzle and cold. An owl hoots in a nearby tree.

When finally I'm listening to the hiss of tyres on the grey road and watching the trees rush past, I sit with my hand on his chest feeling the breath, in and out.

It stands complete. Four doorways lead to paths which open into the inner sanctum of the circle. Clockwise they walk around the mandala to a deep rolling chant.

Later at home I pull back the blankets. Slowly. One by one. Knowing in that one long frozen moment of blind panic that I will never feel his breath again. And with two simple words, *I'm sorry*, the ambulance man confirms this and my heart is torn from my chest.

They are sweeping it away now. Gone are the lines and curves of symmetry and perfection. Beginning at the outer edge they work in towards the centre, pushing the coloured sands before them along the four paths. Their hands sweep the entire intricate design into a pile of sand grains. They scoop up handfuls and place them in the carved brass urn.

There is a brick lodged in my chest. It has sharp edges which scrape against my insides as I move through this reality. And I move quietly, carefully, like one recovering from a long illness. I am fragile, as if made from tiny grains of sand and moving will cause me to collapse. But move I must. The Catholics tell me, *He is with God now, safe in Heaven.* The compassionate optimists tell me, *Time is the greatest healer.* And the more Zen amongst them tell me, *This too will pass.*

They stand on the pier, their robes fluttering in the breeze. One tips the urn and the sand falls. The waves roll in, washing up shells, grains of sand and seaweed, and flow back out again.

Keren Heenan

Out of vogue

The pregnant ones are fashionably dressed in red and black.
She is wearing tracksuit pants, a loose top.
She is waiting, sitting on her own.
A baby cries out to be fed.

She is wearing tracksuit pants, a loose top.
She smells guavas. Mums come and go.
A baby cries out to be fed.
The receptionist looks up a name.

She smells guavas. Mums come and go.
The clock on the wall shows the date.
The receptionist looks up a name.
Some children are drawing with crayons.

The clock on the wall shows the date.
The woman beside her reads *Vogue*.
Some children are drawing with crayons.
She keeps her hands still in her lap.

The woman beside her reads *Vogue*.
Outside, the guavas are ripe.
She keeps her hands still in her lap.
The baby inside her has died.

Outside, the guavas are ripe.
She is waiting, sitting on her own.
The baby inside her has died.
The pregnant ones are fashionably dressed in red and black.

Carol Millner

Benjamin

Benjamin was born twelve weeks premature. We went through it all – contractions, breathing – without having gone to classes. I stood next to Wanda, utterly stunned, while a motherly nurse wiped her forehead saying *Good girl* and white-coated doctors fiddled with equipment. He was delivered, not into his parents' arms, but into the arms of technology – oxygen mask, humidicrib and countless tubes and monitors. They said he was *viable*.

This wizened little creature with transparent skin and dark curly hair was the culmination of our love. A love that had grown from a university friendship – a date at the film festival, late night coffee at Genevieve, a mattress in a student house in Carlton, backpacking in India. A love that matured as we became people with proper jobs, a mortgage, people who ate bagels from Glick's on Sundays and who occasionally shared a chocolate pancake from Scheherazade.

When Wanda discovered she was pregnant, I wanted to tell the world: the tram driver, the people in the cake shop, the lady in the flower shop near the terminus. Life was golden. We walked through the park and watched children playing – soon our child would be there, climbing the slides, being pushed on the swings. We read with delight instructions from a well-thumbed book on pregnancy that we found in an op shop: 'to help morning-sickness each morning the husband will make his wife a cup of weak tea and a piece of dry toast'. We started our own ritual, but dispensed with the dry toast.

We borrowed a friend's campervan and drove to Adelaide to see Vera, Wanda's sister. Wanda wanted to be with her when we announced the good news. We camped at the edge of the Little Desert. In the evening, a family of kangaroos grazed near our van. Whenever we moved, they stood like statues, blending into the bush. In the early morning, we sipped tea as the sun rose to the 'too-whip' call of the honeyeaters. It was there that we started to call our baby 'Roo'. We spent three days with Vera in her snug flat at Glenelg cooking garlicky soups, walking along the beach, the sisters going into huddles over baby things. Vera promised to come over for the birth.

We returned home on the coast road and camped at Port Campbell. We sat on rocks looking down into the Loch Ard Gorge watching the tide come in, sharing a sense of awe at the power and mystery of all that was happening within and around us.

Soon Wanda needed loose-fitting clothes and we would caress and talk to the little mound that was Roo.

One evening, she started to experience cramps. We naively thought she was just a bit tired. She put her feet up and I got us Chinese takeaway for dinner. In the middle of the night, she woke me. The waters had burst. We raced to the hospital in a taxi and within minutes Wanda was being examined by a doctor who said, 'You are going to have this baby. I can't stop the labour now.'

Our world had revolved around camping, walks on the beach, digging the garden. Suddenly it became the neonatal intensive care unit. There's a smiling Thomas the Tank Engine on the opaque plastic doors. On the other side you are thrust into a place where there is no distinction between day and night – it's always abuzz with bright lights, beeping machines and young medical staff bending over cribs, adjusting equipment. The momentum is increased by the perpetual 'tap, tap, tap' accompaniment of cardiac monitors, never quite in unison. Everything is monitored and measured. Colourful mobiles that the babies cannot see hang over them and soft toys wait hopefully in the corners of their cribs.

At first they called him 'Hercules' and we clung to reports that suggested he would grow into a normal healthy child. He started to drink Wanda's expressed breast milk from a tiny bottle, almost like a full-term baby. Vera came over and one weekend we painted the new nursery and decked it out with Beatrix Potter curtains.

Then the severe setbacks started: pneumonia, a brain haemorrhage, a pneumothorax. Wanda and I started to retreat into our separate worlds.

She had room in her life only for Benjamin. She seemed to be obsessed by him, clutching at his possible accomplishments, trying to bury the reality of diminishing hope. Nothing would stop her from catching the tram each morning to be at his bedside. While he was asleep, she searched in the nearby department stores for the elusive perfect toy.

But the world of life-threatening events was too much for me. Benjamin's pneumothorax seemed to be treated as though it were no more than a routine common cold. There was a procedure – drainage tubes were inserted, when his heart slowed down the incident was almost brushed aside, they tried a different drug regime and said, 'You need to smarten up there, Hercules.' My son's heart had come close to stopping! I found solace in returning to work in the library, escaping to familiarity, where the most serious problem was a missing book or a deleted file. And what I was doing appeared to be acceptable; the father going off to work while the mother attended to the baby.

At the end of each day, I'd catch a tram to the hospital. I'd walk slowly up to the rambling red-brick Federation building with its contradictions of closed-in verandas and streamlined technology. I'd walk through the stale tobacco smell at the main entrance where flimsily clad patients in wheelchairs sucked casually on what may have been the cause of their illness, and then along the bright squeaky corridors where vending machines violate dark wood panelling and prestigious Edwardian surgeons glower from their portraits.

Up I'd go to the seventh floor, not really wanting to be there, yet finding it compelling. I'd sit with him on my lap, his tiny hand wrapped around my thumb, as I read him Chekhov short stories.

The nurses didn't get it. One of them said, 'Do you think he understands?'

I said, 'Yes!' And I think sometimes he did. His baby innocence had been replaced by the wisdom of being close to death – something beyond my own experience.

Occasionally, Wanda and I would eat at home together, sitting sullenly at the table.

If things got too uncomfortable, I'd read the paper while she prattled on. 'I think he smiled when I tickled his toes today.'

And, with one eye on the paper, I'd mutter something like 'You know, it's probably just a reflex reaction.'

One day she said brightly, 'One of the other premmie babies, it was his birthday today. His mother brought in a cake.'

And I said, 'Surely being in the NICU for a year isn't something to celebrate!'

There was a silence. Wanda started to clear the dishes.

*

I spent more and more and more time at work, finding excuses to stay back. Excuses not to go into the hospital. Excuses not to see Benjamin who, day by day, looked more like a startled, scrawny chicken, and less like a cuddly newborn.

Gretel worked back too. At first we just chatted around the coffee urn. She seemed to understand that I needed to be distracted from the world of the hospital, so she talked about her music – something I know nothing about.

One afternoon we went out for coffee. For the first time, she asked about Benjamin – but not like the others who seemed to assume that he was like any other baby but just a bit small. She said, 'It must be a terrible disappointment – a kind of loss.'

'Yes,' I said. And I wasn't embarrassed that I had tears in my eyes because I knew she understood. I didn't have to play the proud father role.

'What's it like?' she asked. Not, what's he like? What milestones has he achieved? Smiling? Sitting up? Those prurient questions that seem to be the only things people can ask about a baby. No. She wanted to know how *I* felt. She cared about *me*.

It was such a relief to escape the platitudes: two steps forward, three steps back and the false jollity – Hercules, the smiling Tank Engine. I poured out how I felt – and things I hadn't even realised; the conflict of loving him yet not wanting to be there, the battle of instinct and reason. We got into the habit of meeting for coffee after work and she was usually the one to say, 'You'd better go now,' and I'd get to the hospital later and later.

One afternoon Gretel said, 'Come home and hear some music. I've got a terrific new recording of Bach's *Musical Offering*.'

Of course I went. It was so good to be in an ordinary home without vases of dead flowers, old Christmas cards and dust. We sat together on her sofa and the layers of musical sound seemed to bind us together. It was the first evening that I didn't go to the hospital at all.

I got home late – terribly late. The moonlit sculptures in the community gardens seemed to leer at me as I walked down our silent street. My key grated in the lock – a hollow sound that echoed through the house. In the bedroom, Wanda's dour form was well over on her side. I chucked my clothes on the floor and climbed in, keeping carefully to my side. I knew she was awake, but she made no comment. There was no energy left for an argument.

The next evening, I did go to the hospital – mainly out of duty. Wanda had just left, they said. A play therapist was there trying to get Benjamin to reach out for an assortment of rattles that she waved in a rough fashion only an inch or two from his face. She stood aside while I picked him up in my usual manner. But she didn't go away. Had she been told about the Chekhov? I decided it would be prudent to read *Poppy Pig*.

'Good eye contact,' she said, as I sat with Benjamin on my lap. 'Yes – yes! He's reaching out towards the picture!'

It reminded me of a sports commentary.

A few minutes later, a group of medical students came in on the evening round and I had to listen to yet another interpretation of Benjamin's medical history as the students grimly took notes.

I'd intended to go straight home. But, on the way out, my pulse racing, I used the public phone in the lobby to phone Gretel. I hadn't meant to see her. I was so churned up. Could she meet me for a drink at a nearby bar?

Half an hour later, I was telling her about the play therapist.

'You seem so angry about it. Isn't there any way you could take him home?'

Sitting there in her cream silk shirt, cut low enough to reveal the lace of her bra, she suggested to me what any rational person would do. I had become inextricably reliant on an institution. I could barely think for myself. I was critical of the medical staff but it hadn't occurred to me to defy them.

'He'd need twenty-four-hour care,' I said lamely.

'I'd be prepared to help.'

I could tell she really meant it. Yet the whole hospital situation seemed so intransigent. I was locked into it. For me, that's what having a son meant; visiting an institution and having people observe your interactions with him. She helped me to see this more clearly, and I melted.

In her tiny bedroom, we flicked the venetians shut so the world outside was just a dim glow around the edges, and I became lost in the cushions of her body, breathing in her gentle lavender scent.

Walking home, I felt free – something I hadn't felt for a long time, yet I also felt guilty.

I looked at Wanda lying clenched in her private space and felt as though every pore of my body was shrieking, 'He's been with another woman.' Surely I looked different, smelled different?

'You're late,' was all she said.

I switched off the lamp and stared at the patterns made by the lights of occasional passing cars as they slowed down for the speed hump. I pretended to sleep.

*

The phone. Wanda answered it. 'Yes. OK. We'll be right in.' She turned to me as she scrambled into clothes. 'He's had a cardiac arrest. You must come.'

I admit, I faltered. My child had had a cardiac arrest and I was reluctant to go to him. I couldn't muster any more compassion.

I fumbled with the buttons of my shirt, gave up and pulled on a T-shirt.

Wanda was intent on getting there. I followed her to the car. She drove – speeding headlong down St Kilda Road. I touched her hand. Her sharp profile seemed like a desperate greyhound pursuing its lure.

We ran down the familiar hospital corridors and I grabbed a Coke from a machine, trying to deny, for a few moments more, the confrontation. But Wanda jabbed at the button to summon the idle lift, then she dragged me through those Thomas the Tank Engine doors.

White-coated people surrounded his crib. His face was blue. He was hooked up to a multitude of monitors. They had taken swabs to test for an infection.

A young doctor took us aside – no seniors on at this early hour. 'There's nothing much more we can do.'

We could have demanded a more senior specialist. But this stark situation drained even Wanda of all energy and initiative. The medical staff disappeared. They pulled flimsy blue curtains around our little family and we sat nursing Benjamin – just us – as the click, click, from the second hand of a clock on the wall in this timeless place measured out his final minutes. At peace, he looked more like a baby; eyes gently closed, a shock of black curly hair, neat little ears.

Wanda and I were unsure of what to do. Together we put him back in his crib and covered him with a blanket. Together we walked out of the curtained cubicle. No tears or anger; we were numb. This was new. Bewildered, we signed some forms, received a brown paper envelope with information about funerals and picked up a plastic bag of his belongings. There was nothing more to do here, although the hospital had been Benjamin's home for his whole life. We wanted to linger. But suddenly it was as though we were trespassers.

No need to talk as we drove home down St Kilda Road, cocooned in our car, bereft.

As we parked, our elderly neighbour, Theo, looked up from his pruning, said 'Good morning', then seemed to sense he shouldn't say anything more.

Still silent, we headed for the beach. It started to rain. We walked to the end of the jetty. The sea was grey and choppy. A solitary gull was buffeted across the bay. The cold rain sliced into our faces and mingled with our warm tears. Somewhere a dog barked. We sat there on the end of the jetty, our legs dangling as we stared into a murky distance. There was suddenly nothing that we had to do.

I hauled Wanda back to the beach and we struggled up the sand to the scrub on the other side of the bike track. We sheltered there in the tea tree, sweeping aside discarded cans and cigarette butts. And in the bushes, to the occasional staccato of the pedestrian crossing lights, the rain stinging our bare skin, we made love.

Jennifer Bryce

Flesh and blood

I lock myself away from him, in the bathroom, turning the key, not answering, so he worries, calling, pleading at the door, not yelling as he was before, as he usually does – powerful yelling that alerts the neighbours and frightens Matty.

Matty slips a note under the door, 'Plees kum out'.

I can't, I cry silently.

Shadows shift like moths across the wedge of light; I hear them whispering. I crouch in a corner, against the cold clean shower screen. Eventually there's only an unbroken strip of light. I hear the car starting. Gone to his mother's, again.

'You didn't love her,' he said. 'Bronwyn. When she was born,' he said, 'who cuddled her, held her, mourned her?'

He did. I'd just had thirteen hours of distressing labour – the drip-drugs working painfully slowly, the eventual epidural slipping out soon after he'd gone to arrange evening care for Matty: all the pain coming back, hours of it, while I called and called for someone. Watery blood overflowing onto the sheets. But the baby was dead, had been for twenty-four hours, no one knew why – these things happen, one in a thousand – and why worry about the mother who could give, had given, birth naturally once already, with no complications?

The anaesthetist came back eventually at nine o'clock at night, the midwife apologising to him, trying to massage the baseball of pethidine she'd injected clumsily into my thigh: *Sorry to get you out, doctor,* as I panted and groaned. It'll be painless, they assured me, quick – better to have it induced… who would want to wait until it decayed, turned to muck, only a little putrid skeleton to be born?

Then as he tried to reinject the needle in my spine, 'Lie still', he said as I doubled up again.

I gasped, 'I can feel the head.'

*

Yes, we have a photograph of her being held by him. He gripped my hand, eyes petrified, as I gave the last push and the midwife said, 'Look, a girl. A beautiful little girl.' *Dead, though*, she didn't add.

Yes, we have a polaroid of him cradling her, wrapping her warmly, as if it mattered, me white-faced beside his shoulder, eyes side-slanted. She looks like Bronwyn, I said cautiously. Bronwyn, my sister. So we called her that. You couldn't saddle a *live* child with Bronwyn Brookes, of course – keep the better names…

Held her only once myself. Tentatively. Then put her in the cradle trolley cushioned for newborns. Had to give birth to the other dead thing. The placenta. Squatted under his direction to deliver it: I was numb from pethidine at last, or shock. The midwife pounced on the bloody mass.

Eventually got wheeled out for a shower and bed. Alone, in a ward undergoing renovation. *So she won't hear the other mothers, the babies*, I heard them whispering. Kindly, I suppose.

Kept feeling I'd left something behind.

'Lovely flowers,' the nurses said. 'What lovely flowers you've been sent.'

Tracey-Ann Forbes

Necrosis

Dragonfruited sphere,
shining tissue,
black spotted ball,
bloodless moon.

You are nestled in bowel.
You are torsing. You double me
over. You double what I see:
the folded blanket that rucks
nastily behind the back
behind the back of my head,
the wall spouting tubes,
a chair prickling out from the corner;
whiteness glaring at whiteness.

They have run out of pillows.

He (the doctor, the one with the wand) can't find you.

You bloom, necrotic, spotted, carrioned.
Dead egg carrier you torse, you double, you
shout at the tear that is my
groin back ribs leg knee throat back
back back back back.

He can't find you. They talk
about us in the third person not knowing
we are fourth person poetic split by pain.
They want to send us home.

Dragonfruit: bloom, split, tear, twist, turn.

But they do. Find you. They spear
you and bag you. Pull you through
a hole in my belly after their metal scissors
snip at your stalk. Dead moon. Distended.

And then.

And then you are gone.

You are gone already and I have never seen you.

You were mine. You were opening and closing,
globing, the light that is thrown by belly dreams
and babies.

And when I wake, with a drain and a drip
and a pillow and a morphine button
to press, you are gone.

You are black tissue in a bag.

You are hazard, removed, the absence of pain.

Ovary. Egg layer. Possibility thrower.

Gone.

Quinn Eades

Dr Douglas and the baby rabbits

One

The pouch of Douglas is a small area in the female human body between the uterus and the rectum. It has a name and a shape but the essence of it, the point of it, is that it is a piece of nothing. It is a negative space. It is the empty air in a cup or a bottle. We don't have a word for that territory; we let the vessel speak for it. The pouch of Douglas has a name, a border, but no land. The territory of the pouch of Douglas is infinitesimal, because when all is well the surrounding organs slide against each other like two slugs in a mating dance. The pouch of Douglas, like the pouch of a mother kangaroo or a coin purse, can expand to accommodate growing or multiplying things.

The pouch takes its name from the first man to explore and name this piece of true *terra nullius*. At the time, other men were planting flags in distant places on the globe; Dr Douglas worked closer to home in Scotland and England. He worked as a man-midwife, wrote treatises and held public dissections in his own house. Here is the uterus, the fallopian tube, the ovary and vagina. And here – can you see it? This is my own discovery. I have named it after myself. Ah, there is the bell for afternoon tea.

In 1726, a woman by the name of Mary Toft, who lived in Surrey, announced that she had given birth to baby rabbits. Her local doctor was astonished and ran off to let everyone know. She had been in normal labour, he said, with regular contractions. And then appeared the baby rabbits. The woman enjoyed her celebrity.

But Dr Douglas smelled a rat. 'A woman giving birth to a rabbit is as likely as a rabbit giving birth to a human child,' he said. He went to see her himself, to put an end to the nonsense. He examined her and declared her a fraud.

Afterwards, William Hogarth made an etching of Dr Douglas

172

standing at Mary Toft's bedside, gesticulating, with the rabbit children running off in all directions, unmasked and embarrassed.

Two

Rabbits came to Australia with the First Fleet. Like currency lads and lasses, they grew healthy on fresh air and good eating. They eloped into the bush and ate the crops that were planted for them and built burrows in the new estates that opened up as far as the eye could see. Australia's emblem bore the kangaroo and emu, but the continent was in fact governed by rabbits. The anti-rabbit wars, when they came, were conventional and chemical; mass slaughter and hand-to-hand combat. By the time I could walk and talk, I knew that rabbits had to be caught and killed. Even the family cat could do its bit. 'Go and catch a rabby, Ginge,' my mother urged the big hard tomcat that went with the dairy farm my parents worked for a while.

That was in the south of Western Australia, where it was green and lush and muddy. That's where my sister and I had the job of herding calves. We always stopped to examine the hot pats of manure. We noted that some were sloppy, some firm. We wore plastic galoshes. Dad was always hosing out the stalls where the cows had been. Mum grew tomatoes at the back door of the weatherboard soldier's settlement cottage that we rented from the farmer. My parents had come from Queensland on a working holiday that was already stretching out towards a year. I started school at a one-room schoolhouse, where I open and shut my mouth pretending to chant the times table with my peers. Older children carried me around like a baby. We weren't on that dairy farm for long. Winter was coming and my Queenslander parents were drawn north, following the sun.

I believed in the Easter bunny. We were surrounded by rabbits, so the idea of a large one carrying chocolate eggs wasn't too much of a stretch. I also had hard evidence. Before we left the dairy farm, Mum and Dad and my little sister and I were sitting together when we heard an interesting thump and scamper.

'I think that was the Easter bunny,' said Dad. 'Go and have a look in your room.'

There, on the bed we shared with pillows at either end, where my feet would sometimes reach a cold wet patch that was my sister's wee, were chocolate Easter eggs.

Three

Carnarvon was a place where red earth met white beach sand to create pinkish sand-dunes sparsely covered in acacia scrub. There were utes piled high with kangaroo carcasses. There was the pub where Wilson Tuckey smacked an Aboriginal patron with a coaxial cable and got fined forty dollars for assault. There was a NASA tracking station on the red sand dune just out of town, getting ready for the moon landing. And there were rabbits. We had a grey cat that dragged home a partly disembowelled rabbit. The rabbit was long, as long as the cat.

Four

My partner Steve walks over land near Bathurst, in New South Wales, that was box gum forest then eaten-out farmland and now a land-care reserve. He stops at likely spots and takes coordinates with his pocket GPS. These are rabbit burrows. Rabbits eat the delicate native grasses being coaxed back onto the land. Someone else will come by, later, to gas the burrows. The rabbits will lie there, dead, under the ground. We go walking with our black Labrador, Bertie. Bertie is getting old and pretends not to see rabbits because he can't be bothered to give chase. Kangaroos stand stock-still as we approach. The full, hanging pouch with just the joey's legs sticking out.

There's something in my own pouch. Cells are multiplying, well-fed and happy, burrowing down in new estates. They're going wild, like rabbits.

Five

Dr Douglas blessed that pouch of nothing with his own name. Nothing is a magnet for something. Nothing is a blank page with a pencil beside it. Nothing can be a blessed relief. There is nothing there. I slide on my conveyor belt into the big white doughnut. The warmth of radioactive fluid is strange at the back of the neck and around the bladder. 'Breathe in and hold,' says the machine, in a woman's voice. Pause. 'You may now breathe normally.' I have not yet heard of Dr Douglas or Mary Toft or her baby rabbits. They belong to the new country on the other side of the doughnut.

When did it occur to Mary Toft that she might gather baby rabbits and put them up herself? The vagina is an empty tube. It calls for something to go into it. Perhaps she was bored, and she had an empty space to fill. And then she spied a baby rabbit.

'I'm bored,' I used to whine, back in the dairy farm days. 'What can I do?'

I would be told to go and find something to do with myself, and stop whining.

I took a hair from my head and asked Mum for a glass jar with a lid. I put the hair in the jar. I was thinking that this was the hair of today and today would not go on forever, but I would always have this hair. I could trap a hair's worth of time. The hair did not look impressive in the glass jar. In fact, it looked like an empty jar with a hair caught in it by mistake.

Was Mary's first baby rabbit already dead, or did her attempt to birth it kill it? Did she practise on a series of rabbits, perfecting her fraudulent labour groans, the use of muscles for expulsion, before calling her local doctor?

There's that name: Mary. And another highly unusual birth. I'm doodling, now, into the empty page.

Nothing asks for something. From nothing comes all of creation. We can't seem to leave nothing alone.

The radiologist's report described a five-centimetre tumour in the pouch of Douglas. And another bigger tumour, in another spot. I couldn't listen to this. I let my friend, who had insisted on coming with me, take notes. Tell that other person that looks and sounds like me who might turn up later today or tomorrow but don't tell me. I need to stay here in my glass jar of time, in my ignorance, while other people open and shut their mouths like goldfish.

Six

The night before last, I dreamed that Steve and I were talking to a woman, a stranger. She was about our age. She suddenly said she was miserable because no one would marry her. Steve immediately offered to marry her. He said it the way he'd offer to help someone move bricks around to the side of the house.

As soon as he said these words, he was gone from me. He had shifted over, just like that. Now that he'd made the offer, he had to follow through. This somehow made sense. I spent the rest of the dream wailing and gnashing my teeth.

Seven

Mimi the rabbit is astonished. A giant cabbage has been set down before her. She circles it, looking for a way in. A rabbit has prehensile, grasping lips and strong incisors. Rabbits gnash their teeth at every meal with a wide side-to-side movement. Their teeth grow continuously through their lifetimes, to make up for the erosion.

Mimi the rabbit lives near the Bathurst railway station, a few streets away from us. She is a wanted rabbit. When she took ill, lying paralysed and hopeless on the floor, my friend Helen spent hours feeding her through an eyedropper and spent a ridiculous amount of money at the vet. Gradually, Mimi began to move again. She began to drag her body around. She'd tip sideways and be unable to get up. She'd be set gently back on her wobbly feet.

Mimi and I took ill at about the same time. We're both still here. Our days are numbered, of course. We just don't know how many numbers, how many days.

In the meantime, Mimi chews the many-layered cabbage of life. It is vast. It will be unfinished.

Tracey Sorenson

Small black cardigan

While you are away
I sleep in your small black cardigan
with the diamante buttons,
the top one gone.
Little by little
I shed your glamour,
these sharp paste stars.
I am putting it on
and taking it off
in dreams where the ground
glitters with buttons and tears.

Lambswool, it holds my breasts,
gives me back a waist, of sorts.
You've gone north, somewhere warm,
I'm heading south – snow
on the Stirlings
the weatherman predicts.
Days before we fronted the mirror,
sisters sharing glimpses
of wintered skin.
You said, *Here – take it,*
I won't need it were I'm going.

Lucy Dougan

Poultice for the shock

3.

naturally, suicide
gives way to carrots – plucked from a winter
garden, just in time, thinned
to promote growth in the up-swing.
i rinse them of their burdens, tenderly
we bundle together to honour up-rooted truth.
orange and purple skins mirror
my sentiments, the violence and the salvation –
grate them up and swaddle them
in mother-tongue muslin. here we are,
at long-last in the quiet afternoon.
she ebbs lovingly
at my neck and i exhale past the picture
show of other people's dreams. i carry
my own now, alone
and alive.

2.

i remember the moment i ate his
impossible grief – peel and tops and all –
with my starving love. after words
i didn't understand and tears i couldn't
damn and the natural anaesthesia that comes after
these bitter things.
in a dusk lit only by flickering
television, he sat
beside me
staring straight ahead
and for the first time spoke to me
with heart – *i can't believe i'm watching cartoons.*

angry anvils fell around us, howling, and that rabbit
offered up his carrot. i was just
so fucking hungry.

1.

in earliest light i had a brother. in the big backyard
he walked on his hands to make me burst
into bubbles. i sat on a princess throne – black vinyl
backseat of the old datsun – while he grappled
with his slipping clutch and not-breaking
precious cargo. *green means go*!
i decreed with glee and those over-loaded eyes met
mine in our kindred mirror. sometime too soon
it shattered under the dead
weight we had elsewhere promised to shoulder
together and his unbearable honesty was buried
by hands almost like ours. yellow
years later, after the initial shock subsided, i finally tried
to jump-start the getaway car
he left behind. by not
swallowing anything for anyone
any more.

Anna Minska

Don't break the bunny

for Lyndon

Seventeen years of enormous eggs (the largest you can find at Safeway)
and bunnies in beds, on pillows, outside my door and popping up
in unexpected places, you like a big Easter bunny and a magician,
hiding birthday and Easter and Christmas presents in your car and closets
and under your bed, as if I was a child, or a lover or a life-mate –
someone you loved at least – and I have been and you have been
all of those, and more, and less, and up and down and round and round
and back and forth down a rabbit hole as strange as the one Alice
went down (but she came out of it in the end). Now, you send a box
of bunnies and eggs hidden beneath strips of paper that fall through
my fingers like confetti and all over the floor and everywhere,
making a mess in my silent kitchen. I pick up the gold Lindt bunny
carefully, as if he might break, but he has stayed safe and solid as the ship
that has sailed all the way across Bass Strait to bring him here, home,
where you used to be. I sit alone in the kitchen. I break the bunny.

Gayelene Carbis

Conservation status

I *Vulnerable*

Gouldian finches at South Alligator River.
You snapped at me, then took their photos
    – tiny rainbows at sunrise.

II *Endangered*

One time you took me shooting, down that track.
No tourists there. Patonga mob, sometimes,
hunting magpie geese, wallaby, even
buffalo then. Lots of green cans
on the ground, good for target practice.
You realigned the rifle scope,
handed it over. *Here, you have a go.*
You showed me how to look
and sight and pull. Bulls-eye first time
and a faint vibration singing in my blood,
in the hot and humming air. You took
the gun back, didn't offer it again.

III *Critically endangered*

On holiday in Borneo
you were smitten
with an orphaned orangutan.
Your face then was a boy's –
younger, kinder, more loving
than any you showed me.

I knew then
we'd already begun
the slow process
of extinction.

IV *Extinct*

When I left it was with two pairs
of your work socks, your morning taste
for double-boiled Twinings
(leaf tea, had to be)
and an olfactory memory of you, stripping
off your smoky overalls on nights
in bushfire season. It stirs me still.

V *Identification of new species*

Back in this northern town I think of you
and wonder if we'll meet, and what I'd do.
Approach you? Or pretend I hadn't seen,
just like the last time I was here.

It was as if, despite being so near,
our separation had transformed me
into something strange and new
not yet pinned down or named –
but free of you.

Virginia Jealous

The Railway Hotel

He headed out towards the pronged gates of the cemetery, flicking his cigarette to the gravel. His trousers didn't quite reach his desert boots. He left the family to make their small talk about flower arrangements, to comment on how lovely the service had been. *Life moves on*, he thought.

Davo's song stuck inside his head. It was the only part of the service that resonated with the bloke he knew. He remembered the last time he saw Davo. The Metallica concert in July, the two of them sliding around in the gutter on the way home. A yellow car had driven past and he'd put his arm out to stop Davo from falling into its path. Good times. After a night on the razz, they used to muck around in the shed. Davo was tone deaf, like most metal fans, but brilliant on the drums.

The body had been buried on consecrated ground in a less-frequented part of the Catholic cemetery. An open coffin was out of the question, according to the priest. Luke waited for the boom gates to lift and let the bells fill his ears. Clang, clang, clang. Friends were saying Dave had thrown himself onto the track, right in front of passengers waiting to board the 8.05 to Frankston. Apparently the driver had taken it hard. But after three suicides, drivers can be pensioned out.

Tomorrow would be an ordinary day. He would be back on the road crew shovelling asphalt. They would break for morning tea at seven. Sit with legs apart on crates outside Lee's sandwich shop, passing folded egg and bacon sandwiches from hand to mouth. They would slug sweet iced tea, exchange a few words about the game. Monosyllabic nods would suffice. Tomorrow he would relieve the stinging in his eyes with a pair of sunnies bought from the servo. Take hard swigs of Carlton Draft to dull his headache.

The boom gates lifted and Luke felt the last whisper of the train up his back. It made his kidneys ache. He plodded up to the mini-mart, stiff in his borrowed suit. It was closed. Sunday. The window was plastered with ads for washing powder and discount dog food. A few more blocks and he'd be at his local where the boys all knew his name.

As he walked up the busy road, he felt something wet at his ankle. He looked down to see a mongrel breathing its wet nose onto the cold flesh between his pants and his boots. He kicked it away with his boot. It let out a whimper like a whistle but continued trailing a few paces behind, occasionally wandering onto the road to sniff at an empty pizza box in the gutter. Its ears stayed back and it wouldn't look him properly in the eye. Its fur was matted in bits along its back. It followed him all the way to the KFC.

He ordered a meal deal from the girl. She was wearing heavy blue eyeshadow and not really listening to what he was saying. It annoyed him to have to repeat his order. He ate most of his meal, nothing in his stomach since hearing the news. He took out the last drumstick from the box and threw it to the dog. It was gobbed with mashed potato and dipped in packet gravy. But the dog didn't seem hungry; instead it carried the fat drumstick along in its mouth.

The face behind the bar was hard and unfamiliar. Her blonde hair was half falling out of its ponytail and scattered round her neck like a mane. She was stacking glasses, barely glancing in his direction. Luke tapped the edge of a ten-dollar note on the counter. She began wiping down the far side of the bar. He picked up a coaster and studied the slogan: *because sometimes you're the only one in the crowd.* Cheering started up from around the wide screen, first half well underway. The boys hadn't even noticed him come in, all so absorbed in the game. *The bitch must be deliberately ignoring me,* he thought, *it's beyond ridiculous now.*

He stuck two fingers in his mouth and blew a sharp whistle. The hard line of her jaw stiffened.

'Beer, sweetheart. If that's not too much of a hassle for you.'

She poured him a pint, slicing the top off it with the back of her cold hand.

'Fuck sake. Do I look like I need a shave?' He raised his eyebrows at the few inches of foam in the top of the glass.

She glared at him, muttering 'Arsehole' under her breath.

He slammed back the bitter stout in a few quick gulps and called out for a whiskey chaser. A cross hung from the silver chain low over her breasts. Luke stared at it, thinking of the bland carpet in the church, the crucifix on the prayer booklet, cheaply printed, ink streaks through his friend's face. Each drink brought him closer to nothingness. *Think you know somebody and then they go and end it without two cents of it to you.*

She reached past him to replace a soggy coaster from the counter. He followed the swing of her chain, the bounce of her breasts.

Suddenly, she was in his face. 'Hey, arsehole, got a good enough look? You not seen a pair of tits before?'

The other waitress was laughing at him. Her lipsticked mouth making a noise that could break up pavement. One or two of the boys glanced over in their direction.

'Don't flatter yourself, slut.' He took a step towards her, his suit jacket sliding off the bar stool as he got up. He raised his open hand.

She grabbed hold of his half-empty glass and threw its contents in his face. It was cold and familiar but didn't bring him to his senses. The cross was dancing now, teasing over her breasts.

He felt a hand on his collar. The cotton constricted around his throat. A big bloke, Islander of some sort, had him by the armpits. He was thrown off-balance, dragged backwards off the stool. Its wooden frame made a cracking sound on the hard floor.

The woman continued yelling right in his face, 'Now who's a big man? You're nothing.'

The men stood back as he was hustled through the sports lounge and hauled down the pub's steps. A pain split down his right shoulder as he tumbled. He put out his elbow to save himself but it twisted with the force of landing.

When he came to, the street lights were blurry. He dragged himself into the gutter to vomit. The mutt was still there, loitering beside a pole. It sniffed around him, ears down in sympathy. Together, they dragged each other home.

Bronwyn Evans

Jordy

Should have learnt early,
Jordy and me,
there's a place to go
inside your head
when the monitors came round,
the 15-year olds came round
at night –
how to play dead.

I said if we jumped
we'd land in the clouds.
Jordy said
we'd hit the rocks,
not the sea.

Jordy's dead.
He was braver than me.

Peter Macrow

By his own hand

I left him weeping
at the corner of the street.

How could I know –
death by his own hand
so soon?

Mary Kille

One last time

She looks in the window
sees the garden reflected
behind her

and the single eucalypt
from which her lover
hanged himself.

His father, out to fetch the paper
saw the shape – strange fruit
dangling against the dawn

dangling
as the grass strained up
to reach, console, the limp bare feet.

Too late for a father's breath
yet still warm in the chill
of an autumn morning.

Her mind lurches
to the heavy-scented arums
she carried to the graveyard.

How someone led her to the chapel
fetched a flesh-coloured oblong box
laid it with her lilies at a window.

Thirty years. Still she lives those moments.
She'll let the sadness surface
just this one last time.

Liz McQuilkin

Cut

i.

things you didn't : & things you did : a distance
with so much light in it : wintertime : a dark wood-

grain : a slow turn of hemispheres : into colour:
into two cupped hands : sheltering a flame : things

that enter in : through the space left in a moment:
memory granulated : cold that held us like parent-rock :

urging you back into diamond : into a darkness
i could not fathom : a light i could not strike :

ii.

night with its dark carriages of hours : in a hotel room
in dili a telephone is ringing : & shadows in a first-floor

room : its view out over the suburb : in the minutes after
midnight : as the tides of light & dark reverse their pull :

i am kept awake now by the sound of someone singing :
by the dark gift of her song : one room of that house

will remain unfurnished : every word is an expectation
extinguished : i am speaking of things that are gone :

Thom Sullivan

Buried

I have buried us
in an unmarked grave

dug over a few untruths
and the odd infidelity

covered us with earth
and barbed wire

I have put to rest
all our smashed glass confessions

then read out aloud
again and again

my eulogy of self-pity

to whoever is left
to listen

before walking solemnly back over

our own
dead distances

Jules Leigh Koch

An autumn mourning

It's better to go to a funeral than to attend a feast; funerals remind us that we all must die... A sensible person mourns, but fools always laugh.

Ecclesiastes 7:2, 4

My aunt died suddenly. The autopsy – six days later – found the blood clot in her lung. A small plug that caused her to stop, unexpectedly but seemingly peacefully. But it was too late to find it then. And, at sixty-four, too soon.

Three weeks later, a group gathered to place her ashes beside a newly planted port-wine magnolia – *Michelia figo*. We stood in the freezing mistiness of late morning and early winter. 'Ashes to ashes...' but more like dust to mud.

It was the first time our small collection of cousins had been all in one place in more than twenty years. And we asked that question so often asked on such occasions, 'Why do the best parties happen in the worst circumstances?'

*

Our big dog died slowly but also too soon. The bigger the dog, the sooner they fall. Bred to be big but their hearts are too small, fraught with genetic dangers. We were told our wolfhound, she was only eight, was suddenly old – with cancer gnawing at her bones. It began with a limp, then a lump. And progressed, if that's really the right term for it.

'Nothing to be done,' said the vet. 'It's now a question of quality of life.'

Increasing doses of painkilling tablets gave her – and us – a few more weeks.

As the leaves turned bright then flamed out, each floating falling seemed to count off her remaining days. Letting go was about us being

191

ready, if that were possible. She simply goes to sleep; it's us that have to miss her. And we're never ready for that.

*

My dad had a blood clot, too. His looked like a stroke – a cerebral-vascular accident. Which he has now survived for eleven years. He was sixty-one, now seventy-two. But he has significant disabilities. Suddenly old, he has lived in an aged-care facility these eleven years.

Like so many others there, he doesn't belong. He's not like *those* old people. If only he could coax his arm and leg to work and walk again. That he is mentally alert makes his frustration greater. He feels his limitations and can articulate his annoyance.

The fusty smells of the old, mixed – not masked – with the hospital-grade disinfectant, the night-time cries of distress, the nappy he is expected to wet rather than use a bathroom, the wheelchair, his pain growing with his inability to move himself.

*

'She was only a dog,' some sensible voice tries to tell me. It might be in my head or it might be the reasonable voice of a friend. Or the brusque voice of the world around me, already busy with so many other sorrows.

'Yes, I know,' I try to tell myself. There are bigger griefs, tragedies, horrors in the world, each one of which gives a *sense of perspective* and could cumulatively swamp my sense of loss like it's not even there. But does that make my loss less?

'But she was *our* dog,' I reply, 'and her death is exactly what is wrong with the world.' A small splinter but accurately representing the forest of sorrow. A taste of the same loss, the same anguish, the same grief that feels like fear.

*

My aunt was one of the healthiest people I have ever known. To the point

192

of fanaticism. Organic, vegan, gluten-free, home-cooked everything. One cousin suggested my aunt had not put anything unhealthy in her mouth in at least two decades. But she was frail and unwell. Her bones steadily eroding. Was her strict diet a response to the weakness she felt in herself? Or was it somehow lacking, cruelly, ironically, feeding her mortality? Even the healthiest super-vegan, mega-athletes die.

Twice-divorced, she was afraid of being alone. When the one cousin still living at home worked away, she would go into respite care. Leave her solitary country home in favour of her occasional carers in town. That's where she died.

*

On clear, frosty-sunny days, autumn leaves make sense. Their rusty orange-red warmth seems to be squeezing the last warmth from the dying summer. The colours vibrate against the deep blue skies. The drying crackle underfoot has an aliveness.

When the autumn wind grabs the departing leaves from the trees and sends them dancing and whirling down the footpath, the leaves are given a brief but manic energy, a new kind of life they could never have while still tree-bound.

But autumn leaves don't fit with the first misty rains of winter. The dull days do nothing for their best attempts at colours. The damp renders the leaves limp and sludges them into cold piles, blocking gutters, congealing into mud.

*

The aged-care facility is a strange kind of home. Schooldays for the other end of life. The daily and weekly rhythms give a sense of time, of belonging, of familiarity to something that seems strange to almost any other stage of life.

They joke about it being *God's waiting room* – the last stop on a journey to no one quite knows where. But mostly it's just waiting.

Waiting for a nurse, waiting to get moved, waiting for the next meal, waiting for a visitor, waiting for whatever comes next.

It is not often spoken but there are some who are ready and waiting to die. Life has outlasted living. Death is not resisted. Each soft-cooked meal has literally and metaphorically lost its flavour, a generic mush of another day alive.

*

The evergreen to memorialise my aunt seemed out of place amid nearby riots of autumnal trees. But they had chosen a tree that promised prodigious flowering. In another season. And ever larger as the tree grows to fill the gap by the fence.

The box of ashes was slightly larger than a house brick but heavier. Can our bodies really be reduced by fire to such a small volume? This service had no pallbearers, just a single carrier of the brick as the rest of us watched dumbly.

As the cold seeped into us and dripped over us, my oldest cousin picked a single red-orange-yellowed leaf from the neighbouring tree to adorn the remains of her mother and placed the box in the ground. Autumn now, spring hoped for.

*

My younger brother is concerned about blood clots. They seem to run – or, more correctly, block – in our family. Sudden punctuation in our lives. He has been reading online about blood clots and what they do to bodies.

'Bad circulation' is my dad's explanation. He recites the family history of heart trouble and weakness across generations. It's a grim prognosis that offers little in terms of how to avoid them and the silent, sudden damage they inflict.

Of course, we can try to be healthy. My brother has recently taken up cycling. I chide him that his worry about the risk increases stress levels and that increases the risk – and that good medical advice is not usually found online.

*

My aunt's memorial service also serves as an excuse to visit my dad. Frustrated by his physical limitations, our visits depend on me finding time to travel there. I am glad we can talk by phone regularly but visiting takes planning and commitment.

Each visit, I am reminded of his reality, something I can usually, easily, half-guiltily, avoid. The singalongs, chapels, other *diversions* give shape to their communal waiting but these increasingly intrude on the brief times he and I spend together.

But he has deteriorated physically since Christmas. He jokes about 'getting old' and complains that moving himself is becoming more difficult, while sitting still is increasingly painful. His hands are shakier. He seems more tired.

*

I wonder if sickness is an important part of life and death, and particularly the transition. Perhaps that's why sudden death is so brutal. It isn't only that we didn't get to say goodbye, it's also that we haven't had time to adjust.

For weeks, I had been learning how to go for a morning run without our big dog. It was an unusual kind of *walking the dog*. We would walk to the park together, then tied up, she would watch as I ran laps. She exercising me, it seemed.

And, sadly, in other activities, she had also ceased to be present some time before she was gone. These incremental adjustments help a little. But there are still so many spaces, things not noticed until undone, unfilled. It still hurts.

*

As my aunt's eldest brother, my dad dictated a message I was asked to read on his behalf at her memorial service. Like leaves from their childhood yard, he raked together a small pile of memories that brought laughter to the funeral.

A 1950s, small-town, central Victorian childhood. Five children and two acres in the bush. Sandpits and a home-made swing, then school and piano lessons. 'She was my pretty sister,' he says but, as older brother, he is the hero of his memories.

Later, she was the one who cared for the older generations – my great-grandmother, grandfather, then grandmother as they aged and became less able to care for themselves. Perhaps a rehearsal for an old age she never attained.

*

I wondered when we would know it was time. How to draw the line that says life is now too hard, not worth another day. But we suspected it was better to err on the side of sooner, as callously merciful as that might be.

The vet said we had made the right call. But he was unlikely to tell us otherwise. She was terminal, a couple of days either way made little difference to anyone but us. A few less leaves on the trees, a little colder and darker.

She was never good with vets. Nervous at best, she was rightly suspicious of their needles. As he searched for a vein, I lied to her, telling her it was going to be OK, when I knew it wasn't. She let out a final howl as she relaxed into sleep.

*

The first flowering of my aunt's small tree came in the form of tributes of various colours, sizes, shapes, tied to its branches with garishly pink ribbons. After the service and tree-planting, guests were invited to write their tributes and add them.

Slowly, braving the bitter cold one more time, many of the group returned to the tree to add their message, their voice, their memory.

The bold colours had an autumnal but festive feel, particularly as they fluttered in the freezing wind.

Some tributes came from family and friends unable to travel to the memorial. As a group of cousins, we tied these extra cards to the tree. Then we posed for family photos with the laden tree, an echo of Christmases past.

*

We prepared to bury our big dog under a large deciduous tree in our yard. It takes more work than might be expected to dig a grave, even when the earth is muddy softened with early winter rain. Each shovelful of dirt a wound and a tribute.

Graves under trees might be the expectation of movies and poetry but this ignores the real-life intrusions of tree roots. Large woody arms and tentacle fingers reach into the space, clutching at the clay, where we are wrestling to make a hole.

By now its early-winter dark. A waning torchlight offers little. We work by a Shakespearean gravedigger's instinct previously unknown, untried. But the work is soothing, the tired muscles comforting and the blisters seem fair.

*

Is it wrong that I seem to mourn my dog more than my aunt? That I work harder at this grief? Is it simply proximity, immediacy? Or is it truly the same grief, expressed differently but jumbled together, different burnt leaves from the yard full of autumn trees?

*

My dad was and is a pastor. He no longer 'works' but he hasn't stopped preaching. The chaplains and staff at the aged care facility use him to talk with and comfort fellow residents from time to time. It gives him a role.

But his faith has been strained by stroke, by incapacity, by frustration.

He questions me every visit. 'Why?' I deflect his questions. 'You're the preacher' – and his questions usually lead to faith, even as they remain unanswered.

To his memorial notes, he adds a two-sentence sermon. John 3:16: 'For God so loved...whosoever believes...not perish, everlasting life.' Those who believe die, but somehow they don't perish. 'That's our hope,' he says, certainty belying circumstances.

*

I have a new definition of friend: someone who helps bury your big dog in the shivering dark. Her large, still-warm weight is too much for us alone. Two friends answer the call to help with our solemn task. Their presence more than muscle.

For all our digging, filling in the hole happens too quickly. And she is gone. Now a place, a memory, rather than a life. Yet – hole filled, job done – it is so hard to walk away, to turn back to life. That final wrench seems disloyal.

Almost bare, the tree above still has a few coloured leaves to offer the fresh-turned earth. Next morning, the dirt is sprinkled with fallen colour, as if to hide this new scar. And the wintering sun plays on the heavy dew and crimson leaves.

Nathan Brown

Murphy versus Descartes:
Domum invenio, ergo sum

As a young Australian academic I was employed on what was then called a 'greenfields' campus: a small – intimately small – quasi-university (a college of advanced education). It was newly built within a grove of hoary macrocarpa on an erstwhile dairy farm outside a small rural city. I was deeply insecure. No one in my large extended family had even attended an institution of tertiary education, let alone gone on to teach in one. Insecure, then – but outspoken, aggressive, articulate (within that context). Among my colleagues I suffered no fools, though I knew myself to be the most bumbling of fools, even within that assemblage of academic misfits. I was, by contrast, unfailingly considerate and patient with those who struggled in my classes (that, at least, was my determined intent).

To this place of intellectual employ came, each day, my border collie cross, Murphy.

I would pull up in the windswept car park, routinely note the dreary monotony of the flat, dun, macrocarpa-dominated vista and the functionality of the new campus buildings, trudge past the crumbling sandstone base of the farm's old water tank – it must have been an extraordinary edifice in its day – and slosh through red lava-flow mud to the main building.

With Murphy at heel. At the door she would proffer her day's farewell and trot, in her beautiful prance, her white-tipped tail bannering jauntily, back to the car park. There she reigned, queen of the campus. She was the wise and gentle spirit who gave unity to this unlikely place. There weren't many of us, staff or students, in this raw landscape with its scarcely hallowed halls, and Murphy knew us all. Students who had no dealings with me joyously called her name, stopped and communed with her. She was an institution, and much loved. Much more loved than prickly young me, and with a wider circle of acquaintance.

She was also illegal.

Small my campus may have been, but that was no protection against the pernickety pettiness of bureaucracy. At regular intervals a memo would do the rounds, reminding staff that they were not to bring their dogs to work. It was aimed at me – but its author, presumably not wanting to tackle me head-on, generalised and broadcast it. That didn't work – I would reply with as much pompous acerbity as I could muster, calling the memo's author a 'wee tim'rous beastie', suggesting that he should try to grow a spine and talk to me personally, and informing him that, until then, I would treat his instruction with contempt. There would be no response, the edict would be ignored as promised, and months later the entire charade would be replayed. I must have been insufferable. The wonder of it is that I have so many dear and lasting friends from that time.

*

I hold certain minority views about academic pedagogy, though they are, I am gratified to observe, now deemed much less heretical than they once were.

I have spent a long and satisfying academic career as a sort of a stateless person – 'stateless' in the sense that I call no discipline 'home'. I was trained in political science, but only at the beginning of my career did I actually work in a department/school of political science/ government. For the rest, I was employed in academic enclaves that were proudly trans-disciplinary, and which suffered acute discrimination on that account. I came to believe in trans-disciplinarity – to believe, indeed, that the disciplines are useful paradigms for the organisation of knowledge only at the most basic level, beyond which they become a serious constraint upon intellectual progress. I couldn't even call myself an all-purpose social scientist or a non-specific scholar of the humanities, moving, as I did, seamlessly between the two.

And I have long contested the convention within academic publishing that forbids deployment of the perpendicular pronoun. The fiction is, the name(s) below the title notwithstanding, that the paper has somehow managed to write itself. This has always seemed to me to be utterly cowardly – to enable the author to hide from view; to eschew responsibility for his/her scholarship. It is time to put this iniquitous fiction out to pasture – as, indeed, has largely occurred now within the humanities, though it remains tenacious in the social sciences, and supremely unchallenged in the physical sciences. I have bristled over this for more than a quarter of a century, and it will be a day of joy when there is no longer a need to argue it out with journal editors.

I do, of course, know the origin of the convention that academic writing should be depersonalised. It stems from the abrupt split between subject and object that is one of the most potent legacies of the Age of Enlightenment in general, and Cartesian dualism in particular. For Descartes, the radical separation of subject and object was the principle that cleared the decks for scientific inquiry, the epistemological mode that would set humankind on a trajectory of endless, technology-fuelled progress, truly rendering us 'masters and possessors of nature'. The 'subject' – he who would know (it was emphatically a 'he' in Descartes' day) – is radically separate from, emotionally remote from, and unaffected (or 'uncontaminated') by the 'object' – that concerning which knowledge is sought. It is from Descartes that we derive the fundamental principle of the scientific method – the notion of the sanitised experiment in which the scientist dispassionately 'interrogates', 'dissects' and 'reduces' the experiment's 'object'.

Well, OK. I'm neither anti-science nor in the front rank of its cheerleaders. But Descartes didn't stop there. For him, dualism was a universal principle. Not just an epistemological device. Not merely perceptual: a separation of observing subject from observed object. It also separated, in a fundamental way, that small component of the brain responsible for rational thought (in Descartes's understanding of human anatomy) from the rest. Humans think. In the act of thought they live. *Cogito, ergo sum* – 'I think, therefore I am', the best known of the Cartesian aphorisms. Not 'I cry, therefore I am.' Not 'I run, therefore I am.' I think. If I do not think, I do not exist. Literally. Only the thinking brain is truly alive, truly immortal. The rest of the human body is mere machine, functioning in accordance with certain God-derived mechanical principles.

And then there are the animals. Which don't think. Only humans think, and, thus, only humans have souls, these being synonymous. Animals have no share in immortality, no soul. They are *entirely machine*, acting, Descartes tells us in part 5 of the *Discourse on Method*, 'according to the arrangement of their organs, just as we see how a clock, composed merely of springs and wheels, can reckon the hours'. And they do not feel pain. As I have written elsewhere (of the Cartesian paradigm), 'as only the soul, the living part of existence, can experience pain – mere machines cannot do that – it follows that animals can feel no pain'. But how can that be? Animals seem to emit the sounds we associate with experiencing pain. Ah, no. Such apparent expressions of pain (again borrowing from myself) actually 'have the status of the discordant noises that emanate from any faulty or damaged machine'.

My dogs, not just Murphy, also Dougal, my shrewd and loving little canine fluffy slipper; my second border collie cross, timid, bewildered Duffy; gentle, curly-haired Bill; and feisty, grey Flossie, they have prised me loose from this way of thinking. Descartes should have had a dog – as a companion, not an experimental 'object'. He would have come to understand that in dogs exist the same variation in intelligence and personality, and ingenuity in communication and problem-solving, as are to be found in humans. To observe the complexity of a dog's cognition as it manifests in subtleties of behaviour and mood is to render ludicrous the notion that here is a mere machine, functioning according to strict mechanical principles.

Descartes's own lame explanation for demonstrations of intelligence in animals was that these are matched, in the same animal, by demonstrations of stupidity; and besides, that only humans possess the gift of speech. Let's take this matter of 'shows of intelligence'. I'd already long since lost truck with this argument when I read, not many years ago, Mary Midgley's marvellous book *Beast and Man* (written in 1979, though I read it in Routledge's 1995 revised edition). Midgley exposes the partiality of Descartes's 'standard' of intelligence'. 'People', she writes, 'are also capable of acting both intelligently and stupidly, and relatively stupid conduct by a fairly intelligent being on an off-day is not in the least like the "stupidity" of a machine. A car cannot even try to find its way home; a clock will not make even a bad shot at identifying danger. Stupid solutions [at least] show a consciousness of the problem.'

Brilliant. Wish I'd written that. In knowing that it has to get home, and in recognising danger, a dog will show an intelligence that clearly cannot be equated with the 'intelligence' of a machine. It may, like a human, make the wrong decision in response to the problem, but in identifying the problem the animal deploys an intelligence that is closer to that of a human than it is to that of a machine. As for the criterion of language, this, too, is easily dispensed with, and Midgley does just that, pointing out that science itself has now shown that 'language, or the power to speak it, is actually not the unsplittable, single, unmistakable thing people had supposed'.

I could never have identified the problem with the Cartesian distinction as forensically as Midgley has. But just now my two current dogs, Flossie and boisterous, mischievous Ollie, have scampered, nimble-footed, along the very edge of the sea cliff just down from the shanty in which I'm writing. I hold my breath. One false step and that's it for them. But there isn't a false step, of course, just as there never was for their predecessors, either. No humans could do this, though. Why do we valorise complexity of speech and thought over this ability? Aren't we being just a tad self-serving? The cheetah can run faster than any living creature. Why does this not entitle the cheetah to claim the species championship of the world? Isn't it just a little disingenuous to fasten upon the one activity in which humans seem so plainly superior to all other species and claim this as the criterion upon which claims to superiority objectively lodge?

So it was that I left the Cartesian paradigm behind and went in search of more grounded theories of knowledge, of explanations for emotional and bodily intelligence, of systems of ethics based within notions of a democracy of species and the primacy of ecological relationships. Phenomenology rather than positivism. The indeterminacy and flux of the new physics rather than the rigid certainties of reductionist, mechanistic, old-paradigm science. The subject as research informant – subject and object in dynamic interplay – rather than emotionally remote, 'uncontaminated' investigation. Story and description in synergy with, rather than precluded by, analysis. At the heart of these choices – big important choices – lies the quiet wisdom of Murphy, the border collie, and Dougal the bichon-westy, and their deep, complex companionship. I loved them then and I love them still, and they will walk beside me now as I take my beachcomber's constitutional around Killora Bay.

*

All this knowledge registered and absorbed within my brain – even the understanding that the entire body and all the senses contribute to knowing – was a cerebral understanding. But I also became aware of sub-rational modes of knowing through interactions with my dogs. Much of this occurs sub-linguistically – it is the nature of the communication that takes place when a dog locks eyes with you, holds your gaze and concentrates meaning into that gaze. It is a mode of communication that, at best, proceeds by suggestion and hint, persistently reminding you how deep the gulf that separates the species, how emphatic the deficit in cross-species understanding. It is, nevertheless, my window – my misted-over window – into the essence of animal being.

But dog–human communication is not entirely sub-linguistic. There is compelling evidence that the dog, the first species to be domesticated, developed its barking range to communicate with us, and that we developed a commensurate vocal range to make our needs known to them. This included the precise communication needed for herding, for without the dog we would have remained hunter-gatherers. It may not be going too far to observe that the development of the symbiotic relationship between humans and dogs was a necessary prerequisite to civilisation itself. Perhaps, as a consequence, dogs and humans are uniquely attuned to each other, their understanding of each other more superior, probably, than that between humans and chimpanzees, our closest genetic relatives.

Do I talk to my dogs, then? Absolutely – and they talk to me. It is a primal communication, sometimes fraught, the capacity for misunderstanding ever-present, especially when vocal communication is mixed with that more ineffable communication that transpires through the silent locking of eyes. There are those who are critical of dogs – even antagonistic towards them – because the dog is seen to be incompatible with the principle of, and the presence of, the wild. The late Australian philosopher Val Plumwood took this view. And it is undeniably true that to be in the bush with a dog is to greatly reduce one's chances of significant encounters with wild creatures. But, as briefly thrilling as such encounters can be, their 'significance' is mostly tenuous – it is the thrill of the voyeur, and not to be compared with the deep, electric, uncertain window into animal being that I gain from canine communication. 'With friends like this who needs enemies? Bah, humbug', writes David Quammen in his mean-spirited essay 'The Descent of the Dog'. Quammen may be the most perceptive of men on most of the topics on which he chooses to write, but on matters canine he simply doesn't get it.

*

Occasionally I'd forget Murphy. As one forgets one's shadow. I'd drive across town to play sport, say, and I'd let her out of the car to nose about and explore the ground. Then I'd get back in the car and drive home. An hour or so later Murphy would turn up, having successfully negotiated her way past busy freeways and determined dog-catchers. Domum invenio, ergo sum – *I can find my way home, therefore I am.*

Once, when she was very old – she lived to almost twenty – it took her a day to get home, and she was spent. I was thoroughly irresponsible, then. I did not do well at her death either, nor at that of loyal, quizzical Dougal. I know they'd forgive me, but that's no comfort, and I live with the guilt of having been found wanting in their hour of need, after all they'd selflessly given me. The last and hardest wisdom gifted me by my soft-eyed companions is this: how easy it is, in the juggle of life's pulls and its pushes, to act with an innocent shoddiness towards others. Murphy, Dougal, Duffy and those who now run in their stead taught me the complexity of relational ethics, and the struggle to do right by others that is the measure of an honourable life.

Pete Hay

The second-hand bookshop has closed

'Books without movement. Yet books that find their way lithely into our days, / let fly a lamentation there, begin dances.' René Char[1]

The bookshop is closed,
the notice says.
The entire stock is sold.

We thank our patrons
we wish to announce the dismantling
of our long wall of fiction

paperback and cloth
Asimov to Zweig
also Art. Photography.

Literary Biography.
Penguin Classics are gone.
Postwar Recipes. Regional wines.

Natural History. Philosophy and Religion.
Pacific History. Poetry.
Economics. Health. Crafts.

Books, having been interlocutors
for months or decades,
have no further tenure.

The bookshop, former sanctuary of fonts
habitat of moulds
cabinet of aromas

archive of papers
the mustering place of inks and glues
could become a pharmacy or florist's

thus the light entering
the front windows on winter mornings
will in future be mediated

by the cathode tube
browsers' bags will be shopping trolleys,
and, therefore, may no longer

be left unattended at the front desk.
We were expecting some new stock
in February but the bookshop

is now closed.
Expressions of interest in the furniture
may be made during January.

Tim Bass

---

1. *'Livres sans mouvement. Mais livres qui s'introduisent avec souplesse dans nos jours, / y poussent une plainte, ouvrent des bals'* from *'La bibliotheque est en feu'* ('The Library is on Fire', 1962). This quote and its translation is from *Poems of René Char*, translated and annotated by Mary Ann Caws and Jonathan Griffin, Princeton University Press, 1976.

The man who never forgot how to dance

for my father

That day you tried to walk through walls –
what did you see beyond the opacity
of brick? You were so sure it would absorb
you that moments passed before, furious,
you pushed the boundaries of that curious border,
grazing palms and skinning knuckles.

Taking your arms – just like they'd said to,
or perhaps I'd read somewhere – I put one of your hands
at my waist, one of mine on your shoulder
and clasped the other, hummed a little.
You calmed and smiled and started waltzing,
me following and following your unfaltering lead
towards the armchair by the window where you sat
and, quite suddenly,
fell asleep in the afternoon sun.

Virginia Jealous

The black kite

Over Manus Island,
a black kite flies.

Young hands –
with energy still
to bear the difficulties
of this prison camp –
made it.

The black kite flies,
a messenger of freedom
for us, the forgotten prisoners.

It circles
higher and higher
above the camp,
above the beautiful coconuts.

Our eyes follow its flight.
It seems to want to tear its rope.
It breaks free,
dances towards the ocean,
flies far and again farther –
until no one can see it.

The youths stare into the empty sky
after their impossible dream.

Behrouz Boochani

Translated by Ali Parsaei and Janet Galbraith

Luke

I'm looking at the label on his glasses case.
He wrote it himself –
the first name written bold,
the first syllable of his surname also
but dwindling towards the end,
almost to a dot,
as if it was a name he didn't expect,
    even then
to live all the way into.

Deb Westbury

White coffin notes

Drifting motionless in a hot room
it's all you do
somewhere between the life
you know, and the life
that ended –

almost two years since
you sat beside his father
and your lover, a stranger
asking what colour you wanted
for your only
your half-grown
son,
and waiting –

You were expected, anyhow,
to answer this
and also the next thing
and the next
whatever it was,
all things being possible,
after all –

the white hot room,
one mile, then another, becalmed,
deathstruck.

Deb Westbury

Journey to my son

July 2006

I fly to you

oh so slowly
oh so slowly

and I search each cloud for your face.

I think I see you,
with your hair combed, neat, dressed in white,
looking slightly awake
slightly different in sleep
dressed in white as delicate as cloud
and your hands
folded
as I knew they would be
your long, slim fingers.

Quiet all the strings.

And I dressed all the clouds in your white.
And I dressed all the clouds with your face.
And I carried you with me as I flew to you.

But you were already there, in that faraway place
where the waves and the sea and the planes
and the clouds carry people to
when they go so far away.
More clouds,
more waves,
waves.
How is this so?
What can I make of this journey?
Will you know I saw you out at sea
on the waves of the world
as you dream
in the cloud of unbeing?

How will you make that journey
home? How foreign are we now,
all apart,
me in the sky,
you in the heavens,
your brother on one continent
your father another
and your lover
journeying home
to grieve you.

We are fractions of ourselves
factored out into cloud

not seeing
not feeling
being cloud-light.

Anne Kellas

Sudden death

we walk past
the daughter's school uniform
pegged in the front yard
kissing unmown grass

past the son wandering
room to room remote
control under arm
searching unknown frequencies

in the hallway we hear
love's echo
walls sighing   *we miss*
you   miss you   miss

the father bids us sit
while he fills tiny plates
with broken chips pickles
week-old grapes

we've come to read poetry
he leans forward
to read a line
catch her voice

Barbara Kamler

No closer to land

not this turn but the one where we meant to live
   with a newly built clean-washed
      rah rah of a life
you've been back to Scotland
   family not what you expected
   you shrug it off
   I'm here   that's that
there's a decision we're coming to
   if our son is too sick to play
   so much time now
      to wonder why I had to leave
   in order to start again
I can hear the flap

flap in my head
   the anxious hurry-up
      over the edge of worry
the low wall of the car park   that windowsill in front of us
   day after day as we think aloud   wait
   wait   he might tell us what he wants to do   he might
   recover   coming towards it but no closer to land
will we ever wing it again like Credence Clearwater Revival
   or any of those songs he loves
   capping each other's lines about rolling
      on the *Proud Mary*
   or getting back from Illinois
getting anywhere in this fog

I pass an older couple on the grass verges
   stretching their arms into the dark-leafed cover
      black juice on their hands

I can't say to him that *life sucks*
            it could be worse
   you and I tick off the good things we know
   the spring in his step before we left
the coaches' assessment
            the unbelievable saves in goal
   mirror each other's smiles about everything
            except this
   have we taken a wrong turning
coming here

in front of him we bottle it up
   fold everything into smaller boxes
            don't expect to hold on
   to anything for long
                    aloud we say   *can't rain forever*
   it's not how you start but how you finish
that's what our parents said to us

a winter ago   my son and I
   stood on the bridge over Brayford Pool
            canoes slipping below us into the mist
we leaned over at the same time
            broke into the chorus
   of *Smoke on the Water*
            now   a lone hawk soars above the roofs
   settles on an aerial
pulls its wings in

                                        Alana Kelsall

Behind the fence

Behind the fence
the Boy wonders,
gazing through the
eyes of the metal fence.

A question is raised,
too far and too faint for me to hear,
but it seems he got the answer –
the smile on his face tells me so.

But the mother's face says
something else,
   a different story.

I write down every detail
of the curious child
and his mother.

I look down as I write a few words.
I look up to write more
but they're gone

vanished behind the fence.

Kumar

State of the heart

The phone call came at seven in the morning. Tessa thrust a hand from her doona and reached for it.

'Joe's rung. He's ill.' It was George, her ex-husband, talking about their twenty-two year old son.

'Ill? What's wrong with him?'

'Didn't specify.'

'God, George, didn't you ask him?' She was fully awake now.

'Can you get up there, you're on holidays, aren't you?'

'To Jacky's Marsh!'

'He'll want you.'

'He rang you.'

'You can drive me up, then.' Not that she didn't want to go to her son, but there was a point to be made.

Tessa hung up before he could protest further and lay back against her pillows. So, Joe was sick, again. She remembered when he'd hitched home from Sydney last year. He'd been staying with his uncle, her brother Tom, in Glebe, working out what he was going to do with his life. So much for that.

Sorting through the dirty clothes in his pack, she'd found a bill from the Big Ben Medical Centre, and a repeat prescription for antidepressants, and a folded summary of admission to the Royal North Shore Hospital. Her heart in her mouth, she'd skipped down to Final Diagnosis, and read *acute asthma. ?intercurrent viral URTI*. He'd responded rapidly to nebulised ventolin, the notes said. No risk to his heart. His heart? She read up on it. An acute asthma attack can stress the heart, resulting in heart problems, and in extreme cases, a heart attack.

'I'm okay!' he'd shouted, when she'd confronted him. With every gloomy look she'd worried that he was depressed, with every cough that he was asthmatic. Next thing, he'd gone to Jacky's Marsh, squatting in a friend's owner-built house in the rainforest. A marsh? In the rainforest? She couldn't believe it. Determined as usual, he'd waved her goodbye one morning, and set off, hitch-hiking north.

The clock radio clicked on. She caught the last of the Tasmanian weather forecast: fine and cold, snow on the highlands, sheep alert, bushwalker alert. She dozed a little, then got up.

Under the shower, she thought again about Joe. She'd lost him well before he'd left home, she knew that. One Sunday morning she'd come down to the living room and found him, a ten year old, crouched on the big red cushion, still in his pyjamas, watching television. Through the French windows rain soaked black the ivy on the wall, dripped from the ferns onto the pavers. In the television, figures were moving, colours dimming and brightening, tinny television voices dulled by the beat of the rain. He'd looked up at her, then back at the screen as if she didn't exist. Her heart had ached for him, he seemed so lonely, but what could she do?

She got out of the shower. Water steamed from her body in the cold air. She snatched a towel and dried herself as she walked back to her bedroom. George would be here soon.

'You could've let me know you'd be late,' Tessa complained, thinking cheapskate as usual, won't even use his own car to go to his sick son. She threw her pack onto the back seat and dropped a stack of compact discs into a space beside the gear box. 'Joe's music.'

'You mean he's got the electric up there?'

'Batteries. Anyway, he's coming back with me.'

'And where might he be coming back to, the stately ruin?' George smirked, pulling away from the kerb and accelerating down the hill. Tessa looked back at her house, glimpsing the curlicues of its weathered bargeboards through the trees

'When are you putting the place on the market?'

'Never,' she said. Then, 'How's Sharon?'

'Sharon?'

'Sorry, Shannon, Celia? Your girlfriend.'

'Ancient history.'

She suppressed a smug grin and turned to look out of the windows. They drove without speaking, cruising through the outer suburbs, through strip development, then to the country, rural towns. Travelling everyday between home and the school where she taught, it was years since Tessa had come out this way.

At Spring Hill on the Midland Highway, road works were underway. A truck hosed hot asphalt and a road worker in an orange jacket held up a stop sign. They approached at speed.

'Slow down George, George!' The road worker rapidly switched the sign to 'Go.'

Despite herself, Tessa laughed. 'Exercising his power,' she said.

George said, 'Him or me?' Pleased with himself.

Typical egotism, she thought and couldn't be bothered with an answer.

'Whereabouts is this place Joe's holed up?' He asked.

'Jacky's Marsh. Past Deloraine. It's alternative country.'

'Alternative to what?'

'Just about everything, I suppose.'

'Including us?'

'Looks like it.' She reached for a CD. 'Billy Bragg. Now Valentine's Day is Dead,' she read. She pushed it into the player and Billy Bragg sang *When she first spoke to me my nose began to bleed...*

'Joe's all right really, d'you think?' She leaned towards George.

'Probably out of money,' he said.

'He isn't into money.'

'Everyone's into money. You've got to be, to survive.'

'So that's why you're so tight. Just surviving.'

'That's right, sweetheart.'

They drove off the highway at Ross, parked opposite the Man o' Ross Hotel and went inside. A dining room of dark wood and diamond paned windows, odours of steak and gravy.

They ordered a counter meal each. 'I'll shout you,' George said.

'I'll pay for myself, thanks.'

'Be independent, then.' I certainly will, she thought to herself. They ate schnitzel and chips with gravy and swallowed a beer each, then left. As they drove away the music started up again. *I thought about her until the bath water went cold around me...* Tessa laughed, George smiled, and she laughed again, relaxing in the warmth of the car.

The road to Deloraine took them through the back blocks of Cressy with the blue flanks of the Western Tiers on their left mottled with cloud and cloud shadow. A hawk floated above a line of bare poplars. Reaching Cressy, they turned west into rain blurring the countryside. The roads were edged with hawthorn hedges through Bracknell, Cluan, Osmarton where they once again turned north and she sang along with Billy Bragg: *One day it happened, she cut her hair and I stopped loving her...*

The farmland gave way to scrubby paddocks and they passed houses, a golf course, more houses and suddenly, Deloraine. Skirting the town, they took the road beside the river.

'Keep a lookout for a weatherboard church,' George said. 'If we reach Meander we've gone too far.' They drove beneath Quamby Bluff marking the northern end of the Tiers, and reached the turn-off to Jacky's Marsh just before the church. George slowed and pulled the car onto the gravel shoulder. 'How're we going to handle this?' he asked, as he yanked on the hand brake.

'Handle what?'

'Joe, of course.'

'For heaven's sake! It's our son you're talking about.'

'Could be out of it on drugs, you've got to face up to things, Tessa.'

'He's sick, that's all!' She was so cross, she turned her shoulder to him and stared out of the window. He started the car and they drove along a gravel road through farmland. Ascending, the track deteriorated further. Soon they were tunnelling through dark-leaved undergrowth, water dripping down yellow clay at drain cuttings, the car straddling ruts. George veered off track when a granite boulder protruded from the track. He parked the car and they got out.

'Can't take this vehicle any further.'

'Okay.' Tessa got out, grabbing her back pack. The air was fresh on her cheeks as she started off, walking up the track.

'Know where we're heading?' George caught up with her.

'It's not too far,' she said, trying to sound confident. The ground was spongy underfoot, making for easy walking, and their breath curled in the cold air. High up wind moved through the trees, the foliage scrolling against clouds touched pink by the sunset. Evening was falling. Tessa hugged herself in her parka, sensing snow. A light shone through the trees.

'Here we are.' The track continued on, bordered with wattles in bloom to a garden fenced in wire. They veered up a path through the trees to a cottage, and crossed a verandah to the door. As George banged on the door, Tessa looked through the window. A Tilley lamp glowed on a wooden table, fire in a brick fireplace smouldered. Mugs hung on hooks in a dresser, two kitchen chairs were pushed in at the table.

'Looks lovely,' Tessa said. 'So cute.'

George banged on the door again. 'No sign of a welcoming party.'

'He must be close by, he's left the fire.'

'Close by!' George shivered, and looked at the forest rising above the cottage into the night. 'Where might close by be, exactly?

The cold seeped upwards and Tessa stamped her feet on the boards. She tried the handle of the door and pushed. It opened, a mat slid across the floor, and inside it smelled of wood smoke and dried herbs. A kettle simmered on the hotplate of a combustion stove. She hesitated.

'Better take our boots off.'

'You're sure this is okay?' George waited at the open door.

'Of course it's okay.' Tessa eased her feet out of her boots and placed them outside the door. George wrenched off his boots, they clattered to the boards, and he came in, stooping through the low door. Tessa placed the bag of compact discs on the table, slipped off her coat and back pack, stood with her back to the fire. She couldn't think why Joe wasn't here, but there was nothing they could do but wait for him.

'We could have a cup of tea.' She lifted two mugs off their hooks, grabbed a teapot and took them over to the stove. She found the tea caddy and made the tea, the steam from the kettle billowing upwards. She refilled the kettle and put it back on the stove. She placed the mugs on the hearth. George stood awkwardly, his back to the fire, his hands clenched in the pockets of his sheepskin jacket. Tessa pulled a cushion across with her foot, sat on it and gazed into the fire. She took up her mug, warming her hands. George crouched beside her.

'Surprisingly snug,' he said, 'for an owner built place, especially with that mezzanine. Whoever built it must've insulated properly.' They sat in silence for a while, sipping their hot tea. Through the window the foliage was lit a vivid green by the Tilley lamp. Snowflakes twirled down, slowly at first, then faster, settling on the foliage.

'Snowing now,' she said. 'I hope he isn't out in it.' With the warmth of the cottage about her, Tessa felt safe, and at the same time vulnerable, as though only a transparent film lay between her and the freezing night.

'We should've stocked up on snacks before we came up here,' George said.

'There's something in a pot on the stove.'

'Not lentils!'

'Could be broccoli soup.'

'Tempting.' They laughed, then fell silent.

'Something's happened to him,' Tessa fretted. 'He's up on the Tiers with a broken leg.'

'He rang us, remember. He's okay.' George drew close, comforting her.

'Why did he get us up here, if he's okay?'

'Your guess is as good as mine.'

She stiffened. 'Look up in the mezzanine, George,' she ordered.

'For Christ's sake Tessa, he would've heard us arrive.' But he climbed the ladder and peered into the space beneath the roof. 'It's a while since he changed the sheets,' he said and jumped down to the floor. Tessa pulled her sleeping bag out of her pack. George stretched out, leaning on an elbow, and she spread the sleeping bag across him. 'No. You keep it.' She ignored him, tucking it up, edging closer to him for warmth.

'George, how did this happen?'

'You mean Joe? He's just an independent bastard. Like his mother.'

'Me?'

'That's why you never got on.'

'We always got on.'

'Tessa, I didn't say you didn't love him.'

'And us? What about us, George?'

He faced her. 'I never said I didn't love you.'

She ducked her head and stared into the smouldering fire. 'Why did it happen, then?

'Dunno.' He looked at her. 'My fault. Should've given you more…'

'More what?'

'Space, time, support… More of everything, I guess.'

She couldn't answer.

The door opened suddenly. Snowy air gusted into the room. A young man stood in the doorway. Snow speckled his head and shoulders, highlighting his clear skin, bright eyes.

'G'day guys. Made yourselves comfortable? Great!'

'Joe!' Tessa jumped up, the sleeping bag falling around her feet. They hugged. He looked over the top of her head at George.

'Hi, Dad.'

'How are you, son?'

'So you got here okay?'

'Sure,' George said. 'Not much choice…'

'Lovely trip up here,' Tessa said, interrupting him.

A girl appeared from the darkness behind Joe, walking into the light.

Joe turned to her. 'This is Crystal,' he said. 'My olds, Tessa and George.'

They stared at her. She was slight, with sharp eyes that glittered against her white skin and red cheeks. A woollen caftan hung on her shoulders, dusted with snow.

'Hello, Crystal,' Tessa said after a moment.

George grunted, plunging his hands into his pockets.

'I thought you were ill,' Tessa said to Joe, suddenly. 'Is it your asthma?'

'No, Mum...' Exasperated, he turned away from her.

The girl coughed, hacking. She shuddered, and bent over. Joe strode to the tap, ran some water into a glass and handed it to her.

'Would a hot drink help?' she said. 'There's tea in the pot.'

'That's for guests. We don't take caffeinated drinks,' Joe said.

With this answer, Tessa knew there was nothing to be done, it all lay with them. 'I've brought my sleeping bag,' she said and even as she said it, realised this was a mistake.

'Mum...' Joe indicated the lack of room with his head, 'love to have you. Maybe when I've built another room, hey?'

'You bring us all the way up here?' George turned away.

'There's a good pub down in Deloraine,' Joe said.

'Include me out.' George pulled his coat about him. Tessa held him back with a hand on his arm, looking from one to the other.

'Call back up tomorrow. We'll have a chat,' Joe said.

George shifted. 'Sorry mate,' he said. 'Next time. I've got to get back.'

'You do?' Tessa was surprised.

'Work you know.'

'Right,' Joe said.

There was no offer of food. Tessa picked up her bag, smiled at Crystal, then Joe. George threw the sleeping bag over his shoulder, stooping to pick up the back pack from the floor.

'I'm glad you're well,' Tessa said, and bit her lip. It was clear that right now Crystal was the one not well. 'I brought your CDs up. Love that Billy Bragg.' She looked at him hopefully.

'Billy Bragg? Go Mum!' and he hugged her. 'Thanks for coming. See you, Dad.'

'Down in Hobart next time, son.'

'Maybe. I'm a bit... Want me to guide you to your car?'

'No. You stay inside in the warm, darling.' Tessa kissed him before turning to go. George bent to pull on his boots and she stumbled into hers, her eyes on Joe. She walked a few steps down the path, looking back. Joe drew Crystal to him. She gave a little wave, he waved back. Tessa remembered again the child watching television that rainy Sunday morning. Her son seemed only able to communicate fleetingly with meanings she grabbed from the night.

'So that's what he wanted us to see,' she understood, now.

'What might that be?'

'He's found someone to care for.'

'Coulda fooled me.'

It wasn't simply that. The burden of illness, deciding what to do with his life, all had been thrown off.

'And he's found this.'

'I'd have taken his word for it,' George said, 'without charging all the way up here to find out.'

'It's the only way he could tell us. It's his way, hey George?'

'Maybe.' George was grudging. He draped the sleeping bag around Tessa's shoulders, lifting it up to her cheeks, tucking it around her chin. Before them the landscape was luminous with snow and the moon hung above in its own radiance. Down at the track, a movement of air gusted through wattles already drooping with snow, and they exploded one by one, tossing the snow upwards, revealing their dull gold blooms. George's arm was around Tessa's shoulders, and she leaned into him.

'I can see how this could get a hold of you,' George rumbled.

'Yes,' she said. 'It's so beautiful.'

The vast night poured down from the Tiers. They turned and walked down the track, entering a black and white forest of moonlight in snow-hung trees.

'This is exquisite,' Tessa murmured. 'Thank you for bringing us here, Joe.'

'Myrtle stands over there, sassafras, leatherwood…' George intoned.

'You know the names of the trees?'

'Course I do.'

She'd forgotten that about him. 'It's much too late to drive back home, you know.'

'Weather's too bad for driving, anyway.'

'What about your work?'

'Bugger that. I'll take an RDO.'

'Let's go find that pub in Deloraine.'

'You sure?'

'Call back here, on our way home in the morning, George?' He stopped and gazed into her face. 'To say goodbye to Joe.' He smiled, she took his hand and together they walked on, into the snowy night.

Carol Patterson

Fallout

Suppose you are a woman in your forties. You are at the kitchen sink washing dishes. The furrow in your ring finger refuses to go away. Light from the window is making the bubbles gaudy. The warm water and the whirling hands help you think. Suppose this is the only good reason you do the dishes. Mother Mary in her green, radioactive skin sits on the windowsill, one foot on a snake. Even as a kid, you couldn't warm to that terrible stripped heart and the arms, wide open. She lost her glow years ago but there are some things you can't throw out. You lay her face-down as the hard memories roll around in your brain like black marbles.

You can see your reflection in the glass and it's not what it used to be. Past and through the glass, a garden also needs attention. There is a young girl, your daughter. She is picking peaches. Her whole world is ripening. You hadn't noticed, caught up with all the bills and dishes, that irrevocable swelling under her T-shirt. You tear-up, blame the hormones and slap yourself. You remember anyway, seeing as the washing is piled up. The washing is piled up. You have to do something different.

*

Now suppose you are an eight-year-old. You're belly-down in fresh-turned soil. It is the closest thing in your world to lying on a cloud. It smells like ground pepper and mixed herbs. You watch an ant negotiate a path home, a challenge, since the soil was turned only yesterday. The sun is warm on your back. You give the ant a hand shadow. You smooth a path here and there, guessing at his direction. You haven't brushed your hair or teeth. You're still in your pyjamas, Cinderella hand-me-downs. You crumble bread for him. You know the sky is deep blue, just from the green of the grass. You turn your ear to the ground, one more time. Tears, one after the other, flow from one eye, over your nose bridge, through the other eye and into the soil. You remember how the tomato plants will sing their spicy scent by Christmas, and it is just as well. You stay there for a long time, and finally, raise your fist. You bring it down hard onto the ant, down deep into the dirt.

*

Imagine now, you are a sailor. Your only mission was reconnaissance to Nagasaki, two weeks after the bomb. You've been on dry land twenty years. You wear a back brace and work shifts as a postal clerk. You have a Catholic wife and six kids, none of whom have grandparents, on account of Gallipoli, Turkey and childbirth. You're taking out loans each year for books and school fees. You're standing ankle-deep in the garden about to turn the soil for the summer vegetables. Your fourteen-year-old son is leaning on his spade with a cigarette in his mouth, just as you draw deeply on yours. You shake your head and click your tongue. Your other son is leaning on his spade too, mopping faux sweat from his brow. Your youngest daughter is leaning on her spade, smiling, as if it's an adventure. You shake your head, issue instructions, and go back to work.

It's hot; sweat trickles into your eyes. You pause, wipe your face, take your singlet off, swing it onto the fence. You barely notice that three other shirts swing onto the fence, as you put the spade in repeatedly, lifting, turning, breaking up clods. The fourteen-year-old stops, laughs. You follow his eyeline to your youngest daughter. She is looking around for the joke. You look at her a second time, see the irrevocable swelling and have to look away. You shake your head and click your tongue. *Knock it off, son*, you say, in that tone you've mastered. To your girl, you say, *Get your shirt back on, and go inside to your mother.* You go on with the spade, lifting, turning, breaking up clods. You know you just broke something. She's red, confused, stomping back to the house. She'll be shutting the door when she dresses. She won't be gardening with you, or sitting on your lap. You know she just sailed into fallout and you have nothing to say about that.

Now suppose…you'll be dead in five years, along with all your old shipmates.

*

If you are not sick of supposing yet, suppose it wasn't like that. Maybe you came back from the war with nothing but postcards and ticker tape. Suppose love was as reliable as your first piece of real estate, suppose no one had to be ashamed of their body, or of dying too soon, or of never having spoken up. You can go on supposing for years, but it doesn't get you anywhere. You are not all these people…you are just one.

I'm at the sink.

My daughter comes in from the garden with her T-shirt bulging, mostly with peaches. *Mum, I just found a bug cocoon.* She smells like green grass and peaches. *Have you been crying, Mum? What's wrong?*

It's wonderful, I say, *a sink full of ripe peaches, and these black pearls. They hang around for years, ugly and lumpish, and make no sense until they go around your neck at just the right time. It's hard…but it's the only way things can change.*

You're talking weird, Mum, she says, biting into a peach and setting Mother Mary back up straight.

We're gonna have a celebration soon, me and you, your grandmother, and your aunties. I don't know the details yet, but it will make you feel as though you can do anything. I beam and wrap her in my arms.

I'll give her that string of black pearls one day, when she's grown. When I am belly-up in the black soil, smelling like ground pepper and mixed herbs, I'll be glad I did something different.

Carmel Williams

231

What we wish for

Any day my daughter will announce
she's moving out
to start a life she fully owns.

No more lunchtime breakfasts,
greasy plates left in the sink;
no more coming in at 2 a.m.,
key careful in the lock so I won't wake;
no more agonising over essays, boyfriends,
raging at her parking fines.

Dreams of tranquillity
at last come true:
my music undisturbed,
computer access any time,
the cups and cutlery all washed,
the house at peace –
and empty.

Bob Morrow

On fifty-three

Give way

Is it possible that it has taken me fifty-three years to discover that life is essentially a project of loss and letting go? That the trajectory is one of dispersal. That what we must learn is how to grieve.

Half a century to discover something so obvious, so fundamental.

In my darkest days, I found strange comfort in just a few lines from the Inferno section of Dante's *Divine Comedy*:

> Midway upon the journey of our life
> I found myself in a dark wilderness,
> for I had wandered from the straight and true.

I didn't read any more; it was simply the image of being in a dark forest halfway through my life (I was about forty at the time) that sustained me.

The other image that stayed with me was when I heard someone on the radio say that experiencing grief is like driving through a town. Eventually you get to the other side. This sounded reassuring, but I didn't find the reality matched. I seemed to be forever driving (and slowly). Was my road circular or was it just a really large town? I suspect now that I was misremembering C.S. Lewis's phrase about grief being a long valley and conflating that with the fact that the car was one of the few private spaces in which I could cry without anyone else knowing.

Nonetheless, I see it is common for us to use a journey metaphor in talking about grief and loss, even though the experience isn't linear. And I still enjoy the luxury of driving by myself, when I am free to sing along with the radio, rehearse a lecture, argue with hypothetical others, laugh or, if I should so desire, cry.

Night works

A slick of Australian olive oil, two crushed garlic pods, some diced ginger, a squeeze of red chilli paste, turn on the flame and wait. This is all it takes to animate desire. If I sip a glass of New Zealand Sauvignon Blanc, still cold from the fridge, the moment is complete. I cannot prevent myself from smiling. My smallest finger slips up to my lips, rests between my teeth. I lean against the kitchen bench, stirring the pan, sipping my wine, smiling.

Strangely, I cannot remember the actual meal that triggers this response. I remember the lover, of course, his hands, his body, his humour. Over the years, we have had quite a few meals together, many of them Asian. I expect he would be mildly pleased that the mere smell of garlic, ginger and chilli cooking triggers such fond reminiscing. If he walked in the door this moment, I'm sure he would share my wine and my pleasure. He would be pleased also that I feel only mild sadness that he no longer walks in my door.

The first time I noticed that the smell of these ingredients had this effect on me, I told myself to savour the moment, because it wouldn't last. I avoided the mix, sure that I would become immune to the reaction if I smelt it too often. I was wrong. It happens every time, at home or passing a Thai restaurant, or at a friend's house. Months, years, go by, and still, my limbic system is reliable. I have the memory of pleasure even before I notice the smell or think of the man.

Is this middle age, to enjoy memory as much as experience?

No exit

Some days I yearn to focus on what things are like, not what they mean. The academic project, of course, is about meaning, about naming and explaining. That is my job as university lecturer. It seems my home life projects as mother and as daughter are also that: trying to work out what everything means and what I then have to do. I want to stop and see what things are *like* instead. To live phenomenologically. To shift my focus from understanding to experiencing the thisness of the bits of life around me.

This project of cataloguing in order to analyse was started so young in my life that I have no memory of a time before. There is no childhood memory of texture or vision or movement or sound that is not already overlaid with a gloss of meaning. An image of our first paddling pool came into my mind the other day and I know I was in it, cooling down one English summer afternoon, with my youngest sister. The thought arises that we must be quiet in our enjoyment or we will disturb our parents. I can see the stones that edge the flower beds. We used to walk along their odd shapes, practising our balance. My sister was always better at that than me. I was strangely attracted to that row of stones but their meaning was about my weakness; how, in the physical world, my little sister was already more adept. They represented my attraction to, but discomfort with, the world outside my mind.

It strikes me now that nothing was simply an object or an experience in my childhood. Everything stood in for something abstract, of the intellect. This can't be true. It must simply be an artefact of memory, a kind of retrospective glaze that spreads backwards over my past. Before language and abstractions, children have experiences. But we rarely remember them. I may be conflating the propensity of early language talk in my family to be rather intellectual or analytical with the way we forget unworded experiences.

Detour ahead

'The University is where ideas come to die.' This is the sort of sentence my colleague says in passing, without much emphasis, though with feeling, usually just as I am stepping out of his office. Only the next day I read Peter Robb's essay in *The Monthly* about not becoming a scholar. He says, 'Literature ruined the lives of many young people. Not literature, but the study of literature. Like a fool, when I was young I thought the university was where to take a love of art in words. My life has been full of mistakes, and this was the greatest.'

Like Robb, I escaped academia at a young age. I was tempted by an academic life – by the warm glow of leather-bound books and endless debates about Virginia Woolf – but more tempted by travel, by book publishing, by what I called 'real life'.

Now, three decades after I finished my first degree, I'm back at a university. It's not the same university and the name of the department has changed from English Literature to Communication and Cultural Studies, but it is still a return. The corridor I work in is only slightly more modern than the one in which my tutors worked when I was a student. It has a similar echoing feel to it. Most days there are only three or four offices occupied, and my office door might be the only one open. An administrator was heard to comment that you could use this corridor as a bowling alley and not a single academic would be struck! (This, I think, is a good dramatisation of the abiding divide between professional administrators and academics.)

I am told that in the 1980s a postgraduate student lived in the roof space just outside my office (there is a handy person-hole for access), using the tea room as a kitchen and the toilets for washing. Apparently this student is now a professor at a Melbourne university, so his homelessness was temporary. Or perhaps, he was never homeless in his heart. Perhaps academic life provided his home.

It is old-fashioned to use books nowadays. There are colleagues here who have no books on their shelves and rarely use the library. But I still visit the university library often and every time I do, I find myself inhaling, deeply, slowly. I feel once again that combination of anticipation and serenity, that feeling that I have once more returned to the source of contentment. Like the roof-dwelling postgraduate, I have found a home in the academy and the morgue-like atmosphere of my corridor is part of this pleasure.

Occasionally, as I walk from my office to the car park, I glimpse a middle-aged man in a brown corduroy jacket. I am always thrilled to catch this sight, because it is a throwback to my student days when academics looked like academics. There was never the chance they might pass as 'normal' citizens in those days – they had a different, seemingly a charmed, life. Perhaps even then the shades of the managerial revolution were falling upon them, but I didn't see it. I believed they slumbered through their days reinterpreting *Finnegans Wake* or the Augustan poets.

The colleague who said that ideas are killed off at universities is wrong, of course. He is wrong in the most fundamental way because he is a living demonstration of true scholarship at the university. He continues his research career while meeting the many administrative and teaching demands on his time. But his comment reflects Peter Robb's observation that 'Today's scholars are academic bureaucrats.'

There is a deep sadness among humanities academics that scholarship is dying and that their life's work is no longer valued. This is rarely expressed as loss; more often, it is expressed as anger or cynicism. As a previous generation of scholars leave the system – some retiring, some being pushed out – those of us who remain must try to find our own way of doing intellectual work within a changing world. From my office window on the fourth floor, I can see across into the next building, which is being renovated to create new open-plan offices. The top floor is completely gutted now, only the walls stand. I can see through the windows to the trees beyond, as if the renovated academy is empty.

Falling objects

In the books of my childhood, all the exciting and transgressive things happened around midnight. Feasts, adventures, escapes... All the horrors, too, happened then – ghosts, deaths, strange visions, sounds in your bedroom or down the stairs. An empty house suddenly, except for the rats chattering hungrily in the attic above your bed.

In adulthood, though, it is under the harsh light of the sun that the momentous things occur. Betrayals happen over lunch, loss flies at you as you wait for the bus, despair lodges in your stomach as you sit staring at a cup of tea at four p.m., wondering if you have the energy, the will, to lift it to your lips. Wondering what your lips are for. Expecting always to be lonely.

'Loneliness is the natural companion of the writer.' This is Helen Garner, who can say such things without sounding pompous or self-indulgent. Who can say such things in front of one hundred people and half will nod and feel somehow reassured.

Double curve

Some years ago, I presented a paper on ambiguous loss at an academic conference. My interest came because I recognised that the grief I felt about my son's diagnosis with a disability was a kind of ambiguous loss – I hadn't lost my son but I had lost some of my expectations and beliefs about him and about mothering. After I spoke at the conference, I was astounded at the number of people (mainly women) who came to ask me for details about the Pauline Boss books I had cited and to talk about the value of naming an experience of grief as ambiguous. It was as if giving it a specific name helped people feel their grief was valid or understood. This may be similar to the way I took comfort in Dante's image of the dark forest.

I still sometimes feel loss about my son's disability – because he experiences challenges, because we live a life in the margins, because he is different from me and I sometimes struggle to bridge the gap between us. At other times I am happy and fulfilled as a mother. When I think about his future, I feel uncertainty and fear and, if I let it, those feelings can immediately be closed over into a kind of blankness that is similar to feeling depressed. I'm getting much better, though, about allowing myself to feel the uncertainty and fear and to accept those confronting emotions without closing down.

In her essay 'Memory and Imagination', Patricia Hampl notes that 'Pain has strong arms.' I love this phrase and how it can be understood in a variety of ways. In the essay she is making the point that we retain images that are associated with painful or negative experiences from the past, but that over time the emotion and the image may become separated. Memoir, she says, 'seeks a permanent home for feeling and image, a habitation where they can live together'. Writing memoir allows us to fasten our loss to the page with an image, a process which, paradoxically, holds and releases grief.

One way

My mother is eighty-seven. I am part of the generation of 'career' women who care for ageing parents and young or teenage children at once. Like my own ageing, like mothering, like being single, and like working in academia, watching my mother age is an experience infused with loss but containing much else as well. It is a privilege to witness someone confronting their final years with such determination and courage. It is also hard to watch.

My son and my mother get on well, as they always have done. They are both at their most gentle with each other. Their conversations are a little surprising at times because of my mother's deafness and my son's unusual take on life. Some years ago, my son became interested in death. We visited the Fremantle Cemetery several times and had various conversations about death and its aftermath. He was inclined to accept the possibility of heaven in spite of my atheism. He created a cemetery in our garden, using a patch of dirt and cutting out cardboard headstones with the words 'Henri Matisse 1869–1954 RIP, Claude Monet 1840–1926 RIP' and so on. When my mother visited us (she was still mobile in those days), he took her on a tour of the cemetery. As I went to make a pot of tea, I heard her commenting that it was a bit bare. By the time I had returned, my son was looking a little startled.

'But they don't grow, do they?' he asked.

'Yes, dear, of course they will, with a nice bit of fertiliser and water,' replied my mother.

'Is that how they get up to heaven?'

'Oh, does he believe in heaven?' my mother asked me, shocked.

Later that night, my son asked me whether bones did in fact grow out of the ground in cemeteries if you watered them. I explained my mother had been suggesting he plant some flowers in our cemetery. He looked unconvinced, as children so often do when we try to explain either muddles or mysteries.

Nowadays, my son does jobs around the house for my mother or talks to her about school while I do the jobs. They are both very matter of fact people, so when we have been there for precisely one hour and fifty-five minutes, they start saying goodbye to each other, regardless of what I am saying or doing. They both know that the right period for a visit is two hours.

Because of this forthrightness, I have talked to my mother about dying, though it is not something we discuss often or in detail. She says she is ready to go; I say that I am not ready for her to go. She just smiles, as if to say, 'You'll learn'.

Under construction

I wanted to write about being fifty-three, about middle-age and how I begin only now to understand that loss is central to our lives and to becoming ourselves. I wanted to write about the haphazard nature of our journey – that the road never takes us through the town. I wanted to write about how recording loss is like returning to the self. I wanted to write all this in fifty-three short paragraphs; that would have been so neat. But instead I have learned Bret Lott's maxim first-hand: 'Form follows necessity'. I know really that there is no neat way to describe the relationship between middle-age and learning to grieve, between everyday loss and identity. The closer I approach my topic, the further it is from my grasp.

This is why we have poetry. This is why Dante's work spoke so clearly to me. This is the reason I have gravitated back to the academy and its library. Like pain, poetry has strong arms.

Rachel Robertson

Works cited
Boss, Pauline, *Ambiguous Loss*, Harvard University Press, 1999.
Dante, Alighieri, *Inferno* (translator, Anthony Esolen), Random House, 2002.
Garner, Helen, Keynote at the NonfictioNow Conference, 21–23 November, 2012, RMIT, Melbourne.
Hampl, Patricia, *Memory and Imagination, I Could Tell You Stories*, W.W. Norton, 1999.
Lewis, C.S., *A Grief Observed*, Faber and Faber, 1961.
Lott, Bret, *Rethinking Memoir*, NonfictioNow Conference, 21–23 November, 2012, RMIT, Melbourne.
Robb, Peter, 'The Life Not Lived: Reflections on Scholarship', *The Monthly*, December 2011.

The museum of menstruation

1975

At first blood I cried.
You found a spare belt –
grey elastic and two
gold safety pins.

Your face, pinched at my tears –
you had forgotten your own.
The way a mother can preside
at her daughter's circumcision.

Wes Lee

Unborn

I am quiet – my body leads me.
The night pads I change hourly
are full of such food. The sleek clots,
dark, like liver, from this child's broken bed,
are sewn into my vision – for months
I will feel them, the vaginal canal
tattooed with the suddenness of their slide.
The ache bears down, and the spill slips
and spasms, the womb a blood lake
in a ruptured valley, the silt half-congealed.

I cannot sense it, but our tiny mollusc
of a child clings on, its stubborn hold
stronger than its heart. We find
its thin sac in the emptiness, a grey line
in a grey image, ten days later,
and the surgeon explains how they'll
probe their way through the tight
lips of my cervix to scrape it out.

There is no illness, no fever.
The breasts feel nothing
where they have felt, till now,
everything. And low down, in each
bone of my pelvis, leaching into my spine,
the cry – wrapped up in its silence,
the mute tangle of its noise... I fold
in my lover's arms, the space he held
closing on the small arc of my body.

Kristen Lang

A short history of eggs

On Sundays my mother passes around the eggs, one for each child, one for her and two for my father. She cooks my father's first in the frypan alongside a butter-soaked slice of bread. Then my brothers each take it in turn to cook theirs. My older sister prefers to boil her egg, hard-boiled, the yolk yellow as the sun. Finally, my mother scrambles my baby brother's egg into a buttery spread at the bottom of a saucepan. I am in the middle, sixth-born, old enough now to cook my own egg.

I take it to the corner of the kitchen away from the others and crack it gently on the side of a teacup. I ease apart the shell with my thumb and finger, so that the inner skin holds like a hinge when I pull the shell back. I then tip the yolk from one half of the eggshell to the other, letting the white slide into my cup. All the while I keep a close eye on the yolk, not only for blood blisters that might signify a fertilised egg gone wrong – one I will not eat – but also for ruptures. The yolk glistens and slips from one side of the shell to the other.

When all the white slides away into the cup, I offer the yolk to one of my brothers to cook alongside his own, as if his egg had twins. Then I take a fork and two spoonfuls of sugar and begin to whisk. I tilt the cup to one side to get maximum egg-white under the whisk without spilling any. I do this for an hour or two. I do this till the kitchen is empty of breakfast eaters. I do this till well past the time when we must leave for church and it is too late to eat. I must fast for three hours before Mass and Communion, otherwise I will be in sin.

*

I found the eggshell on the nature strip in front of my therapist's house. I had walked down her path at the end of my last session before Christmas, my head down, eyes to the ground. The shell was white against the green of the freshly mown grass and stood out against the yellow summer daisies sprouting there. I picked it up and cradled it in the flat of my hand. Its edges were torn and cracked in places. There was a creamy stain in the centre. Otherwise there was no sign of life from the bird that must once have lived inside.

In my fragile state, on the eve of a therapy break, I imagined the little thing had fallen from the nest still in its shell and when the egg hit the earth hard, its shell broke open and the bird's life was aborted, before it ever had a chance to fly. I had come into therapy to make sense of myself, this person who felt things too deeply and could not soothe her conscience long enough to get to sleep at night.

I carried the eggshell to my car and wrapped it in a tissue. I put it in a corner of the glove box. I kept it there as a souvenir, an accompaniment to my sorrow, a way of getting me through the long summer break.

Each day during the holidays, I measured my therapist's absence by counting the pills left in my contraceptive pill packet. I had only started back on a light dose of the pill after the birth of my third daughter. This baby's presence was a greater pleasure than any broken eggshell and yet the tiny piece in my car seemed to represent a part of me that felt broken. And having it there tucked away in the glovebox of my car became a comfort even after the Christmas break was over and I resumed weekly visits to my therapist.

In time, I almost forgot about the shell as the months and years rolled by and my third baby grew. Three healthy daughters now and still I hoped for a son. Six years later, now in my late thirties, I tried to conceive again and succeeded. For ten weeks, my husband and I were delighted but we kept the news to ourselves, wary of the possibility of loss. One in five pregnancies ends in miscarriage.

I had learned about miscarriages when I was still a child. My mother had one once, somewhere between my two younger sisters. I saw it but did not see. The sudden rush of pain, premature contractions, the doctor in the morning. The blood on the sheets. My mother passed the foetus into a potty and kept it safe in water in the sink for the doctor to examine. Later, she described a little creature cocooned in a bubble of jelly. Her lost baby.

It was a Tuesday. I remember the walk across the car park and back to my car, the slow drip of blood between my legs. I remember squeezing my pelvis, as if by this simple movement of my body I could hold on, hold onto my little Horatio.

Horatio, I said under my breath. *Horatio, hold the bridge.*

The doctor had told me it was too soon to know. It was not unusual to bleed in these first few weeks, she said. It might not spell the inevitable. The inevitable, she said, was not inevitable, though to hold my grief, or to help me to focus on something else, some greater grief perhaps, she offered her own story, of how she, at forty-two years of age, had stopped IVF, and finally made the decision to accept her fate.

'You already have three children,' she said to me. 'Think on it. Even if the inevitable happens, and you lose this one, you have something to fall back on.'

I fell back on my past.

*

A ten-year-old girl, I stood beside my mother in the front garden of our house. The geraniums had wilted under the summer heat, and my mother picked at them carelessly. She plucked off the dead ones and threw them away.

Mrs Bruyn from up the street stopped at our fence. 'I was sorry to hear about your baby,' she said, and my mother's eyes filled with tears. 'But you still you have your other children,' Mrs Bruyn said. 'They must be a comfort to you.'

My mother nodded, her eyes misty with tears, and Mrs Bruyn walked away. I watched her floral dress billow in the breeze. I heard the clip clop of her heels on the concrete path. Like my parents, Mrs Bruyn came from Holland, the land of babies, my mother told me, the land of large families, even if there was not enough room.

Mrs Bruyn had room for babies but she had not made any. It was not her fault, my mother told me, something to do with her eggs. Eggs, I thought then, like chicken eggs that sit under the warmth of a fat hen for days, then one day crack open and out pops a baby.

*

'You must not leave it too late to have your babies,' the doctor told me. 'Once you reach forty, your chances halve.'

The doctor had accepted her fate to be childless and I had waited too long for this last one, just as she had waited too long for her first. Our eggs were old. I worried then about the possibility of an early menopause, that I had lost all chances for another baby, for a boy.

The lottery of pregnancy, the doctor said. *The later you leave it the less chance of success.* I did not tell my mother about my miscarriage. She did not tell me of hers until later, years later when we could share our grief. She had lost this other baby in the toilet, like a penny doll, she said. She could see its arms and legs, its little eyes. My unformed son, Horatio, could not hold the bridge. Ten weeks into the world and he was gone.

My husband has white lumpy bits on both his ankles. That is where the babies were attached in utero, he tells me, as his mother once told him. All the dead babies that he had managed to outlive, as if his life cost theirs. And Mrs Bruyn who lived up the street and wished my mother well. She had no babies at all. I think of Horatio often, of who he might have been had he lived.

The day after my miscarriage, after I pulled my car over to the kerb in front of my therapist's house, I took the eggshell out of its hiding place. I unwrapped it and carried it up the hill. My therapist stood at the door of her consulting room as usual and as I walked past I held out my hand to offer its contents. Instinctively she opened her palm and as the shell passed from me to her it cracked completely and fell into her hand in pieces.

Today, nineteen years later, my youngest and fourth daughter, whose birth followed Horatio's loss, tells me she is in trouble because of my eggs. 'Your eggs were too old,' she says. 'They've given me allergies.'

I did not plan to have this daughter so late in my life. At the time, I called her an afterthought, almost by way of apology. Should I have felt guilty? One of those impossible thoughts. If I had not had her then, she would not now exist.

Put off the best till last, my mother said. *Always save the good stuff.* Do all the hard and horrible jobs first while you still feel the pleasure of anticipation. All those years ago when I came home from Mass and went to collect my egg white from the fridge, it still sat in the cup like a fluffy white cloud, but the cloud no longer stuck to the sides of the cup. The cloud had come away and slid around the inside of the cup afloat on a trickle of liquid that had leaked its way of out, like a rain puddle. It no longer tasted of meringue, but had a raw egg flavour that curdled my stomach.

*

When I think of the warmth of a freshly laid egg in the cradle of my hand, the warmth of the egg that has just slipped out from its hen mother's body onto the straw of the henhouse, only to land in the cold outside air, I remember my last daughter's birth. How she hung there upside down in the doctor's hands, after a quick labour that had surprised us all. Her body was slimy and purplish blue. In her first few moments in the world, I wondered through the fog and haze of a painful labour, will she ever breathe?

And then came the cry, the loud scratching sound that is a newborn's cry, and I could let myself think the unthinkable. If she had left the best till last, if she had held off that first breath, then she would not be here today to complain about her mother's old eggs.

Elisabeth Hanscombe

Desiccation

You know what I did today? I went and made an appointment to have a pair of eyebrows tattooed. You probably think that's pathetic, at my age, but I haven't had a decent pair of eyebrows since the seventies, when I plucked them to death. And I just feel like, well, I'm fast running out of youth now and it would be good for my morale to look a little bit nicer for a little bit longer. So I had my hair cut and coloured too. I just love the bright pink streaks.

Ted hasn't said anything. He's OK with the idea of the eyebrows, but I don't think he likes the colour of my hair. I reckon he's embarrassed. He always gets embarrassed when I do anything out of the ordinary, like the time I put Christmas baubles and bells on my boots and flashing earrings in my ears and tinsel all through my hair and he said he wasn't walking into the pub with me looking like a tacky Christmas tree and sounding like Santa's sleigh. I was just having a bit of fun, but I suppose if I'm honest it was also a last-ditch attempt at grabbing a bit of attention. You know that poem about growing old disgracefully, well, I want to be noticed, but I don't want to look silly. I was being careful not to make a laughing stock of myself. But what would I know? Maybe they were all laughing at me anyway, despite the smiles and the complimentary comments when we did finally go out that night.

Well, after the eyebrows, next week I plan on getting my teeth whitened. This is my three-step programme to make the most of what's left of my looks.

Ha, that's a joke, calling them looks! You wouldn't believe how quickly what passes for youth disappears the moment you hit the menopause. I've gone past that now. You could say I'm well and truly post-post-menopausal, and it's no joke at all. They don't tell you about all the zillion nasty little physical effects of running out of hormones. Never mind the hot flushes, everyone knows about them – standing in the middle of the office with sweat suddenly pouring off you, feeling like you're being steamed to death, from the inside out. That's the least of it. I could have lived with the flushes, on the assumption they would one day fade away. No, it's the *dryness* that's the real killer with this post-menopausal stuff. It started out, and it's a bit embarrassing to say really, with my knickers feeling like they were rubbing really scratchily against, well, you know, my *bits*. At the time, I thought, *Oh, I'm putting on weight, my knickers are just getting too tight*. So I took to wearing my old knickers, the ones with all the elastic stretched so they were sagging in the crotch. Just as well I kept them really. So that was OK.

I decided Ted and I both needed to lose some weight, so I put us on that 5/2 fasting diet. And I took up jogging because I was beginning to notice how difficult it was for me to bend down or walk up the stairs. So yeah, it's been a bit of a get fit and healthy campaign for a while now, I suppose. Getting old really does bring you face to face with your own mortality. Least that's how I explain it to myself. It scares me, the thought of getting old and decrepit and in pain and unable to get about, trapped in a state of permanent debilitation.

Well, all of that worked OK. I lost weight and got a bit fitter, but the dry stuff just got worse and worse. A few months after I switched to the fat knickers, my bits started feeling like they were burning up and getting really super-sensitive to everything, didn't even need to have to be in my knickers to make it feel like I was wearing sandpaper. I'm not joking; it was just horrible, disgusting and horrible. I had to stop wearing knickers altogether. But even that wasn't OK. A few months later, and I ended up having to stop wearing my usual leggings, the seam of the crotch, no matter how loose, just kept rubbing and burning and stinging. Now I wear skirts and even without any fabric touching me *there*, it still stings and burns and aches and is so unbelievably intolerably uncomfortable and impossible to ignore that I don't know that I can carry on.

But that's not all that dries up. All of you dries up. Your skin and hair, they go all thin and dull and brittle and cracked, my lotions and potions don't work any more, my hands feel like dry paper, that awful sensation like when you rub your hands on carpet, ugh. And your hair just goes mental, that's why I decided to have it cut short. It went all weird and wouldn't go into any style no matter how much I blow-dried it or how many different gels and lotions I used. And your nose dries out, your throat dries out, all your bloody orifices dry out, it seems, backside and all. And worse at night, of course.

And then your eyes. I thought it was my hair, what with it going all flyaway and brittle. It would break so easily and then the shortened hairs would curl in at exactly the right angle to poke into my eyeballs. Well, that happens anyway, but it's the drying out of your eyes – it's like you run out of tears, your eyes go all gritty and you can hardly see properly no matter how many magnifications up you go on your reading glasses, and it feels like there's something scratching them all the time and contrarily they water if you don't blink fifty times a minute. Even eye drops don't help. It's all so unbearable, all these little low-level things that add up to making life one long intolerable nightmare.

But just to be perverse, the one thing that doesn't dry out is your bladder. Oh no, that decides that it can no longer hold more than twenty drops at a time so you find yourself doing mad dashes to the loo a dozen times a day, and just as many at night. Your bladder suddenly has the categorical imperative on your life. Your day revolves around making sure you have instant access to a toilet, at all times. And at night you can't just sleep through, it wakes you up and that's that, you just have to go, no choice in the matter. Talk about being a slave to your body.

I've been to the doctor, of course. She prescribed this hormone cream for my down-there bits. That did diddly-squat. She more or less washed her hands of me, said there was nothing she could do barring giving me HRT to try. Well, no thank you, I told her, I'm not taking substitute hormones just to have to go through all this crap again in five years' time. I found this gel on the internet that seemed to help for a bit, but not much.

Well, dryness, yes. If it's that dry *outside*, you can imagine how it must be *inside*. No sex, that's for sure; haven't had any for ages. Ted hasn't been happy about that, I can tell you. He doesn't say anything, though, except the once when I told him that it was just so dry that it was really painful and I couldn't bear it any more and no there was nothing the doctors could do. It was a big enough palaver for me to have a pap smear what with having to take Valium and lots of lubricating creams and god knows what, just to get the speculum up there without feeling like I was being torn to pieces…well, he got the message. But he said, *So you're saying that I have to go without sex for the rest of my life?* That made me feel really bad.

I'm scared he'll leave me now. How can a man go without sex? It's not the same for us, less of a drive or whatever, and with the menopause, well, I've certainly lost all interest, not that I had much to start off with, I suppose, and to be honest I'm a bit relieved that it's not on the agenda any more. It was getting to the point where we'd be sitting watching telly and some steamy sex scene would come on and I'd be squirming in my seat hoping like hell it wasn't giving him any ideas. I took to avoiding touching him too closely or too suggestively and shrinking away every time he came near me, in case he got ideas. We ended up manoeuvring around each other in this really awkward way, which is pathetic; we've been married for years.

But it worries me all the same. Why should he stay with me, when there's no more sex? What's to stop him wandering off after anyone who offers him what every other man on the planet seemingly gets? We aren't meant to live this long, are we? It's just so unfair.

Well, it all got too much in the end, I can tell you that now. My Sebastian died. You remember him? My little cat, got sick suddenly and upped and died and I was devastated. You'd think at my age I'd have seen enough loss not to be overwhelmed by it, but I just went to pieces. And I couldn't cry – at least I could cry, but the tears just stung and hardly flowed and there was no relief in it at all. The more I cried, the more physically painful it got and I had to control it all in the end. And I thought, this is not OK, this is not good enough, I can't stand living like this any more.

So I went back to the doctor and I told him (bad luck I got a 'he' this time) I wanted to go on HRT. And I got this dismissive lecture about HRT really only being useful for ageing women who only have a few years to go at work and need something to help them with the hot flushes until they retire. Meaning: at which point they just go home and sit in their kitchens and put up with all this physical crap, because they're useless now that they're not 'contributing' to society any more. Made me so angry! You can bet that if men got the menopause, they'd have found a fix for it by now.

Well, I've been taking the HRT for three months now, and I'm happy to say that it's actually improved enough of the horrendous symptoms of this ghastly state of being an old woman that I'm sorry I didn't go on it earlier. But then, that would have meant coming off it that number of years earlier and right now I am prepared to fight to stay on this medication for the rest of my goddamn life! Who are they to withdraw the one thing that makes life for old women bearable? I tell you, honestly, that I was actually becoming suicidal thinking about having to put up with all this dryness and hot-flush stuff for the rest of my life, and, make no bones about it, it does last forever. There's no improvement or remission or tapering off with getting old.

Mind you, the rubbing on my bits, that's still going on. It's better than it was, and I can forget about it for hours at a time. But I still can't wear trousers unless they have the baggiest crotch ever, and I still can't wear knickers. And sex is still well and truly off the agenda.

I told Ted the other day that things seemed to be improving with the HRT, but that I didn't think sex was something I'd be thinking about again, not in a hurry. I told him how scared I was that he was going to leave me. You know what? He laughed and said I was being silly, of course he wasn't going to leave me. Sure it was irksome the whole sex thing, but he married me for all of me, not just for being fantastically attractive and having an amazingly sexy body. He made me laugh. I'm glad he thinks I'm still attractive. And maybe I am too, and maybe that's why I'm happy to do all these things now to make the most of what looks I have left. Five years, ten maybe, then it's back to square one with the post-menopausal stuff. But for the moment, things are OK, bordering on bearable.

I said a little memorial prayer for Sebastian the other day. I can cry again now. Who'd have thought that would be a good thing, eh?

Tamara Jones

Innovations

That sound again, shrill and shrieking and sharp as a fork in a filling. I look up from my catalogue and see Kylah hunched over the table, head bent and hands cupped around her phone. My granddaughter at fifteen: a pink frizz of home-dyed hair with a tablet of dark glass grafted to her fingers. Over and over she taps the phone, and each time it emits that horrible shriek. And tinny music, looping like a long night in purgatory. Something in me shudders. *Not at the table, love,* I say, and she nods but keeps hitting the screen. *Kylah,* I say, hearing my voice harden. *Just let me finish, Nanna,* she says. It's some game about pigs and birds and slingshots and she's been playing it since she unwrapped the phone at Christmas. I shake my head and slowly unpeel her fingers from the device. *It can sit on the bench until you leave,* I say, and she scowls but is still young enough to obey. Give it a few years and she'll swear at me and storm out. *But you're reading your magazine,* she says. Old enough for backchat, then. *That's different,* I say. *It's a catalogue. You have a look while I make a cuppa.*

She flips through the pages as the kettle heats, reading out the titles. *Royal wedding costume ring. Hand-painted wooden cover for your bin. Sound-effects machine: sixteen life-enhancing sounds for everyday use. What is this?* she asks, her scorn bubbling with the water. *It's a mail-order catalogue,* I tell her. *You fill out the form and they send you the products.* She snorts. *So it's e-Bay for old people,* she says.

The kettle clicks off. I swallow my retort and concentrate on pulling teabags out of the tin. She's only a child, I tell myself, despite the day-glo hair, the kohl around her eyes and the love bites on her neck. A child who still treasures the bauble I gave her a few Christmases back: shiny pink glass with her name in glittering loops. It hangs from her dressing table next to the photo of her boyfriend. I don't tell her I ordered that ball from this catalogue. Nor will I describe to her the stillness that comes as I open each new issue and methodically go through it, listing my purchases on the order form in neat block letters. Or the feeling a few weeks later as the parcels begin to arrive: anonymous brown cardboard, discreetly labelled.

It started when my Ern stopped going to work. A neighbour left her copy here and my hands found its pages. Used to ironing shirts every morning, these old fingers had been idle and fidgety since Ern's redundancy – the catalogue returned to them a sense of purpose. And it helped when he got sick. *It's like I've got no skin*, he told me once. *Every touch goes right through me.* Nothing the doctors did seemed to help. So I ordered one of those foot-comfort pillows to stop the sheet touching his toes, and a lap table so he could have dinner in bed. Rainbow flameless candles with a remote control, to make the room cosy. The sound-effect machine to make him laugh. And he read the paper and did the number puzzles as he always had, and only rarely stepped beyond our room. Kylah told me last week that she uses her phone to listen to pop music from Finland, to read the UK music press without paying a fortune for postage, and to watch people shuffle through snow-filled Moscow streets. I wonder now if this portal to another world would have helped Ern more in those last months than the familiar rustle of his newspaper.

Outside, Indian mynas hop along the deck railing, turning their dark and glossy heads to hunt. Eggs, they're looking for, or weakling chicks – they'll swoop in when the parents are on the wing and turf the young birds out of the nest. It's so long now since I've seen the crimson flash of a rosella, let alone a king parrot, green as new grass. They trilled for us every morning in the early days of our marriage, when I bulged with Kylah's mum. I'd cradle seed in my hand, laughing at the feel of the birds' feet in my palm and my daughter quivering within. We'd sold our grimy terrace in North Melbourne and driven Ern's beloved Kingswood out to this wooden cabin beyond the city's sprawl, so that our child would be able to run and roam and yell under a canopy of manna gums. We watched her grow, watched the houses nearby subdivide and sprout units in their gardens, watched the slow creep of concrete and bitumen. And then came the nest-raiders and their screeching Australian cousins – rats with wings, I call them.

They've scared away all the bright birds, I told Ern once when he was still working, so he went to the council and hired a wire trap, built by the old blokes at the local men's shed. He hired a gas cylinder too, and an airtight bag. Every evening for a week he laid out scraps but let the mynas come and go. Sunday morning he set the trap. Hours he was out there that afternoon – I was roasting a chook and it was crisp and close to overcooked before he came in from the garden. He changed his clothes, washed his hands and sat at the table. *I couldn't do it*, he said. *I had the cylinder hooked up and the bag in place, but then I let them go.* I carved the chicken. *It would have been painless for them*, I said. I would have done it, I knew. I would have let the gas still their stealthy movements. I would have wrung their scrawny necks or swung them in a slow arc until their heads connected with the trunk of a tree.

Kylah's phone dings. Her body seems to lean towards it. *That might be Josh*, she says. *Can I have it back now, just to check the message?* I pause as if I'm thinking but really it's because I want to drag it out for a minute, to make her wait. Her mum has never been one for discipline. Natural parenting, my daughter calls it. A term she learnt from the urban hippies she flatted with after she left home. In it, some veiled comment on my own parenting style, as if mine was somehow unnatural. *Don't use that tone with Kylah*, she says to me. *Don't you be stern.* She calls some days and I listen to my daughter's voice in the receiver and feel that she's talking to me from the moon. Now Kylah's foot starts to twitch; her fingers tap the table. *Oh, all right then*, I say, and she lunges. She unlocks the phone with quick fingers, strokes the screen and laughs quietly. Her thumbs rattle out a response and then she watches the phone, expectant, for the reply. How long would she wait, I wonder. What if her Josh gets caught up and forgets to respond? People on the train stare at their phones with the same look: the distant gaze of someone who is always elsewhere. And the tender way they touch the screen, as if it were a newborn.

Since Ern died, I've often ridden the train, gliding from the suburbs to the city and then out along the radial arms of the other lines, encased in a bubble of metal and glass. I stare out the window until I hear a woman's voice crackle through the speaker. *This train will terminate here,* she says, and so I step past the station's generic architecture into a place I have never seen. I always imagine the settlements at the end of the lines will be dismal frontier places, but each time I am surprised to find bakeries and newsagents and families going about their business. I buy a coffee and the newspaper and talk to the people behind the counter. *Miserable weather today,* I say, or *Lovely to see the wattle in bloom,* and the teenage shop assistants nod and smile and turn to the next person. The words in my mouth are as strange as if they were spoken in another language, as if I was a tourist using a phrasebook.

The return journey always seems quicker. I sip the coffee and lay the newspaper on my lap but cannot bring myself to read it. Instead, I watch the other passengers watching their phones. How often I've wanted to reach out and lay my hands on the warm cheeks of those around me – the soft and pouchy powdered ones of women my own age, the stubbled ones of young and suited men who look like boys borrowing their father's clothes. *I'm here,* I yearn to say, *come back to me.*

Across the table, Kylah is still staring at her screen, as if some great mystery will be revealed there. Look away and you'll miss it. Soon she'll be old enough to go on proper dates with her Josh, not just goofing around with their mates at the nearest shopping centre. I can see them now, sitting at a table with starched white linen and candles and both with their hands on their phones. Where is the romance in that? I remember my first evening out with Ern, that pulsing sense of his body close to mine. We sat in a pizza restaurant with red-checked tables and drank sweet, cheap wine. He told me he had just got a new job in the supply chain of a paper company, his hands enacting the process from forest to pulp mill to paper as he spoke. I heard the words but it was his hands that caught me – their long and delicate fingers – and it took all my will not to reach out for them that night. And I had to show the same restraint in his last months, lying chastely next to him in our bed, never able to roll over and reach out, never feeling him press himself into my back. While that stretch of cold sheet between us was new, I realise now the crack had been there long before computers took over the supply chain and took away Ern's livelihood. When did he start to bring the newspaper to the table, turning the pages as he quietly swallowed his food? And how many years did I sit opposite him, waiting for a word? After the meal he always thanked me then went straight into the lounge to watch TV, bathing in flickering blue light until bedtime. When the washing up was done, I'd follow him in there, watching his profile rather than the screen, feeling a gap between us despite the warmth of his shoulder against mine.

Another *ding* from Kylah's phone. Finally. She opens the message and smiles, lit up with the wonder of a girl who knows herself to be loved. Perhaps they'll be OK, her and Josh. *Not long until your birthday*, I say. *What do you want this year, love?* She shakes her head. *Nothing from your catalogue, Nanna*, she says, but she is still glowing from Josh's message and the smile softens her words. And there she is again, my beloved Kylah – first and only granddaughter – beaming as she used to before she cut off her plaits and bleached her hair, as she used to before Ern died. *I'm saving up for driving lessons*, she says. *Maybe you could help out.* She'll be able to apply for her learner's permit once she turns sixteen, she tells me, and has already been reading up on the road rules. *It will have to be money*, I say, and she nods; she knows I never learnt to drive.

Whenever we went out, Ern held the Kingswood's leathered wheel and I was the navigator. I'd plot journeys from our house on the fringe to where our daughter lives near the city, in a crumbling terrace so like our own first place. A different route each time, if I could, just to see something new. Somewhere I have our old street directory, with post-it notes on the pages we used most often and pencilled lists of directions for Ern when he was driving alone. There's the tattered blue RACV folder too, with yellowed interstate maps and the caravan park guide.

I kneel at the kitchen dresser and open the doors. Kylah stands beside me. *What are you looking for, Nanna?* It's in here somewhere, I'm sure. *Your grandfather's Melways*, I say. *Some of the roads might have changed, but it should help when you start driving.* She doesn't speak for a moment, and I can see from her face that she wants to say something but is searching for a way to do it without hurting me. Another glimpse of the old Kylah. *Spit it out, girl*, I say. *Well*, she says, *it's just that I have a Satnav in my phone*. For a moment I think she is talking about a piece of the Russian space program. *I type in a destination*, she explains, *and my phone tells me where to go*. All the pages of the Melways, all the journeys taken and planned, all the notes and directions, I realise, turned into wiring on a circuit-board encased in black glass.

I reach out and hold the dresser, momentarily dizzy. *Take it easy, Nanna*, Kylah says. *You shouldn't be kneeling down. Let me help*. I try to close the doors before she can look inside. *No stress*, I say. *It's probably out in the glovebox of the Kingswood*. Of course, she is too quick. She runs her fingers over the shelves of boxes within – all brown cardboard, neatly labelled, unopened. *What are these, Nanna?* she asks. *Oh, nothing*, I say, and shoo her away so I can shut the dresser. *Just bits and bobs I've got to sort through*. I can't tell her that the boxes contain every item I've ordered since Ern died. Somewhere in there is a solar-powered air freshener, a valuable kitchen compost crock, a pocket telescope and microscope (don't miss a thing, the description said). The catalogue arrives and I fill out the form. When the boxes come, I hold them in trembling hands but cannot remove the tape. Then I put them away.

Let me make you another cuppa, Kylah says. She stands at the sink and refills the kettle and I remember her doing the same thing the weekend I found Ern. She was only eleven but she kept a quiet calm as her mother crumpled into tears on Ern's side of the sofa. I'd been cooking, and the house smelt of roast chook and rosemary potatoes. The undertakers had carried away Ern's body and the police had taped up the garage. They would be back over the next days, they told me, and asked us in hushed and respectful tones not to touch anything. I had told them that I found Ern out there behind the wheel of the Kingswood with the engine running and a pipe from the exhaust to the driver's window. I told them that I turned off the car and opened the garage doors to let the fumes out. What I did not tell them was that afterwards I sat beside him in the passenger seat as I had on all our other journeys, that I closed his eyes and reached for his hand and let it cool until the only warmth I felt was my own. Then I called the police.

Kylah places the mug in front of me then picks up her phone. The tinny music starts, and the shrieks, and something rises within me. *What is that bloody game?* I ask. *It's called Angry Birds,* she says. She passes me her phone and wraps my hand around it. I feel its weight in my palm and the damp heat from her grip. *I'll show you,* she says, and so I let my granddaughter glide my fingers across the glittering screen.

Catherine Padmore

At 86

the carers began to shower him
his wife no longer able
to contain his wandering limbs

he didn't mind
followed them like a pup
smiling and absent

she railed against it –

the bibs they tucked in his collar
the puréed food and the spoons

she flung them all –

fixed a knife and fork
to each blank finger

held his hand   hard
through the long day slide

when they came to change his pad
she tore out the cotton wool belly
strew it on the floor like a bride's confetti

each time the shower started
she pounded her fists on the wheelchair
arm   and shouted

leave him alone –
he's mine   you bitches.

Julie Watts

The stroking

(i)

need to walk the boundaries
tonight, walk the fences, keep

the silence in. need to keep
myself jewelled, spangled, bright for

the hour. is grief tidal? need
to follow a new North, fly

to a season of matt-fin-
ished words. a whiff of kelp a-

bout the moon? need to run a
finger across the creped back

of your hand, across purpling.
need to complete the stroking

(ii)

the night hums and in the interval
between breath and moon and soft focus
we unfurl beside the Sound, islands

dolloped on the horizon, from the
rocks, aquamarine and scrub blurring,
gulls apostrophes cut loose, and there's

wide silence here, bar lines through hours un-
played, sea beneath cloud turning tinsel
to truth and this is, was, our stroking

(iii)

drip feeding you sea, in these last hours, quilt of you
barely rippling, music on the edge of silence.

call it unsewing? bloom on the back of your hand,
tenses knocked from you, nurses hovering like bees.
the diameter of solitude? need to shape

a frame, find safe keeping for the shirt box and pins
holding the ward, hour, breathing waning, the stroking

Kevin Gillam

Dancing with Al Bowlly

The morning my mother died
there was a frost,

you could bite the air
like an apple;

the weather had somehow
frozen a part of memory.

At the nursing home
staff kept their distance,

as if to come too close
might give them frostbite.

My mother lay curled
like a wrinkled foetus

under a thin sheet.
She was somebody else.

My real mother had slipped off
and was dancing,

warm in the arms of Al Bowlly
as he sang to her:

Love is the sweetest thing.

Rob Wallis

Swing Low, Sweet Chariot

Today he felt very small. He often felt small these days, when taxi drivers swung the seat belt over him to buckle him in and he couldn't swell to fit the arc as he once had, or when, with flustered steps, he tried to keep ahead of those stiletto heels which appeared from nowhere to pierce the pavement behind him.

He felt small in this large white room with its three empty beds. Just him in the chair with the blue blanket over his knees. And the old woman sitting near the door, tapping at the clasp of her handbag.

'Are you warm?' she asked.

His lower lip opened slightly to show he was. 'Time?' he asked.

'Soon.'

Why were they waiting? He needed to be prepared.

He drew back his sleeve and looked at his watch. He recognised his watch. They put it on him every morning.

'Can you tell what time it is?' she asked.

He looked at the dial. It reminded him of something.

'What time is it?' she repeated.

He could see the hands and the numbers. They were connected, he knew. 'Twenty,' he said, without conviction. He pulled his sleeve up further in case that would help. The numbers suggested something which made him uneasy. He let the sleeve go.

'She's late.' The old woman sounded irritated. She stood up and opened a drawer. 'Remember the talcum powder's in the top, and I've left you some apples.'

Why was she making a fuss? It didn't matter. Always a fuss. He wished she'd sit down.

She went to the window. 'It's starting to spit,' she said. 'But I brought an umbrella.'

His fingers wandered over the knobbly weave of the blanket.

There were steps coming along the corridor, getting louder, stinging the lino. Someone came in, filled the doorway, then they were looming over him.

'Hello, Gerald. Sorry I'm late.' His hand was being lifted by another hand. Its rings bit into him. 'I'm Esme Butterworth. I'm here to ask you some questions.'

Perhaps he should offer her a chair, but she was already sitting, opening the briefcase on her lap.

'No right or wrong answers, Gerald, and no medals at the end, just a big smile from me.' Clicking her pen and aiming it at some paper, her cheeks rose into a rehearsed smile that stretched behind the lenses of her spectacles.

He was still aware of her rings against his palm, lingering like an acrid smell.

'Now, what's your name?'

'Mr Robinson.' He heard the old woman laugh.

'Your first name.'

'Gerald.'

'Can you remember my name?'

He stared at her, embarrassed. She'd told him, he knew.

'Never mind. What's your address?'

He felt the words come out in familiar shapes, though he wasn't sure. But the stranger was writing them down. Her dress was a flaring green. Her glasses were so thick he couldn't see her eyes.

'Where were you born?'

Again his mouth followed the old habits.

'And the date?'

'Nineteen seventy-two.'

'No, no,' said the old woman. 'Nineteen twenty-three.'

She might be right, but nineteen seventy-two was important too – for some reason.

'Can you remember your first job?'

He thought of the office with Paul sitting on the edge of the desk in his sleeveless jumper. After work they used to play billiards at the pub.

Something jabbed his lower lip.

'He dribbles,' said the old woman.

His hand flapped to get her away from his mouth, but the handkerchief with her fingers bony inside it was rubbing against the bristles of his chin.

'Your first job,' said the green woman.

The sound he managed to make in his throat wasn't firm enough to be moulded into a word.

'Yes, Gerald?'

He didn't like the stranger calling him Gerald. Her voice was thick and shiny, as if it was coated with lipstick.

'Bil-, bil-' he said.

'He was a clerk,' said the old woman. 'He doesn't remember.'

'And what job did you have when you were first married?'

Was he married, then? He remembered Eileen whose sleek sheet of hair broke where it fell over her shoulder. Had he married her? 'Clerk,' he said.

'No, it was the war,' said the old woman.

Why were they asking him questions to trap him? 'War,' he repeated. The uneasiness he'd felt before passed over him again, like a shadow. He wanted the room to be pure white as it had been before. He shut his eyes. Inside his head there were twirling specks of silver and white. Far away the stranger was talking to the old woman. The silver specks whirled like a snowstorm; he could feel himself disappearing into them, being carried up weightlessly.

'Gerald! Wake up!' Fingers with hard rings were shaking him. 'This is an important question. I want you to tell me whether you want to go home, or go to a nursing home?'

It was such an effort to push the words out of his brain. 'Nursing,' he said.

'What?' The green woman was leaning forward.

He could see her eyes now, torn apart by the lenses of her glasses so that she didn't seem to look at him at all.

'Go home or to a nursing home?' she repeated loudly.

He must have got it wrong. 'Home,' he said. 'I want to go home.' This time he must have got it right because they didn't say anything.

The green shape turned to the old woman. 'Can't you take him back?'

'It's impossible!'

What did it have to do with the old woman? He wanted to go home. Why hadn't it occurred to him before? He looked at the large white room with the three empty beds. He wondered where he was.

'I want to go home,' he said again, comfortable now with the words. He thought of the way his own bed fitted him, of the yellow light moving across the floor of the veranda room.

'When he gets out of bed, he can't walk,' said the old woman. 'He falls over and I can't lift him.'

'Is that true, Gerald?'

He didn't know. He couldn't remember falling over. Perhaps it was true.

'He wets the bed.'

He wanted to sit in the old wicker chair that creaked with him when he moved. And to stroke the cat, feel it purring under his hand.

The old woman was breathing in wetly through her nostrils. She must be crying. 'Ask the nurses here,' he heard her say. 'It takes two of them to lift him.'

'Don't you see, Gerald,' said the green woman, 'you need to go somewhere where they'll give you proper nursing care.'

He didn't want nursing care. He wanted to be in his kitchen, reading the paper with the taste of marmalade in his mouth. And then he'd do the crossword and have a second cup of tea.

'You need twenty-four-hour care.'

Why was this stranger interfering with his life? Again he felt the shadow over him. He made a fold in the blanket that covered his knees and passed it from his right hand to his left. The open weave felt satisfying against his fingers. He made another fold and passed that to his other hand too. He was making the blanket into a sea of waves. If he did this right, the shadow would move on.

The old woman was speaking urgently. 'Gerald, don't you see? I can't look after you any more.'

He knew that tone. It meant he wasn't going to be allowed to do what he wanted. He tried to work faster with the blanket, feeling it grow heavier on one side as he fed it through his hands.

'We need his signature,' said the green woman.

'He can't write any more.'

'Gerald,' said the green woman, 'is it all right if your wife signs for you?'

He wondered how long the old woman had been his wife. Was she Eileen from the office? Her hair wasn't sheeny any more.

'We need your wife to sign for you, Gerald.' This stranger was so pushy. 'Can she sign for you?'

His legs were cold. Someone must have removed the blanket.

'Yes,' he said. He felt relieved. Now maybe they'd leave him alone and he could go home.

Stella Kent

Lost and found

Christmas and our home is in chaos. A giant tarp covers the hole that was our lounge room wall. A pair of skip bins overflow with the rose bushes and the remains of our driveway. No matter how much I sweep, the floorboards feel gritty. We don't even know when the tradesmen will finish what ought to have been finished six weeks ago. *After New Year* is all we have to go on. I want to scream at that layabout crew. Mick simply nods, *Have a good Christmas, fellas.*

The cricket on TV glints and shimmers through leadlight glass that seemed to compensate for all the many shortcomings when we first bought this place. Less than a kilometre from the beach, the worst house in a pricey street. I was cooking at the café, Mick had gone out on his own: *Solar: Our Sustainable Future.* We'd never have managed without Dad.

This should be any other Christmas, me and Corinne slaving over lunch, Dad, Mick, Corinne's Garry, watching sport in a home that's trussed up for happiness, not this crumbling fortress sealed in scaffolding. The stupid things I cared about: cracks and missing mortar, our 1940s lavender bathroom, a lounge room that felt too dark and small. Now I'm shuffling through Mick's spreadsheets, a new one a week: budget projections, policy numbers, insurance payouts. Lists and post-it notes to keep my life from tumbling down. *You should be set, Suzie Q.*

Dad's out on the patio egging Corinne's exchange student to try her hand at beachcombing. 'You don't need any of those whizz-bang metal detectors.' He helps her fit flippers and mask.

'Poor Dad,' my sister says. 'Gita's too polite to say she doesn't swim.'

'If you're willing to use your own resources – your eyes,' we hear Dad say, 'be in the water at first light. Anyone can make a go of it.'

I watch Gita baulk at the prospect of wrapping her mouth around a snorkel. She'd never set eyes on the Indian Ocean before coming here.

'God,' says Corinne. 'The beach is the last place. She won't walk to the bus-stop without a sun umbrella.'

'So *smart*.' It doesn't take much to make me peevish these days.

'It's status, the whole beauty thing. Over there, you don't want people thinking you work out in the fields. Whitening moisturiser. She lathers herself with the stuff.'

'Some people would give everything they own to have her lucky skin.'

For once, my little sister doesn't sigh. She doesn't push the other point of view. Corinne rubs my back, the way our mother used to do.

The salads are dressed and glad-wrapped, the turkey resting in foil. Corinne pours champagne cocktails knowing Mick won't touch a drop. We gather around the patio table to exchange gifts.

Mick, bless him, has shopped online. 'All the way from the US of A,' he skites, as we unleash ribbons from robust cardboard boxes that are keepers in themselves.

Corinne and I go, 'Oh, wow,' and even Garry and Dad make suitable noises as each of us, over summer tops and boardies, model our goose-down vests in exotic shades.

'*I'm Juniper Berry.*' I spin around. I'm sweltering.

Mick looks full of himself. 'Should be good for winters, Ern. Down the beach and back.'

Dad gives a sad half-smile. 'Just the ticket, Mick.'

Like the big finale at the fireworks, Dad waits for last to bring out his gifts. A benevolent Father Christmas with a good slug of pirate, our Ern, his treasure chest is a plastic trunk salvaged from the verge throwout, crammed with booty he's combed from the beach. He empties a bag of sunglasses across the table. This is the moment when I find a pair of Raybans and before I've had a chance to look in the mirror, Corinne will go, *Suze, they're too wide for your face. Trust me.* The designer glasses always look good on my sister, while I end up with a thirty-dollar pair stamped with the Cancer Council logo.

Not this year. Corinne picks out the top brands and sets them down before me. 'These ones, Suze.' She opens a pair still in their case. 'Prada.

271

Easily four hundred bucks.' But the Pradas are too tight for me and they don't fit her either.

Gita tries them on and we all sing approval.

'They were made for you,' my lovely husband says.

Behind those Pradas, with her silken hair and pearly smile, she's our very own Bollywood star.

Dad's cobbled together a mismatch of second-hand picnic plates and wine glasses to gift Corinne, piled inside a wicker basket he found after Carols by Candlelight. The things people leave behind on the beach, the precious things lost to the ocean. Wedding bands slip from fingers, chains yank free in dumping waves. Freaky things, the prosthetic leg Dad once marched home. He's a trooper, our Dad. Expensive things, belongings with sentimental value, he'll hand on to the lifeguards. Sometimes they find their way back to their owner, other times no one ever claims them.

Corinne sighs at this year's picnic set. She sneak previews the bag of jewellery Dad has waiting.

'I worry about you down there on your own.'

'Been swimming since I was a nipper.'

'You're not as steady on your feet now. Is he, Suze? What if you get caught in a rip? And every year, not just summer, there's more and more shark attacks.'

Pointy dolphins, Dad calls them. 'Faint heart never won fair maiden. Can't let paranoia stop you living.'

My sister bristles. 'I'm not being paranoid. It's a fact.'

Dad brings out a shoebox of picnic cutlery, amongst them a stack of gleaming teaspoons.

Now it's my turn to scold. 'Dad, I don't want you bringing those home. They're junkie spoons.'

'One man's trash,' Dad starts. 'Give 'em a scrub with the Ajax and they soon shine up.'

Mick comes to the rescue. 'She means drug addicts, Ern. For shooting up. Heroin. Crack.'

Dad gives a little grunt, whatever that means. He reaches into the trunk and pulls out something wrapped in a tea towel. 'Speaking of fair maidens, this one's for you, Suze. Found her on the reef where you and Mick snorkel.' Where we used to snorkel. 'The seaweed opened up and there she was, poking her tongue out at me.'

A small brass figurine decked with a fancy crown and necklaces; two, four, six sets of arms all flashy with weapons.

'Thought she'd be just the go for hanging your keys on.' Ever practical, is Dad.

'How do these things end up at the bottom of the ocean?'

'Finders keepers,' Dad says. 'I call her Shirl the Girl after Shirley Saunders from school. She used to poke her tongue out at me. Drowned in a rip one Easter.'

'My point exactly.' Corinne inspects her fingers, now gleaming with other people's gold.

'Kali,' Gita says quietly.

'Who?' Mick takes the figurine.

'Kali.' Corinne speaks for Gita. 'She's one of the important goddesses.'

Gita turns to Mick. She looks at him kindly. 'Kali gives us the strength to walk the path to a higher life.'

Mick blinks. The table turns quiet. Garry gives up on the strawberry lodged in the base of his glass. Corinne throws a silent *Sorry*.

Today of all days, when we're trying to forget.

'She's boss woman,' Dad chimes. 'That fella she's got pinned to the ground isn't going anywhere.'

'Shiva lies down in Kali's path to subdue her anger,' says Gita.

'Good luck to him,' I say. I'm seething.

'Kali looks a little terrifying but she's the great protector, the most caring of all the deities.' It's the most I've heard Gita say.

Mick gives me a wry smile. 'Perhaps she couldn't deliver. Not for want of trying.'

'Mick.' I take his hand. Skeletal. His forearm is a drop sheet of ginger hair and freckles, a shock of treated lesions. Bitter recognition for all my years of harping.

Corinne refills the glasses. Garry stuffs Christmas paper in a garbage bag.

Dad jangles one of my new Sheridan pillowcases filled with hidden treasure. 'Who's for Lucky Dip?'

I take a deep breath. 'Mick!' I enthuse before this man for whom no luck can alter his course.

*

Mid-January and still not a tradesman in sight. I've pre-cooked dinners for the week, overspent on organic vegetable juices boosted with whatever vitamins and minerals make them eight bucks a pop. The freezer is stocked with lemonade icy poles – the only food Mick now craves. The laptop and phone live on our bedside table alongside the drug dispenser. I've arranged for Corinne to call in each day even though Dad says he can mind Mick on his own.

My husband looks childlike in our bed, propped against a sea wall of pillows.

I feel myself teeter. 'I don't need to go. I'll call them.'

'Do the training, Suze. Get the certificate. All I need is rest.'

'What if you need something? What if Dad doesn't hear you? What if he's out?'

'I have *communications*. I'll manage. I could run an entire country from this here throne.'

'But what if…'

'Suze.'

I kiss his lips, his cheek, his ear, the bridge of his nose. 'Friday, your royal pipsqueak.'

'And don't go phoning,' he calls after me. 'I'll be too busy for personal calls.'

*

On the final day at the Bureau of Statistics, we finish training early.

I graduate as a home-based interviewer equipped with a laptop and phone headset, a job where I choose my own hours. They've taken me on knowing my circumstances. I haven't had to lie.

I pull alongside the kerb where a van and tradesman's trailer is parked on our verge. Two guys in matching shirts perch on ladders, only neither is attending to our house. The garden has had a short back and sides, our perimeter fences stand exposed and shabby. Along the fence tops run lengths of wire and electrical connectors. They've turned our home into a detention centre. 'What are you doing?'

One gives the other a *Here's trouble* look. 'Mick Quinn's order. For the cat.'

'We don't own a cat.' Pair of clowns. 'My husband can't stand cats.'

It seems I'm mistaken. Mick rests on the lounge, across his lap a small spotted cat that watches as I breeze across the room. It's a pretty thing with caramel markings.

'Suzie Q. How'd it go?'

When I pet the cat, it draws back and growls.

'Hush, Mikey.' My husband ruffles its ears.

'Whose is it?'

'Actually,' Mick smirks, 'he's yours. People on Gumtree were giving him away. He's been neutered, microchipped, had his nails filed. Haven't you, boy?'

A purr rumbles through the room.

'He looks like a miniature tiger.'

'He's a *Bengal*,' Mick says as if the cat is royalty. 'Pure-bred.' He scratches between the cat's ears. 'Methink she likes you, Mikey.'

'Mikey, Mick? You come up with that?'

'It's his name. It's on his papers.'

I go to stroke Mikey's ears but he turns his head and flicks his tail.

'He'll get used to you. You've always wanted a cat.'

'You've always hated them. Native birds and all that.'

Mick shrugs. One more fix to set our house in order. To save me from my lonesome future.

'The fellas still out there?'

'The pair fortressing our home?'

'A few wires, Suze. It's still our ocean haven.'

Dad bowls in with a plate of homemade cakes. 'They give you the certificate, Suze?' You can bet he's been at the Autumn Club swapping teaspoons for afternoon tea. 'Mikey!' Dad claps his hands, and the cat bounds from Mick's lap and swaggers, yowling, across the floor. Dad bundles him up and swaddles him like a baby. The thing is growling, Dad's nose only inches from those still-formidable claws. He holds a finger to the cat's nose. 'Don't you even think about it.'

I see Mikey surrender, he lies back compliantly and lets Dad rough him around the chin as you would a dog. God, you've never heard such raucous purring.

'I'll put the kettle on.' I step around paint tins. 'Any sign of a tradesman?'

*

Summer swelters day and night. Mikey sleeps at Mick's side, watches him adoringly. I try to stroke him, win him over, but he flicks his tail at my face. When I slide into bed, he voices his disdain. I lie rigid at my edge, marooned from my husband by a maelstrom of cat.

I recruit my father to extract the damned animal when the palliative team call. They tend Mick, bathe him, change sheets and bedding. When they leave, I creep in and close our door, steal my husband for myself. Interlacing our fingers, I lie quietly by his side, breathe him in.

*

Beyond the bed that now defines Mick's world, the cat and Dad do daily battle. Mikey's tail swishes, his cries fill the house, the hair along his spine turns electric. Yet he caves to the entrapment of Dad's arms; those feline eyes turn liquid.

I feed him, I try to befriend him, but he knows the pecking order, the weakest link in the chain. He pounces at my calf when I dish out his treats. I'm measuring Mick's morphine and he nips my leg and prances away. He's on our bed at night and he's sprawled between us in the morning. I've taken to closing the study door and dozing in the refuge of Dad's old recliner. It's enough to get me through the Bureau work, the monotony of questions about *use of public transport* and *family doctor visits within the last twelve months.*

The voice on the end of the phone can't know that I'm barely hanging on.

*

Mick is listless, too drugged against discomfort to call it proper living. The floors are carpeted with cat hair and gritty fluff. Dad's taken to helping with the laundry – my good tops and bras, his beach towel and gardening shirt merrily spinning knots together.

This morning the builders showed up – two months of waiting and they pick now to grace us with their presence. I stood guard. Wouldn't let them through the door.

*

Mick. My Mick. No more swims to start and end our day. No more meanderings, you jogging the length of the beach, me wrapped in a sarong content to lag and look for shells, your prints my prints patterned in the sand.

The new guard. A cat that bristles at the sight of me. An animal I never chose and never asked for, whose loud opinions penetrate my brain.

I want love songs. You and me, alone, together in our bed. I want to drift, dreamy with foreverings, my hand your hand, a sea of turquoise blue. I want you to get up from this bed and we'll walk to the beach and the ocean will glitter and you'll say, *Come on, slow coach,* and we'll tumble laughing into water that's clear and cool and sweet against our flawless skin.

*

The head-thumping fumes of oil-based paint and newly lacquered floors. It's affected Dad's sinuses and he's gone to stay at Corinne's for the week. Every window is cracked open but June is wet, too cold to properly air the house.

Mikey has taken to sleeping on my goose-down vest, Mick's gift from Christmas. Perhaps it's a protest on his part at my refusal to heat the big new lounge for his convenience alone. Perhaps he senses some kind of link.

I'm yet to honour my pledge. I haven't found the fortitude to scatter ash and bone upon the ocean, our special place above the reef.

Lethargy: you do your best to mask it but it shows in your voice.

Mary, seventy-five, who uses public transport more than once but no more than five times a week, said to me on Friday, *You sound worn out, dear. Are you all right?* One grain of kindness and I was blubbering into the mouthpiece. Then the sleep-deprived guy with five dependents. He stacks shelves for half of what I earn. When I asked, *Have you or has anyone in your household travelled overseas in the last twelve months?* he said, *What do you think?* I snapped right back, *Just answer the stupid question.*

Mikey's bored with only me around. He's on a rampage up and down the hall, doing spin-outs on the newly lacquered boards. Soon he'll be on the hall table, batting at the keys on Kali's many arms. I'd like to poke out my tongue at him the way that statue does. I try to make my calls but Mikey yowls and struts into the study, sets about chewing on the laptop cord. 'Naughty. No.'

His hiss still makes me cower.

I abandon the headset, close the laptop. I try to muster enough enthusiasm to get on with some sorting. Bills. Insurance. A form for the electoral roll. The cat's pedigree papers destined for the bin. Then I hear Mick, *At least look at what you're throwing out.*

So I do. I read aloud to Mikey. 'Your official name, my friend, is *Runamok Mikey.* If the collar fits, bucko....' He eyes me suspiciously. 'That's what it says. Your father was *Runamok Wild Thing.* Your

278

grandfather, *Runamok Jungle Flame*. They'd give you a run for your money.' I scan down the list. Not a Huggable or Lullaby amongst them. 'The ones before that were still stalking the Bengal jungles, tearing the innards from meeker beings.'

Mikey sits on his haunches, unimpressed at my rude tone. I hold out his stamped certificate. 'Shall we hang it above your bed?' I'm feeling slightly manic, as chirpy as the willy-wagtails that perch on our electric fence, taunting Mikey with their waggles. 'Going. Going. Gone.' I chuck the folder in the bin. But there. On the back. A post-it note. From Mick: *What chance does the small fella have with this dodgy lot? Be nice to one another. In case you haven't worked it out, he's all bluff and bluster. You're the strong one, precious girl.*

Mikey ups and swaggers from the room. He has no time for weeping.

I'm making coffee and the cat is underfoot, demanding food while his breakfast sits uneaten in his bowl. I don't mean to step back on his tail. He yelps and strikes with needle-like incisors. A shock of pain arrows up to my skull. I gasp and turn, plant my foot. 'You shit of a cat.' His body lies pinned beneath my shoe. He's snarling, teeth and claws bared, he's primed to tear my foot apart. A wave of fury surges through me. 'Nasty little *shit*.' I press down on him, a dead weight of suffering, the awful endlessness of grief. He's a small cat, light; he's surliness over substance. It's the moment, the brink between reason and revenge, when I jerk my weight and crush his cage of bones.

He stares up at me, glinting contempt, tail rapping at the floor. 'I ought to break you.' I ease my foot. He doesn't move. The throaty grumble fades away. 'What? *What*, Mikey?' He blinks at me with gilded tidal pools. A ripple. A small vibration that burrs against my foot. It grows, inflates, breathes air into my lungs, enfolds my lonely heart. That purr. His song.

Robyn Mundy

Five years and still –

Five years –
and still there are days when
I want to pick up the phone and
call you –
time seeps by,
and though grief
    loosens its cruellest hooks
I remain bereft,
    perplexed –
where are you?

Are you still sitting at your computer
tapping out the stories of your life –
    the boy in the Queensland bush,
            the young man stationed in Darwin,
poring over radar?

Or will I see you
coming into the kitchen –
    a cup of tea in the offing –
joining us around the table,
the arc of your arms
still
wiry and strong?

And if I could get a line
    through to you –
what would I say?
The children are growing,
    beautiful,
I left my job,
the old cracks in the family
widen and groan
like lathe and plaster in the drought –
I admit we are all

diminished
without you.

Most of all,
unreconciled.
I would ask you to
come home –
it's enough now,
            please
come back –

And here it is again –
the persistence of that old,
mad dream of
    restoration,
when the patience of mourning,
the gratitude
for all the rich
    love you left amongst us –
gives way
to the shocking
    need for the miracle:
the past
            intact and
    cupped
in the broad palms of your suntanned hands.

Rose Lucas

On the way to your funeral

Heading to you
(*no longer there*)
the fields and camel-hide hills
seem drawn and subdued,
the road like an offering
at their feet.

Every thought of you
stains the country-side, bleeds
into each boulder and every tree
so you'll be somehow forever
in the calm line of the distant mountains
or the hilltop fence that holds back the sky.

Kristen Roberts

Because she must

after Philip Kobylarz

An older woman. The painter's mother. Sewing. Gentle light filters through the lace curtains. Of a sitting room. A rusty-brown woollen blanket on her lap heralds the end of yet another day. Of waiting. Of autumn. In the garden, her husband is watering the last roses. Maybe or maybe not. She can almost smell the damp earth. She used to be fond of singing. Yesteryear. Her son is in the trenches. Of the Somme. The needle in her thin hand glides through the cotton handkerchief. She pricks her finger. She likes red. Red for the letters she is embroidering in the corner. She imagines lines of soldiers. They are mere ghosts swathed in the pall of their shadow. Soon she will light the candles. She is not hungry but she will prepare dinner. Because she must.

Parce qu'elle le doit

d'après Philip Kobylarz

Une vieille dame. La mère du peintre. Elle coud. Une lumière tamisée pénètre par les rideaux en dentelle. D'un salon. Une couverture couleur feuille-morte sur ses genoux marque la fin d'un autre jour. Encore une journée. D'attente. D'automne. Dans le jardin, son mari arrose les dernières roses. Peut-être ou peut-être pas. Est-ce l'odeur de la terre humide qu'elle respire? Elle aimait chanter. Autrefois. Son fils est dans les tranchées. De la Somme. L'aiguille dans sa main fine transperce le mouchoir en coton. Elle se pique le doigt. Elle aime le rouge. Rouge pour les lettres qu'elle brode dans le coin. Elle imagine un cortège de soldats. Simples fantômes drapés dans le linceul de leur ombre. Bientôt elle allumera les bougies. Elle n'a pas faim mais elle préparera le souper. Parce qu'elle le doit.

Christiane Conésa-Bostock

I have failed with my life

Troubles come
instead of food.

My groans pour out like water.

The thing I fear
has come upon me.
What I dread
befalls me.

I have no rest.
Still my troubles come.
Is my strength the strength of stones?
Is my flesh bronze?

When I remember the past
shuddering seizes my flesh.
'Behold,' I cry out.
'Violence!'
I call for help.
I am not answered.

My days are past.
My plans are broken.

The desires of my heart have flown.

Hear my voice.
Feel my pain.

N.S. Nagaveeran

Four last things

'Already the air grows dark…' Joseph von Eichendorff[1]

These were the last things.
A breeze from somewhere making the leaves
of the calendar fan out, and then subside.
The spire of St Lucian on the corso,
transfixing the balcony wall with a needle
of light kindled on its gilded crucifix.
One motorcycle in the street below,
its pilot yelling at the unruly mob
of sheep traversing; and the locomotive,
stagnant within its girders, and three burly
foot-soldiers abusing the tattered
herdsman, they reel from a drunk symposium
and grimace in glee, each to the other,
over the hapless wench they had arraigned
(officially at first) then shared into the dawn;
their whips swish at the shepherd,
the train gives out a sympathetic hiss,
a sparrow fossicks in the dust. And then
the very last – a threnody uncurls
from an upper window hollowed by a burst
of misdirected gunfire yesterday,
a shadowy contralto, luscious, terrible,
trailing away into the reddened sky.

Alex Skovron

1. *Es dunkelt schon die Luft…* This line, here translated from the German by
William Mann, is from Eichendorff's poem '*Im Abendrot*' ('At Sunset'), one
of the poems set by Richard Strauss for his *Four Last Songs*.

The leaving

After seventy years
it is the leaving
she holds in her hands.

Shivering in the heat
a blonde girl wrapped in black wool
moves towards the gate.

Outside a man waits.
She is to exit on the left
remove the star, walk out.

Behind, from a broken window
the mother and father will her
beyond the gate, pray she does not look

back. She is to walk alone. They stay
she will go, they have decided
she says no but they will not barter

with their child's life. She glues
their photos in the soles of her shoes –
father   and   mother

each step grinding to a future,
to a mother's voice: *You will go.*
You will see. You will survive.

Barbara Kamler

Nearer my God to thee

I was born in 1923. We lived in Lachlan, which is out back of New Norfolk. Dad worked at the asylum. I had two sisters. We were close in age. That photo was taken when I was thirteen. My elder sister is that one, Thalia, and this is the baby – Dulcie – just two years younger than me. We normally tied our hair back with wide ribbons, but, that day, my father let us have a photograph. You can see that we all had hair long enough to sit on. Dad didn't like us to think too much about our looks. People paid us a lot of attention, and my father, he didn't like it.

Dad worked at the asylum. Sometimes, he would tell us stories about some of them in there, but he didn't like to do that. After they let them out, he would say, *Don't go near him, if you see him walking along the Lachlan Road.* You see, there were some who walked to Lachlan every Sunday from the town. That was a long way. The cemetery was there, and they came to visit the cemetery.

My hair still grows fast. Now it's completely white, but it still grows fast. It's a nuisance. I haven't been to Lachlan or New Norfolk for many years. I can't get on a bus. It would make me too sick. I can't go on a bus and I can't listen to music. I can't listen to guitar music. It's because of this disease. No, I haven't seen Lachlan for many years.

New Norfolk is a town with a black, black river where its feet should be, and a terrible black thorn in its heart. The river, if you ever see it, flows almost black, and it's a cold river. You can feel the cold coming up off of it, though science people say there is no such thing as cold, as such, there is only an absence of heat. They have probably never stood or sat under the weeping willows along the banks of the Derwent River. When you're there under the willows, the cold is a real thing, as solid as you standing there.

I have sat on the grass under one of those willows with an old boyfriend, and I remember singing 'A Robin Built a Nest on Daddy's

Grave', and I sang 'Wyldwood Flower', and I longed for him to crack open or set alight the way I needed him to. He was not that kind of a man.

The Derwent River is one of those rivers that makes you wonder what it's like to be on the other side. There used to be a house there – well, it could still be there, as far as I know – and I used to think about it a lot. It was long and white, and there was a cross-hatched fence between it and the river. The fence was stained where the flood waters had come up at one time or another. I used to sit under the oak trees and watch the old house and wonder who lived in it. I would have given anything to have gone there, to have walked through the house. Once, I saw a white dog sniffing in the yard. It didn't seem to belong there. There was a feeling of tragedy about that house. I don't know why.

The people who live there, in New Norfolk, or who grew up thereabouts, don't like to talk about the hospital – the asylum. Mostly, they don't go and stand by the river. You can't do that, if you have to live there. You have to get on with your life. It was a different era back then. We can't judge.

When they let them out of the hospital, you'd see them walking along the road or going into town. My father used to say, *Don't go near them!* There was a lady. We used to see her. She used to walk out to Lachlan every Sunday. She'd climb up to the top of the hill and she'd sit on a rock and she'd sing 'Nearer My God to Thee'. Dad would say, *If you see her, make sure you hide in the trees.* So, when we saw her, we hid behind the trees and watched her. She'd sing 'Nearer My God to Thee' and then she'd sing other hymns. I never hear that hymn, 'Nearer My God to Thee', without thinking of her. *Don't go near her*, my father told us. *Hide behind the trees...*

There was a Gypsy Man, a real gypsy. He lived out the back of Bothwell. I remember him. He had a shock of black, black hair. He lived in a blackberry patch – in a corrugated-iron humpy down near the river. He'd walk miles. To Bushy Park or Ellendale. Right out along to Plenty. I think he had a cart. He collected old metal off the housewives. Us kids were scared of him. He hated the sound of a shotgun or a firecracker. Sometimes, the boys let off penny bungers behind him.

During the war, I worked at the hospital. I was a nurse. If the air raid siren went off in New Norfolk, we had to leave our beds in Lachlan and run all the way in the dark to the air raid shelter. That was two miles.

I don't like to think about some of the things I've heard about the asylum. They say about girls coming in with babies that should never have been born – things like that happened back in those days, in some of those places right out back, behind the mountain. Nobody talked about it, but they knew. People knew. There was ignorance. You wouldn't know. Back then, things went on. The girls went and worked in the asylum laundry. The babies were hidden away. There were stories that would make your hair stand on end.

Even in Lachlan, there was a boy not so far from our place who used to be tied by the hands to the front gate. If we had to walk past him, he would bark at us, and spit. The kids at school said there was a man out in the scrub with no arms or legs. They said he was carted around by his brothers in a wheelbarrow.

It was when I was at school that I first heard the word Black Bobs. I didn't know what it meant. I asked my father what they meant when they called one of the boys from way out behind the mountain a Black Bob. Dad was very upset. He told us to never mention it. It was something we shouldn't talk about. Black Bobs.

There was…still is…a place out west of Bothwell called Black Bobs. Some of those places, you know, they still have a feeling, a strange feeling. You'd see a house in a paddock, set back from the road, and it would be hard to know if anyone lived there or not. It might seem that someone was watching you as you rode past on your bicycle. Sometimes, it gave me goosebumps up my arms, when it seemed that a raggedy curtain moved in a window when we were riding our bikes past.

We loved to ride out to the hop fields. Once a year, we brought strings of hops back to decorate the house – around the door frames, over the mantelpiece and so on. That was way out at the Styx River. I loved the smell of the hops when they were ripe. We used to look into the front gardens as we rode past. There were great, tall hollyhocks, roses, raspberry canes. We loved to take a billycan and fill one with raspberries picked from along the fences. Nobody minded. There was plenty for everyone.

Well, Bushy Park was a long, long ride from Lachlan. Normally, we stopped by the river where it ran over the boulders, and we lit a little fire, and made billy tea, and we ate sandwiches of butter, or butter and sugar, with thin slices. Did you ever try honeycomb? If Dad had just robbed the hives, we would put chunks of the comb on our bread, and the wax would be there to chew all the way back to New Norfolk.

People go back there, now, and look at the asylum. The vandals get in and spray things all over the walls. Break things. I can tell you, now – even if I could go there, I wouldn't. People go there and they want to see the underground tunnel, the bathrooms, the places where they did that shock treatment. I don't know why. I don't know why people want to see those things. I remember Dad talking about a room back there. Nobody would go in it. There was nothing in there, but it was where they put the Dog Boy. He was from way out, and they found him living with the farm dogs in a pen. That wouldn't happen these days. Things like that don't happen these days. There are laws.

We had a funny little dog. It had three dog legs and a fourth leg that was a queer shape. One day, the doctor came to see my father, and Dad asked him to look at our little dog who was limping around the house. The doctor looked at our dog and he asked my mother, *Where does the dog sleep, Mrs Cole?* My mother told him the dog slept in the fowl house with the chickens. *Just as I thought!* said the doctor. He said, *Your dog has three dog legs and one chicken wing, from sleeping with the fowls.* That's true!

Funny, the things you remember. As the crow flies, you know, Lachlan is only about seven miles from Crabtree, across the mountains. Well, there was never any road, back then, but some of the men went up there with chains to bring down the timber. Some of them remembered seeing hyenas out there in the scrub. One man, Claude, followed one for four hours, right up into the hills. I never saw one, in the wild, but sometimes I thought I heard one out on the mountain, yipping at something. They don't bark, those creatures. They say all they can do is yip. We had lambs taken, sometimes. If the corpse of a lamb was left behind, because the beast was frightened away by a shotgun, the kids of the poor families would come and collect it for the wool. It was fine wool, but not as fine as the mainland's. There was too much feed, you see.

Some of those poor families – it was nothing to see a whole wallaby stewing in a big, black pot in the front yard. Traps everywhere, including the roofs of the houses. They lived on chip potatoes and gravy. There was an old lady, so fat and so crippled, she lived in a big chair in front of the kitchen stove. The doctor said, if you went in the front door, you just kept on out the back door, the floor was on that much of a slope. They used to put sleeping medicine in the baby's bottle, and Lord knows who the parentage of that poor wee thing was. Well, it didn't seem to care. It slept almost all the time. The doctor said they were a grand old family, once, and lived in a beautiful house with Tassie oak floors and carved banisters, but, generation by generation, they pulled apart the old house and moved into the one I knew them in. All that was left when I knew them were some old foundations.

If ever you walked up the old road to the tumbledown house, there was a frogs' hollow near the creek where the fog hung late into the day, and there was always an eerie feeling there. Some Hobart folk once tried to build a shack there, but they only stayed in it just the one time. After that one night there, they never stayed there ever again. Some cranky people used to live in huts and humpies out the back of Lachlan, after the war. Sometimes, when we were playing in the bush, we'd come across a campsite. It made you feel queer and frightened, when you found someone's camp right out the back of the town like that. Sometimes, the camps were abandoned, and there'd be possum droppings all through the humpy and the bedding...possum droppings through everything... everything strewn about...

I reckon you can feel it, a place like that. There's a feeling there. We used to say something bad must've happened there, maybe even way back. Oh, there were places, all right. There was Dead Horse Gully, Ghost Gully, Big Stump Butt, and others. There were spots where the fog or the frost never lifted, where the sun never got to, all covered in moss, and the ground seemed to breathe a coldness up at you. There were roads you never rode to the end of on your bike. Funny, that! You'd just feel the strongest urge to turn around and head home. And you did.

You'd hear voices, sometimes... *What was that?* you'd wonder. Later, you'd tell yourself it was, maybe, a parrot that someone had taught to speak, escaped from its cage and living in amongst the old black pine trees. You'd hear noises that weren't human noises; words that weren't the King's English. It'd make your hair stand on end.

Sometimes, I just imagine I'm travelling out there, back to Lachlan, though I can't go any more, with this disease. I close my eyes, and I can picture the black swans on the Derwent – black swans everywhere, and those little spotted ducks. I picture the reeds at the edges, and the shape of Mount Dromedary across the other side. In some places, wild apple trees have been left to grow along the sides of the road. There are rose hips and hawthorns all the way along. And the river gets blacker the closer you get to New Norfolk. The town is full of antique places, now, they say. It reminds me of my great grandma. *I'll come back and harnt yer!* she used to say. Oh, I was frightened of her. And, of course, I believed her. All those antique places they've got there now – it feels as though the whole town is haunted.

And I never knew what happened to those three children. She lost all three. No one told children things like that, in those days. They whispered, but they never told you, and you knew you weren't to ask. All three of her children, lost. It still makes my heart ache for the poor creature. We'd be hiding in the trees, just like my father told us, and there she'd be, singing 'Nearer My God to Thee', sitting there on the big rock on top of the hill. 'Nearer My God to Thee'. And Dad told us, *Hide if you hear her! Hide in the trees!* Because they were about our age, see. Those three.

Philomena van Rijswijk

Jetsam

The same griefs that cut:
your brindle cat, stiff, rolled
in velvet, put into that April
earth; the silky-furred dog that
dragged you from in front of the
gun, his last breath in your
mouth; the not-born, kick-missing
boy you never touched, his blue
flesh wailing silence.

These same griefs that cut longer,
harder free-bleed – nothing can
mend the ruffled flaps; muscle and
skin temporarily grasped until proud-
flesh un-numbs, and you breathe
all
the way down
to the pubis.
Your eyes unfilm and the green door
is finally an exit from the house, not
something that keeps the world out.

Zan Ross

Seized

she writes this poem
as a prophylactic
against loss and darkness
descents are many
she travels
like a particle
along two paths
one a tendency towards existence
sense and memory
the other towards non-existence
nonsense and annihilation
she carries the energies
of a dark universe
visions of an underworld
long past and rising
she is the lamb in the sheepfold
wolf in the forest
virgin violated
lupa levitated
madonna whore
lesbian lover
her transitoriness
is as permanent
as memory and invention
she falls and rises falls and rises
like a wave

Susan Hawthorne

After rain

After rain
there is your smell
on the footpath
of my place.
Still, still
after rain
when everything is gone
and everywhere is clean.
I do not yet know
what can clean your name
from the wall of my heart?
No rain.
Nothing.

Ahmad Aienjamshid

Biographical notes

Ahmad Aienjamshid is an Iranian poet currently living in Australia. His work has been published in journals, newspapers and magazines in Iran. In Australia his poetry has been published in *Writing To the Wire*, and at *writingthroughfences.org*. His work was exhibited as part of *Our Beautiful Names: an exhibition of art and poetry*, Castlemaine State Festival, 2015. He co-wrote and performed *Through The Moon*, a poetic conversation with Janet Galbraith, Castlemaine State Festival, 2017, and represented Writing through Fences at the Queensland Poetry Festival, 2017. He performed an adaption of *Through The Moon*, titled *Heart's Tongue*, alongside Samantha Bews for the Castlemaine Children's Literature Festival, 2017.

Susan Austin is a poet, mental health occupational therapist, mother and activist. Her first poetry collection, *Undertow*, was published by Walleah Press in 2012. She has published in numerous journals and been a featured reader at various literary festivals in Tasmania.

Tim Bass is a painter and poet living in Sydney. He worked as a book editor and university lecturer before teaching painting and drawing at the Victorian College of the Arts, Melbourne. His poems have been published in *The Bulletin, Poetry Australia, Hobo*, and *The Age*.

Rosemary Blake holds dual Australian/Canadian citizenship. She has published in *The Fiddlehead, The Antigonish Review, Grain, Best Australian Poems* 2012, and various anthologies. Her poetry collection, *Wintering*, was published by Ekstasis Editions (2007). She was a residential fellow at the Banff Writing Studio.

Ann Bolch is a writer, editor, and story coach. She regularly publishes her fiction, non-fiction, and copy writing. She won the 2013 C.J. Dennis Short Story Prize with an excerpt from her first novel, *Fourth Drop*. Ann provides editing, ghost-writing, and coaching through her business: www.astorytotell.com.au.

Behrouz Boochani graduated from Tarbiat Moallem University and Tarbiat Modares University, Tehran. He holds a Masters in political science, political geography and geopolitics. He is a Kurdish-Iranian writer, journalist, scholar, cultural advocate, and filmmaker. He is currently a political prisoner incarcerated by the Australian government in the Manus Island Regional Processing Centre (Papua New Guinea). Boochani was writer for the Kurdish language magazine *Werya*; is an Honorary Member of PEN International; member of Writing through Fences; winner of an Amnesty International Australia 2017 Media Award, the Diaspora Symposium Social Justice Award, and Liberty Victoria 2018 Empty Chair Award; and is non-resident Visiting Scholar at the Sydney Asia-Pacific Migration Centre (SAPMiC), University of Sydney. He publishes regularly with *The Guardian, The Saturday Paper, Huffington Post, New Matilda*, and *Sydney Morning Herald*. Boochani is co-director (with Arash Kamali Sarvestani) of the 2017 feature-length film *Chauka, Please Tell Us the Time;* collaborator on Nazanin Sahamizadeh's play, *Manus*. Boochani's poetry has been published in *Cordite, Writing to the Wire* and *The Guardian. No Friend but the Mountains: Writing From Manus Prison* (Picador, 2018) won the Victorian Premier's Prize for Literature.

Liam Brooks lives in Melbourne and writes short stories, historical essays, poetry, creative non-fiction and memoir. He teaches English and Spanish at a public high school. He has published with the Australian Society for the Study of Labour History, *Seed Magazine,* and the *Port Melbourne Historical and Preservation Society.*

Nathan Brown is a writer and editor, based in Warburton, Victoria. He has written as a magazine editor and columnist, novelist and blogger, and continues to write regularly for publications around the world. 'An autumn mourning' was first written as part of his MA at Deakin University.

Jennifer Bryce lives in a Melbourne seaside suburb. After a career in educational research she is now fulfilling her passion of becoming a writer. She has just completed her first, Australian Gothic, novel. She is a founding member of Elwood Writers and runs her own literary blog: http://jenniferbryce.net/.

Gayelene Carbis has been shortlisted for various poetry prizes including: Montreal International; Fish (Ireland); Martha Richardson; Adrien Abbott; MPU; and ABR and The Age Short Story Awards. In 2017, her play won Best Premiere Production, Sarasota Festival (USA); and her first book of poetry, *Anecdotal Evidence,* was published by Five Islands Press.

Liana Joy Christensen is the author of *Deadly Beautiful: Vanishing Killers of the Animal Kingdom* and two poetry collections, *Wild Familiars* and *Unnatural History.* Liana's essays, poetry and short stories are published nationally and internationally. She was shortlisted for the 2014 Newcastle Poetry Prize.

Ali Cobby Eckerman won the 2013 Kenneth Slessor Prize for Poetry for *Ruby Moonlight.* In 2014 she was the inaugural recipient of the Tungkunungka Pintyanthi Fellowship at Adelaide Writers Week; and the first Aboriginal Australian writer to attend the International Writing Program at University of Iowa. Her memoir, *Too Afraid to Cry*, was published by Ilura Press, 2014. In 2017 she received the Windham Campbell Award for Poetry from Yale University, USA.

Dr Christiane Conésa-Bostock is a French-born Australian. Her writing has been widely published. In 2011 she published her first poetry collection, *De passage de France en Tasmanie,* and with The Grove Road Poets (4 other poets) published an award-winning collection, *Of Things being Various.* She was made *Chevalier de l' Ordre des Palmes Académiques* by the French government.

Lucy Czerwiec was born in rural WA of migrant parents and now lives in Perth. She has been a member of OOTA Writers group in Fremantle for many years and writes short fiction as well as poetry. She has been published in Australian anthologies and journals. She has worked in different nursing specialties.

Lucy Dougan works as Program Director for the China–Australia Writing Centre at Curtin. Her books include *White Clay* (Giramondo), *Meanderthals* (Web del Sol) and *The Guardians* (Giramondo) which won the 2016 WA Premier's Prize for Poetry. She is co-editor (with Tim Dolin) of *The Collected Poems of Fay Zwicky* (UWAP).

Jane Downing has published short stories and poetry in many prestigious Australian journals. Her novels, *The Trickster* (2003) and *The Lost Tribe* (2005), were published by Pandanus Books. Her next novel, *Yack* was Commended in the Jim Hamilton Unpublished Manuscript Award, 2016. She can be found at www.janedowning.wordpress.com.

Quinn Eades is a researcher, writer, and award-winning poet; the author of *all the beginnings: a queer autobiography of the body* as well as *Rallying*; and currently is working on a book written from the transitioning body, *Transpositions*.

Adrienne Eberhard has had poems published in Australia, USA, UK and France; and in anthologies such as *Motherlode, Best Australian Poems* and *The Indigo Book of Modern Australian Sonnets*. Her fourth collection is *Chasing Marie Antoinette All Over Paris*, Black Pepper, 2019.

Bronwyn Evans is an award-winning writer based in Melbourne. Her play, *The Hand that Feeds You*, was performed in the Ten in 10 Festival in 2013 and her work has appeared in various anthologies and journals. She holds a Grad Dip Arts in Creative Writing from the University of Melbourne.

Tracey-Anne Forbes has had numerous stories and poems published in Australian literary magazines and anthologies, including *Award-winning Australian Writing*, 2012 and *One Book: Many Brisbanes*, 6. Ginninderra Press published a collection of her stories, *Crushed Sugar*, in 2007 and a verse novel, *Saving Ginia*, in 2014.

David Francis has published in several Australian literary journals. His first poetry collection, *Promises Made at Night*, was published by Melbourne Poets Union in 2013. Currently, he is a PhD candidate in Creative Writing at the University of Melbourne. Previously, he worked as a transplant surgeon in Melbourne and Kathmandu.

Janet Galbraith is a poet, installation and performance artist living on the un-ceded lands of the Jaara people. Her work has been published in numerous journals, magazines and newspapers and performed at the Tasmanian Poetry Festival, Queensland Poetry Festival, Midsumma, and ArtsOutback. She is founder and co-facilitator of Writing through Fences. Her poetry collection, *re-membering*, was published by Walleah Press, 2013.

Kevin Gillam is a WA writer with three books of poetry published: *other gravities* (2003) and *permitted to fall* (2007) both by Sunline Press and *songs sul g* in *Two Poets* (2011) by Fremantle Press. He works as Director of Music at Christ Church Grammar School in Perth.

Gill Goater lives in Port Macquarie, where she facilitates a poetry discussion group (now in its sixth year). She has been published in various anthologies and magazines and won the 2015 Dangerously Poetic Byron Bay Writer's Festival poetry prize. In 2011 she published a poetry collection, *Occupied by Gods*.

Elizabeth Goodsir lives in Hobart. *Wind Rippling Water*, a collection of her poems illustrated by Bruce Goodsir, was published in 2012. *Blue Pollen Beautiful* was published in 2017 after being shortlisted for the 2015 Tasmanian Premier's Literary Prizes, plus winning the University of Tasmanian Prize for Unpublished Works and the People's Choice Award. It was illustrated by her daughter, Madeleine Goodwolf.

Fran Graham is a West Australian who has published in journals and anthologies including *Best Australian Poems* 2012. In 2017 she won the Norma and Colin Knight Award, the SWWWA's Bronze Quill Award, and the Remote and Regional WA Award in *Poetry d'Amour*. Her first collection, *On a Hook Behind the Door*, was published by Ginninderra Press, 2011.

Susie Greenhill lives on the mouth of a river in Tasmania's far south. Her short fiction has been published in anthologies and journals in Australia and overseas. Her almost finished novel, *The Clinking*, won the 2016 Richell Prize for Emerging Writers. She has a PhD in creative writing and environmental literature.

Debi Hamilton is a Melbourne-based psychologist and writer. Her short stories and poetry have been published in numerous journals and anthologies. In 2014 she was joint winner of the Newcastle Poetry Prize and placed second in the University of Canberra Vice-Chancellor's Poetry Prize. Her second poetry collection, *The Sly Night Creatures of Desire*, was published in 2016.

Elisabeth Hanscombe is a psychologist and writer. She wrote her PhD on 'Life Writing and the Desire for Revenge'. She has published short stories, essays and book chapters in the areas of autobiography, testimony, trauma and creative non-fiction. Her memoir, *The Art of Disappearing*, was published in 2017. Elisabeth blogs at www.sixthinline.com.

Susan Hawthorne has published several poetry books: *Lupa and Lamb* (2014), *Limen* (2013), *Cow* (2011), and *The Butterfly Effect* (2005). She is the author of two novels, *Dark Matters* (2017) and *The Falling Woman* (1992) as well as writing non-fiction and editing several anthologies. Her books have been shortlisted for national and international awards.

Pete Hay researches environmental and place activism, plus the cultural geography of islands, but mostly writes poetry and essays. His books include

Main Currents in Western Environmental Thought, Vandiemonian Essays, The Forests (with Matthew Newton), and four volumes of poetry, most recently, *Girl Reading Lorca* and *Physick*.

Keren Heenan is a Melbourne writer and arts teacher. She is the winner of a number of Australian short story awards and placed second in the 2015 Fish Prize (Ireland). She has been published in prestigious journals and anthologies in Australia and overseas.

Dianne Hicks Morrow was writer-in-residence, Tasmania-Prince Edward Island cultural exchange, 2012. She was poet laureate of Prince Edward Island 2013–16. Her second poetry collection, *What Really Happened is This*, won the PEI Book Award for Poetry, 2012. Her two non-fiction titles are *Kindred Spirits: Relationships that Spark the Soul* and *Fixing Up the Farmhouse: Forty Years of Living, Loving, and Lamenting*.

Virginia Jealous is a West Australian who writes travel journalism, essays and poetry. Her first and second collections of prose and poems were published by Picaro Press (2011) and Hallowell Press (2017) respectively. Her book about a woman who knew much about loss, the extraordinary poet, Laurence Hope, is *Rapture's Roadway*, Ventura Press, 2019.

Tamara Jones is a former languages teacher who now devotes her time to writing, in between gardening and baking cakes. Originally from NZ, she currently lives in the UK. She has published several short stories and recently started writing a novel.

Barbara Kamler is Emeritus Professor at Deakin University and mentors early-career researchers on academic writing and publishing. Her most recent book is *Leaving New Jersey* (Interactive Press 2016), a poetic memoir. She is working on *Late Love*, a collection which captures, in poetic form, the stories of couples who have been together many years.

Anne Kellas is a South African-born Australian. *The White Room Poems* (Walleah Press, 2015) was shortlisted for the Margaret Scott Prize in the 2017 Tasmanian Premier's Literary Awards. In 2018, *The Netted Air* appeared in the Picaro Poets series and her poetry showcased in the *Australian Book Review States of Poetry* (Series Two). Anne mentors poets and teaches poetry classes.

Alana Kelsall writes poetry and short fiction. Her first book of poetry, *The Distance Between Us* (Melbourne Poets Union) was published in 2015. She has been shortlisted for the Newcastle Poetry Prize and won the Ada Cambridge Poetry Competition in 2014. She lives in Melbourne.

Stella Kent is a Launceston-based, award-winning playwright whose works have been produced by ABC Radio, CentreStage, the Australian Script Centre, Ten Days on the Island Festival, London's Old Red Lion Theatre, and the Tasmanian Theatre Company. Dr Kent taught at the University of Tasmania for many years.

Mary Kille was born in England where she trained in medicine, emigrating to NW Tasmania in 1973. She has published three books of poetry: *Proving Flight* (2011), *Happenstance* (2017) and *The Furgling Fairy-wren* (2018).

Karen Knight was born in Tasmania. She has published widely since the early 1960s. She has written four collections of poetry. Her most recent, *Postcards from the Asylum* (Pardalote Press), won the 2005 Dorothy Hewett Flagship Fellowship Award, the 2007 ACT Alec Bolton Poetry Prize and the 2011 University of Tasmania Prize.

Kumar is a Nepalese writer of poetry and prose. He began writing from within Australian immigration detention camps. He finds writing essential to his survival after more than six years in exile. His work has been published in *Our Beautiful Voices* (Mark Time Books), e-borderlands, local newspapers and the literary online magazine, *Communion*.

Kristen Lang lives near Sheffield, Tasmania. *SkinNotes* (Walleah Press) and *The Weight of Light* (Five Islands Press) were published in 2017. *Let me show you a ripple* (poems and photographs) was self-published in 2008. She was awarded a PhD at Deakin University in 2004 for her creative thesis in poetry.

Wes Lee lives on the Kapiti Coast of NZ. She has won a number of awards including the 2010 BNZ Katherine Mansfield Literary Award. She is the author of *Body, Remember* (Eyewear Publishing, 2017), *Shooting Gallery* (Steele Roberts, 2016) and *Cowboy Genes* (Grist Books , University of Huddersfield Press, 2014).

Jules Leigh Koch has published five collections of poetry and received two South Australian Literature Grants (2008, 2011). He is the recipient of many awards and was a regular guest reader at the Lee Marvin readings at the AEAF and a guest reader at Adelaide Writers' Week in 2017.

Kristen Levitzke is a Perth-based writer who graduated with a BA and Dip Ed from University of WA. She has published several short stories. She is a bibliophile with a passion for language, education and literacy development.

Rose Lucas is a Melbourne poet. Her first collection, *Even in the Dark* (UWAP, 2013), won the 2014 Mary Gilmore award. It was followed by *Unexpected Clearing* (UWAP, 2016). She is currently completing her third collection, *At the Point of Seeing*. Rose teaches in Graduate Research at Victoria University.

Georgina Luck has published in literary journals including *Griffith Review, Southerly, Overland* and *Etchings*. She won the Griffith Review/Text Publishing Emerging Writers' Award for Fiction in 2009. Georgina has received two Varuna Writers' Fellowships, an ASA mentorship, and been commended in numerous awards.

Peter Macrow is a Tasmanian writer. His seventh poetry collection, *Fish Tank Circus*, was published by Picaro Press in 2014. Through his Blue Giraffe Press he published poetry journals *Blue Giraffe* and *Prospect*. He continues to publish *Windfall: Australian Haiku*. He writes piano and vocal music.

Robyn Mathison, born Narrandera NSW 1938, co-edited *Past the Poppies* (FAW TAS, 1996 with Megan Schaffner); *Republican Dreaming* and *Moorilla Mosaic* (Bumblebee Books, 1999 & 2001 with Lyn Reeves); *Behind the Masks: Gwen Harwood remembered by her friends* (Ginninderra Press, 2015, with Robert Cox). Ginninderra Press published her books *To Be Eaten by Mice* (2009) and *Still Bravely Singing* (2017).

Mardi May facilitates the poetry group at the Katharine Susannah Prichard Writers' Centre in WA. She is a Life Member at KSP and serves on the Board of Management and the Literary Committee. Her published work includes three poetry collections and two verse novellas. She has received many literary awards.

Liz McQuilkin, a retired English teacher, co-authored the poetry collection *Of Things Being Various* (Forty Degrees South) which won the 2011 National FAW Community Writers' Award. Her first solo collection, *The Nonchalant Garden*, was published in 2014 by Walleah Press. Her poems have appeared in various anthologies and literary journals.

Gina Mercer is a Tasmanian poet who has taught creative writing in universities and communities for thirty years. She was Editor of *Island* from 2006 to 2010. She has published eight books, including five collections of poetry. Her latest, all about birds, is *Weaving Nests with Smoke and Stone* (Walleah Press, 2015).

Suzi Mezei is a Sri Lankan-born, Melbourne writer, interested in social justice, animal rights and the environment. Her work has appeared in *Award-winning Australian Writing* 2014, *Hecate*, and *Quadrant*. She writes poetry, prose and plays.

Carol Millner has published her award-winning poems and short stories in Australian and NZ anthologies such as *Amber Contains the Sun*. In 2015 her first full-length poetry manuscript was shortlisted for the inaugural Dorothy Hewett Award (UWAP). She is currently a PhD student writing short fiction at Curtin University.

Anna Minska is a writer, performance poet and singer who lives in a forest in WA. She has a background in psychology and community mental health work. She currently teaches singing and creative process.

Ahlam Mohamed is a Somali poet who has written poetry throughout her life and continues to write now that she is in Australia. Ahlam's writing brings hope to those who remain behind in immigration detention. She has been published in *Our Beautiful Voices* (Mark Time Books), e-borderlands and has read her work on ABC radio.

Sharon Moore is a writer and freelance editor who lives on a farm in the deep south of Tasmania. She has published non-fiction, book reviews and articles on environmental themes. In 2015, she published her first novel, *The Sea Pool*.

Bob Morrow grew up in Sydney, and settled in Melbourne after ten years wandering the world. His poems frequently explore matters of family, belonging, and a sense of place. In 2013 he published a chapbook, *Moving On* (Mark Time Books).

Robyn Mundy is the author of the novels *Wildlight* (Picador, 2016) and *The Nature of Ice* (Allen & Unwin, 2009), and co-author of *Epic Adventure: Epic Voyages for young readers*. Robyn lives in Tasmania and spends several months of each year guiding tourist voyages to the Antarctic and Arctic.

Rashida Murphy is the author of *The Historian's Daughter*, shortlisted for the Dundee International Book Prize and published by UWAP (2016). Her fiction, poetry, and essays have appeared in journals and anthologies internationally. She was a Writer-in-residence at the KSP Writers Centre and is currently teaching at Edith Cowan University.

N.S. Nagaveeran began writing poetry whilst incarcerated in the Australian-run immigration detention camp on Nauru. Nagaveeran's poetry has appeared in *The Stringer, Writing to the Wire*, and *Our Beautiful Voices* (Writing through Fences). Nagaveeran's first collection of poetry, *From Hell to Hell*, was published by Writing through Fences, 2015.

Dr Catherine Padmore teaches literary studies and creative writing at La Trobe University. Her first novel, *Sibyl's Cave* (Allen & Unwin, 2004), was shortlisted for The Australian/Vogel Award and commended in the first-book category of the Commonwealth Writers' Prize.

Anthony Panegyres is a PhD candidate at UWA. A few of his journal publication homes include: *Overland, Meanjin, Dotdotdash* and *ASIM*. Some of his anthology homes include *Best Australian Stories, The Year's Best Australian Fantasy and Horror* (2011 & 2015), *Dreaming of Djinn, Kisses by Clockwork, Bloodlines* and *At the Edge*.

Carol Patterson lives at South Arm, Tasmania. Her output includes novels and plays as well as short stories (including seven published in *Island*). Her love of the environment resulted in her gaining a PhD in Geography and Environmental Studies, scholarship that enriches her writing about people and place.

Lyn Reeves has published poetry, haiku and stories in many prestigious journals and anthologies. Her sixth collection, *Designs on the Body* (Interactive Press), received the IP Picks Best Poetry Award, 2010. Drums Records released a CD of Lyn reading from it. A collaboration with Hobart artist, Luke Wagner, resulted in a fine print limited edition book, *Small Worlds* (2017).

Johanna Rendle-Short is a linguist, lecturer and writer. As an academic, she has published in refereed linguistics journals for over 16 years. She reviews and edits academic texts. She has a piece in *Press: 100 Love Letters* (University of the Philippines Press, 2017).

Duncan Richardson writes fiction, poetry, radio drama and educational texts. He has published five poetry/haiku collections including *Ultra Soundings* (Interactive Press, 2012) and *Mountains, Plains, Sea* (Pula! Press, 2014). His verse play *The Grammar of Deception* was produced by the ABC in 2008 and he has published several books for children.

Kristen Roberts lives in Melbourne. Her poetry and short stories have appeared in various journals and anthologies including *page seventeen, Australian Love Poems*, and *Award-winning Australian Writing*. Her poetry pamphlet, *The Held and the Lost*, was published by the Emma Press (2014).

Rachel Robertson is a senior lecturer at Curtin University. She is author of the memoir *Reaching One Thousand* (Black Inc), and co-editor of *Purple Prose* and *Dangerous Ideas about Mothers*. Her creative work appears in *Westerly, Griffith Review, Island, Meanjin* and *Best Australian Essays*. She has a particular interest in writing about illness, disability and loss.

Zan Ross is a WA poet. She has published in Australian journals plus a few in Canada, Budapest, Paris, USA and online. She has had two collections published: *B-Grade* (Monogene Press), *Enpassant* (Fremantle Press), plus a chapbook, *Je ne sai quoi* (Vagabond Press).

Megan Schaffner has poems in the Picaro Poetry Prize anthology, *The Green Fuse*, 2010, and the prizewinning collection: *Of Things Being Various* (Forty Degrees South, 2011). She has edited four anthologies for the FAW, Tasmania. Her collection of poetry, *A Poem is a Parachute,* was published by Ginninderra Press (2015).

Pam Schindler is a Brisbane poet, librarian and bushwalker. Her work has appeared in Australian print and online magazines. Her first book of poems, *A Sky You Could Fall Into*, was published in 2010 by Post Pressed. She was a Hawthornden Fellow in 2013.

Maureen Scott Harris is a poet and essayist. She has published three collections of poetry in Canada. *Drowning Lessons*, her second book, was awarded the Trillium Award for Poetry in 2005. In 2012, Pedlar Press published her third collection, *Slow Curve Out*. Her essay 'Broken Mouth' won the 2009 Wildcare Tasmania Nature Writing Prize.

Katherine E. Seppings is an artist, writer, editor, and photographer published in various journals, anthologies, blogs and non-fiction books. She has received awards for her poetry and short stories. Her two poetry collections are *When Embers Dance*, Melbourne Poets Union (2015); and *Love & Death in Castlemaine*, Mark Time Books (2016).

Deborah Sheldon is a professional writer from Melbourne, Australia. Her latest dark fantasy and horror releases include *300 Degree Days &Other Stories, Thylacines, Perfect Little Stitches & Other Stories,* and *Devil Dragon.* Other credits include TV scripts, feature articles, non-fiction books, stage plays, and award-winning medical writing.

Alex Skovron has published six collections of poetry, a prose novella, and a volume of short stories, *The Man who Took to his Bed* (2017). His most recent, *Towards the Equator: New & Selected Poems* (2014), was shortlisted in the Prime Minister's Literary Awards. He was born in Poland, arrived in Australia aged nine, and lives in Melbourne.

Stephen Smithyman lives in Melbourne. His poems have won the Victorian Cancer Council Outstanding Poem Award 2011, the Poetica Christi Poetry Competition 2013, and the Glen Phillips Poetry Prize 2017, as well as appearing in a range of anthologies and magazines. His father was the New Zealand poet Kendrick Smithyman.

Tracy Sorensen is a journalist, fiction writer and documentary-maker living in Bathurst, NSW. She grew up in outback WA. In 2014 she was diagnosed with stage IIIc ovarian cancer. She is currently writing a series of meditations about illness. Her debut novel, *The Lucky Galah* (2018), has been published by Picador.

Sarah St Vincent Welch lives in Canberra and facilitates creative writing in her community. Her poetry chapbook *Open* was published by Rochford St Press in 2018.

Thom Sullivan published his collection *Airborne* in New Poets 14 (Wakefield, 2009). Since then he has edited or co-edited seven books of poetry. His poems have appeared in *Australian Love Poems, Best Australian Poems* 2014, and *States of Poetry 1,* Australian Book Review. He won the 2017–18 Noel Rowe Poetry Award.

Emily J. Sun has published essays, fiction and poetry in various journals and anthologies, including *Island, Hecate* and *Growing up Asian in Australia.* She has studied creative writing at the International Institute of Modern Letters (NZ) and completed a MA in English & Creative Arts at Murdoch University.

Lesley Synge is a Brisbane writer. Her poetry collections are *Organic Sister* (Post Pressed, 2005) and *Mountains Belong to the People Who Love Them: Slow Journeys in South Korea and Eastern Australia* (Post Pressed, 2011). Her novel *Cry Ma Ma to the Moon* is available on Amazon Kindle.

Philomena van Rijswijk lives in Tasmania. Her novel *The World as a Clockface* was published by Penguin, 2001. Her poetry collection *Bread of the Lost* was published by Walleah Press, 2013. Her latest fabulist novel, *The Bishop, the Gypsy and the Dancing Bear,* addresses the themes of xenophobia and border security.

Rob Wallis has published four collections of poetry. His latest is *An Elegant Sufficiency* (Birdfish Books). He has received the FAW John Shaw Neilson Poetry Award, the MPU Martin Downey Urban Realism Award, and been shortlisted for the Fish Publishing International Poetry Competition (Dublin) and the Bridport Prize (UK). He lives in country Victoria.

Julie Watts is a WA writer and has published in various journals and anthologies including *Westerly, Cordite, The Anthology of Contemporary Australian Feminist Poetry* and *Australian Love Poems* 2013. Her first poetry collection, *Honey and Hemlock*, was published by Sunline Press, 2013. Her second, *Legacy*, was published by UWAP, 2018.

Deb Westbury was a fine poet and gifted teacher. She lived in the Blue Mountains from 1998 until her death in 2018. Her poetry collections are *Mouth to Mouth* (1990), *Our Houses are Full of Smoke* (1994), *Surface Tension* (1998), *Flying Blind* (2002), *The View from Here* (2008) and *Winter in Stone Country*, Hope Street Press, 2016.

Terry Whitebeach published her first collection of poetry, *Bird Dream* (Penguin Books), in 1993. It won the Anne Elder Award and was shortlisted for the WA Premier's Award. Her other published work includes cross-cultural biographies, picture books and young adult fiction. *Trouble Tomorrow*, a YA novel (Allen & Unwin, 2017), was co-authored with South Sudanese colleague Sarafino Enadio.

Carmel Williams won the NT Literary Awards Red Earth Poetry Competition in 2004. In 2005 she won the ACT Alec Bolton National Award for an unpublished poetry manuscript, *The Butcher's Window*, which was published by Picaro Press in 2012. She holds a BCA (Creative Writing) from Flinders University.

Acknowledgements

Rosemary Blake, 'Geese', *Prayers of a Secular World,* Albiston, J. & Brophy, K. (eds), Inkerman and Blunt, 2015

Behrouz Boochani, 'The black kite', *The Guardian, Day of the Imprisoned Writer,* 14 November 2015

Ali Cobby Eckermann, 'Ningali', *Inside my Mother,* Giramondo Press, 2015

Liana Joy Christensen, 'Before they fall', *Southerly,* 76, 2, 2016, pp. 67–75

Lucy Dougan, 'Small Black Cardigan', as 'Black Cardigan', *White Clay,* Giramondo Press, 2008. Republished in *The Philosophy of Clothes,* River Road Press, 2009

Quinn Eades, 'Necrosis', *all the beginnings: a queer autobiography of the body,* Tantanoola, 2015

Tracey-Anne Forbes, 'Flesh and blood', *Hidden Desires: Contemporary Australian Women's Writing,* Houen, C. & Woodhouse, J. (eds), Ginninderra Press, 2006. Republished in *Crushed Sugar: Stories,* Ginninderra Press, 2007

David Francis, 'Sis', *Promises Made at Night,* Melbourne Poets Union, 2013

Janet Galbraith, 'Climate change', *re-membering,* Walleah Press, 2013

Kevin Gillam, 'the stroking', *Australian Love Poems,* Inkerman and Blunt, 2013

Gill Goater, 'Journeying to lithium', *Occupied by Gods,* self-published, 2011

Fran Graham, 'The Tao of loss', *Running Through The Stars,* Fellowship of Australian Writers, Tasmania, 2005. Republished in *On a Hook Behind the Door,* Ginninderra Press, 2011

Susan Hawthorne, 'seized', *Lupa and Lamb,* Spinifex Press, 2014

Pete Hay, 'Murphy versus Descartes: *Domum invenio, ergo sum*', *Professorial Paws: Dogs in Scholars' Lives and Work,* Cole, A. & Sbrocchi, S. (eds), Backalong Books, 2016

Dianne Hicks Morrow, 'Prosthetic', *Long Reach Home,* The Acorn Press, 2002

Virginia Jealous, 'The man who never forgot how to dance', *Things Turned Upside Down,* Picaro Press, 2011

Anne Kellas, 'Journey to my son', *Blue Giraffe,* 6, 2007. Republished in *The White Room Poems,* Walleah Press, 2015 and in a selection of Anne Kellas's poems translated into Ukrainian by Hanna Yanovska

Alana Kelsall, 'No closer to land', *The Distance Between Us,* Melbourne Poets Union, 2015

Stella Kent, 'Swing low, sweet chariot', *Voices,* National Library of Australia, Autumn 1993

Mary Kille, 'By his own hand', *The Furgling Fairy-wren,* self-published, 2018

Kumar, 'Oceans of sacrifice', *Our Beautiful Voices,* Mark Time Books, 2015, and online magazine *Communion*

Kristen Lang, 'Unborn', *SkinNotes*, Walleah Press, 2017

Rose Lucas, 'Five years and still –', *Unexpected Clearing*, UWAP, 2016

Georgina Luck, 'Calving', *Overland eBook, Women's Work*, March 2012

Peter Macrow, 'Jordy', *Fish Tank Circus*, Picaro Press, 2014

Robyn Mathison, 'Double mastectomy', *Poetrix*, 13, 2008. Republished in *To Be Eaten by Mice*, Ginninderra Press, 2009

Liz McQuilkin, 'One last time', *The Nonchalant Garden*, Walleah Press, 2014

Gina Mercer, 'After, there are the birds', *Weaving Nests with Smoke and Stone*, Walleah Press, 2015. Republished in *States of Poetry 2*, *Australian Book Review*, 2018

Carol Millner, 'Out of vogue', Smith, Glance, Konrad, Millner, Clarke, *Amber Contains the Sun*, Department of Culture and the Arts, WA, 2008

Ahlam Mohamed, 'Born with no homeland', *Our Beautiful Voices*, Mark Time Books, and e-borderlands

Sharon Moore, 'The trees of Antarctica' (abridged version), *Island Magazine*, 101, Winter 2007

N.S. Nagaveeran, 'I have failed with my life', *Writing through Fences*, 2015

Anthony Panegyres, 'Submerging', *Overland*, 214, Autumn 2014. Republished in *Best Australian Stories* 2014

Lyn Reeves, 'Subdivision', *Designs on the Body*, Interactive Press, 2010

Kristen Roberts, 'On the way to your funeral', *Quadrant*, 44, July–August 2008

Rachel Robertson, 'On Fifty-Three', *Meniscus*, 5.2, 2017

Megan Schaffner, 'Your Fibonacci', *A Poem is a Parachute*, Ginninderra Press, 2015

Pam Schindler, 'After the fires, Kinglake (2)', *Meanjin*, 70, 3, 2011

'Like someone who is leaving', *Australian Poetry Journal*, 6, 1, 2016

Deborah Sheldon, 'A guest for dinner', [untitled] *magazine*, #4, May 2011. Republished in *300 Degree Days and Other Stories*, Oscillate Wildly Press, 2018

Tracy Sorensen, 'Dr Douglas and the Baby Rabbits', published (abridged version) as 'The Pouch of Douglas', *Medical Journal of Australia*, 202, 11, 2015

Emily J. Sun, 'Lacrimosa', published as 'Lacrimosa dies illa', *Westerly: New Creative*, 26 September 2016, https://westerlymag.com.au/issues/new-creative/

Lesley Synge, '124-LUV', *The Hinterland Times*, December 2013

Deb Westbury, 'Luke' and 'White coffin notes', *Flying Blind*, Brandl & Schlesinger, 2002

Terry Whitebeach, 'Nostos' as 'Loss', *Famous Reporter*, 36, 2008

Carmel Williams, 'Fallout', *InDaily ezine*, 2/6/2013, http://indaily.com.au/arts-and-culture/

www.ingramcontent.com/pod-product-compliance
Lightning Source LLC
Chambersburg PA
CBHW031952120726
47898CB00002BA/356